Buck, Gayle
Willowswood match   26.95
                                     7/04

DISCARD

Willowswood Match

Willowswood Match

Gayle Buck

Five Star • Waterville, Maine

Published in 2004 in conjunction with Gayle Buck.

The text of this edition is unabridged.

Set in 11 pt. Plantin by Carleen Stearns.

Printed in the United States on permanent paper.

Library of Congress Cataloging-in-Publication Data

Buck, Gayle.
　　Willowswood match / Gayle Buck.
　　　　p. cm.
　　ISBN 1-59414-208-4 (hc : alk. paper)
　　1. Americans—England—Fiction.　I. Title.
　PS3552.U3326W55 2004
　　813'.54—dc22　　　　　　　　　　　　　　　　　2004043254

Willowswood Match

One

The billowing sails cracked overhead. Miranda breathed in the tang of the salt air. The wind ruffled the edges of her bonnet and tugged playfully at her long skirts. She looked out over the sea in great contentment. It was the first time that she had ever sailed the ocean, but it held no fears for her. She had discovered in herself a love of the endless expanse of moving, rolling water, the crash of the waves against the bow of the ship, the sting and taste of the spray on her face. Since the day the *Larabelle* left the safety of Portsmouth, Miranda had experienced a sense of freedom she had never felt before. In setting foot on the *Larabelle*'s deck, she had left her cares behind her.

A shadow fell across her and she turned her head to find her brother, Jeremy Wainwright, standing beside her at the rail. "I should have you get your parasol, you know," he remarked with a grin.

"Pooh! What do I care if I become as brown as you are? I shan't have Mrs. Calvin and her ilk whispering behind my back in England," said Miranda with a toss of her head.

Jeremy's smile faded. "I'm sorry you are still bothered by that, Miranda. I had hoped being on the sea would allow you to forget."

Miranda tucked her gloved hand into his arm. "And so it

has, brother. I mentioned the old cats only because I was just thinking how free I am at this moment. The ocean is so vast and beautiful that one is quickly aware how small one's problems really are."

Jeremy looked out to sea. There was a sense of wonder and love in his expression. "Aye, you are right there. I would not trade my life at sea for any other."

"How fortunate, then, that you have become a ship-owner. Our uncle could have been a prominent farmer instead of a sailing captain and had no understanding of your inclinations," said Miranda teasingly.

Jeremy grimaced at the thought. "I am indeed fortunate. When Uncle Ebenezer offered to back me in the *Larabelle*, I knew that at last my dreams were to come true." He looked down at his sister. "I hope that you will also find your place someday, Miranda. I do not need to tell you that I have been concerned on your account."

Miranda laughed. Her blue eyes were warm with affection for him. "You need not be, Jeremy. I shall come about, never fear. Indeed, I think that the moment I broke my engagement I started on the mend. When I look back on it, it was the mistake of my life ever to agree to marry Harrison Gregory. We would never have suited and how I could have thought otherwise, I do not know. He wished me to become someone I could not be. As for the resulting scandal, why, I never garnered so much attention in my life!"

"It is not the sort of attention that I could wish for my beloved sister," said Jeremy a shade grimly.

Miranda squeezed his arm. "It is done with, Jeremy. And by the time I do return to the States there will have occurred something far more interesting than my transgressions for the ladies to talk about. So do, pray, put it all out of your mind. I assure you that I have!"

"You have always had the trick of turning to the sunshine, Miranda," said Jeremy. His sister laughed and directed his attention to a school of fish leaping beside the ship. The subject of Miranda's recent unpleasant experience as the center of malicious gossip was dropped and by silent agreement not referred to again.

A day outside England the American merchant ship *Larabelle* was hailed by a cutter flying the British colors. With little ceremony the British ship signaled intention to board the *Larabelle*. Mindful of the cutter's guns, the Americans acquiesced. As an oarsboat ploughed the waves toward the *Larabelle*, the passengers on deck shifted uneasily, murmuring. Since the Congressional renewal of the Non-Intercourse Act against England, the British had become more vigorous in harassing American vessels.

Miranda Wainwright watched apprehensively as the oarsboat tied onto the *Larabelle*. "Jeremy, what do they want?" she asked.

Jeremy Wainwright's expression was grim. "Nothing good; you may count on that, dear sister."

The Americans watched silently as the British came aboard. Six British marines formed a guard for two officers. As the British seamen marched smartly up to the small knot of passengers, Miranda slipped her hand into her brother's arm. His fingers covered hers with a reassuring squeeze.

The slighter of the British officers stopped with a hand resting casually on his hip. The marines flanked him with guns to the ready. The officer looked over the *Larabelle*'s passengers with an unpleasant smile. "Good afternoon. A beautiful day, is it not?"

"Damned puppy!" Miranda dared not turn her head to locate that low growl. The passengers about her stirred, relaxing slightly. Someone coughed, hiding laughter.

The officer's lips tightened when he heard the soft chuckles. His chilly eyes searched for the source of the voice.

"What can we do for you?" asked Jeremy, his voice hard. Miranda knew that tone of her brother's and she glanced up at his deeply tanned face. It seemed carved from the hardest oak, giving nothing away.

The officer's mouth relaxed into a patent sneer. He locked his hands behind him and rocked on his heels. "I regret to say this vessel is found to be in violation of the Orders in Council, which forbid trade with France. The vessel is therefore placed under seizure and is to sail to a British port for impoundment," he said.

Stunned silence greeted the officer's pronouncement. Miranda winced as Jeremy's fingers tightened painfully on hers. Then a babble of protest arose. "France! We've not been to France. This is preposterous!" "You can't seize an American ship. This is outrageous!" "Jeremy, can they do this?"

A high quaver rose clear of the loud confusion. "We are on our way to England, young man, not France!" snapped Mrs. Winthrop. Beneath her wide shading bonnet, her eyes sparkled with indignation. She had to tilt up her head to meet the British officer's eyes.

The officer looked down his long nose at the tiny woman. He drawled condescendingly, "So you are, madame."

A broad elderly man shouldered his way to the front. "This ship is a neutral, sir! Parliament's laws mean nothing to us."

The man's deep voice held a growl that the officer recognized as the one that had called him a "damned puppy."

The officer's voice was cold. "This ship will go quietly or suffer the consequences." He nodded out to sea, drawing attention to the ugly snub noses of British cannon. The sight sobered the knot of passengers. Miranda saw the helpless anger in the grim faces around her and in some, fear. As for Jeremy, his stony expression had not changed. Only his eyes betrayed his rage.

The British officer smiled again. Contempt narrowed his eyes as he swept a glance over the passengers. He addressed his subordinate officer over his shoulder. "Mr. Craige, how many hands are we lacking?"

"Two, sir."

"Ah, that was it." The officer's eyes roved over the American sailors, who were bunched loosely against the rail. His voice took on an exaggerated note of surprise. "Mr. Craige, I believe I have discovered deserters from His Royal Majesty's navy! Two, in fact."

"Aye, sir!" Mr. Craige made an abrupt hand movement. The British marines advanced on the American sailors, who had stiffened but continued to stand immobile in front of the threatening British rifles. Two sailors were herded away from the others toward the side where the British had boarded. One of the sailors chanced to meet Miranda's gaze and she was appalled at the fear shining in his eyes. She recognized the seaman, who was really just a boy. Young Ned Simmons had entertained all on board with his merry accordion. A marine nudged him roughly with a musket butt and the sailor stumbled past her.

"No! You cannot do this!" Miranda exclaimed. She hardly felt the warning pressure of Jeremy's hand on hers as she stared straight into the British officer's surprised face. "You have no right to impress our sailors. These men are American citizens!"

There was a murmuring of support among the *Larabelle*'s passengers and a restive movement toward the men holding the American sailors. The British officer flicked his hand in command. Miranda's breath caught as muskets were trained on the passengers. The moment was suspended. Tense fear curdled the air.

The British officer's gaze passed indifferently over Miranda's shocked face to settle on Jeremy, who stood close beside her with her hand still imprisoned in his own. The officer's voice was clipped, meaningful in tone. "Your wife is admirably soft-hearted, but her pity is wasted on these deserters. It is futile to interfere in the King's business." He started to turn but stopped at the sound of Jeremy's voice.

"Captain!"

"Captain William Daggett, at your service, sir," said the officer with exaggerated courtesy.

Jeremy clenched his teeth. "Captain Daggett, to what port will you escort us?"

"To Falmouth, sir. You will not be inconvenienced long, I trust. There is adequate lodging to be had, as well as transport," said Captain Daggett smoothly. He bowed, then turned on his heel and, followed by his subordinate, strode to the side of the ship. After the officers had disembarked, the American seamen were prodded over the side into the waiting oarsboat. Within moments the *Larabelle*'s passengers had the deck once more to themselves. They crowded to the rail to watch the oarsboat pull away. Jeremy and Miranda stood together, as one in their anger and frustration. Miranda's slim fingers were tight on the wooden rail as she watched the forlorn American sailors in the oarsboat grow smaller with the increasing distance. The event had been awful enough, but she was shaking with the realization of what might have happened. She briefly closed her eyes and saw again the ready British rifles.

"Well, lad, a bad ending for your first voyage," said a gruff voice. Miranda turned her head. The elderly man who had openly protested against the British officer's pronouncement stood beside them. His eyes were on the American sailors, who could be seen climbing reluctantly aboard the British vessel. He sighed regretfully. "Aye, a bad ending for those men especially. Nothing to be done, poor devils."

Jeremy, too, stared out over the sea at the swaying British ship. He grasped the rail so tightly that the tendons stood out white on the backs of his hands. "There is nothing to be done now, I grant you. But once in port, we shall see."

The gentleman chuckled at the strong purpose in the younger man's voice. Shrewdly, he measured Jeremy's hard expression. "It will likely be a hopeless cause, lad. But you've a look of determination that I like. Therefore I am with you."

Jeremy turned to eye the gentleman. He knew from the passenger list and the infrequent conversations that he had held with the gentleman that he was an Englishman by name of Edward Billingsley, long retired from trade and now returning to the land of his birth. At his searching look the elderly gentleman chuckled again. "Aye, lad, I know. What can an old man like myself do? But I've influence of a sort. It is yours when we touch land."

Jeremy's face lightened with a dazzling grin. He held out his hand and the two gentlemen shook hands. "I thank you, sir. Any aid that you may give me will indeed be welcome."

Miranda added her own expression of gratitude. "You are most kind, sir. My brother and I truly thank you."

Mr. Billingsley's eyes twinkled at her. "You are a young

lady of backbone, Miss Wainwright. I admire that quality in man or woman."

"My sister's sense of independence has always been a source of pride to me, but I have never been prouder than when she spoke up in behalf of our sailors," said Jeremy. He put his arm around his sister.

"Aye, it was bravely done," said Mr. Billingsley with a nod.

"Perhaps, but my bravery seemed close to bringing disaster upon us all," said Miranda with a shudder.

"Aye; the insolent puppy had the audacity to offer us harm. I shall not let that go unquestioned, I promise you," said Mr. Billingsley, his gaze frosty as he turned his eyes once more toward the sea. Miranda glanced back at the British cutter. It followed the *Larabelle* like a great winged shadow, its prow dashing spray.

Two

The *Larabelle* landed at Falmouth on the rugged Cornish coast. The green harbor was surrounded by hills, but Miranda thought Falmouth itself was old and ugly. Houses crowded the shoreline and their steps were overgrown with seaweed while the tide washed at their foundations. Miranda's opinion was further colored by the outrageous treatment afforded the *Larabelle* upon docking. Customs officials swarmed over the ship to ransack every cabin, spilling out the contents of every barrel and chest and box in their search for contraband. Surplus stores especially liquor, were confiscated.

Jeremy Wainwright could do nothing but stand by while his ship was summarily stripped of everything of value by the Duties officers. Edward Billingsley stood beside him, once even reaching up to squeeze his shoulder in sympathy. "Don't worry, lad. We'll have our day," he said.

The *Larabelle*'s passengers were set ashore and the small band took a subdued leavetaking of one another before separating for their individual journeys. Miranda and her maid took rooms at an inn that looked fairly respectable and then embarked on an exploration of the town. The people in the streets were ruddy-cheeked and well-fed. Many of the men were wearing the uniforms of the volunteer regiments to which they belonged, reminding Miranda that England was a nation at war. As for the women, they wore extremely thin gowns and their shoes clattered on the pavement as they walked. "I've never seen such gowns, Miss Miranda. It is almost enough to make one blush," said Constance Graves. She could not tear her eyes from the shocking sight.

"Indeed it is," said Miranda, equally fascinated by what she saw. She stopped outside a dress shop and exchanged a glance with her companion. As one, the women entered the shop.

Under the guidance of Edward Billingsley, Jeremy set in motion an official protest. His goal was to have the charges of illegal trade dropped and to regain possession of his cargo, as well as to free his two impressed crew members. Jeremy was met with cynicism and indifference; but he learned quickly that it was otherwise with his ally, who was a wily and informed old man. When Mr. Billingsley made known his identity and mentioned those in certain circles with whom he had influence, he was treated with swift deference. Therefore, the protest lodged by the unknown American shipowner Jeremy Wainwright was given unusual priority in high quarters.

Jeremy was soon caught up in the tangle of bureaucracy and he realized that the struggle would take longer than he had anticipated. Though he and Miranda had taken lodgings at the same inn in the quayside town, he rarely saw his sister. He was aware that she was made restless by the enforced inactivity and he was also uneasy that Miranda was alone except for her maid in a strange town. One evening as they sat over a late dinner, he spoke his thoughts aloud. "I believe that it would best suit both of us if you would go on ahead to our cousins. I should not then be anxious over your continued safety and you will have something better to anticipate than another dull day," he said.

"I do not know that I care to leave you behind, Jeremy. Besides, I wish to know the outcome of the whole tedious business the moment that it is resolved. I cannot very well do that while with our cousins," said Miranda. Even as she protested, though, the thought of leaving the dull, ugly portside town held appeal for her.

Jeremy thought he could read her thoughts fairly well and he pressed his advantage. "Come, Miranda, there is the post. I promise that I shall write to you each day and you will be as well informed as though you were still here. The difference will be that you will not be obligated to stare at these same four walls while waiting on me to come in each evening. You cannot convince me that it pleasures you to kick your heels while I am about the business. That is the crux, is it not?"

Miranda laughed and shook her head. "I do not deny that the patient role does not suit my nature. Very well, then. I shall do as you suggest and go to our cousins."

"Good. I shall make travel arrangements for you and Constance in the morning," said Jeremy. He leaned back in his chair with an unconscious sigh. His face settled into tired lines.

"Poor Jeremy. Is it going so badly, then?" asked Miranda sympathetically.

Her brother shook his head. "It is going slowly, rather. However, without Edward's help it would have been an impossible task to even be granted a hearing. But eventually I think we shall bring it off exactly as we hope."

"And with your worrisome sister removed from the scene, you may concentrate more freely on the struggle," said Miranda teasingly.

Jeremy was obliged to laugh. He stretched out his hand

to her and lightly clasped her fingers. "I apologize, Miranda. I see that is how it must have sounded and I did not mean it to. But yes, now I shall not be anxious about you. I'll know that you are safe and being properly entertained at Willowswood."

The following morning Jeremy put Miranda and her maid into a carriage. He had had second thoughts about the wisdom of sending his sister on the journey without himself for escort, for he had been hearing for days of brooding unrest in the countryside due to the long economic depression, and there were disturbing stories of rioting among the unemployed. But at breakfast when he had voiced his concerns, Miranda pooh-poohed him. "Really, Jeremy, you swing from one point of the compass to the other. I assure you that I am now determined to leave this damp place and nothing you say shall stay me," she said, drawing on her gloves.

"You are right, of course. As a shipowner I should demonstrate more firmness of purpose, should I not?" said Jeremy, smiling.

He had been somewhat cheered by his sister's lack of hesitation. Miranda could be trusted to keep a cool head on her shoulders. But when he shut the door to the carriage he left his hands on the window edge, reluctant to say goodbye now that the moment had come.

Miranda looked down at her brother's frown. "I will be fine, Jeremy."

"I do dislike your traveling alone, Miranda. I wish there was someone we knew to act as an escort," he said.

"What would I do with an escort?" asked Miranda scornfully. "I am hardly one of those helpless ladies who swoons at the least excuse, Jeremy. Between us, Constance and I shall be able to handle whatever may arise."

He laughed, acknowledging that it was probably true. "I am sorry that I cannot accompany you myself. But I shall not know anything for certain for several days yet. In the meantime, we must do all that we can for Ned Simmons and the other seaman. Edward is earwigging every influential person he knows." Jeremy's eyes turned suddenly cold and his jaw hardened. "As for the cutter's commanding officer, our good Captain Daggett, that is another matter that I wish to address."

Miranda squeezed his fingers. "We will win, Jeremy. I know it in my heart. I shall tell our cousins of our misfortune. I should think that they might know someone with influence as well. I may yet be able to add a persuasive voice to the fight."

Jeremy nodded. He suddenly grinned. "I know that you found it difficult not to be able to help. Perhaps at Willowswood you will find a way to do just that."

Miranda smiled back at her brother. "We are from a determined family, Jeremy. Could I do anything less?" Impulsively, she reached over to kiss his lean, browned cheek. "Good-bye and good hunting, brother!"

Jeremy stepped back from the carriage, signaling the driver. A whip cracked and the chaise jerked forward. He put his hand to his mouth and called, "Miranda, just think before you leap, will you?"

Miranda wrinkled her nose and waved. She knew he was remembering her near tragic impetuosity on board the *Larabelle*. "I will, Jeremy!" The carriage got up speed, its iron tires clattering over the damp cobbles. Jeremy watched the chaise until it had disappeared.

Three

As Miranda traveled through open moorlands she was awed by the beauty of hills unfolding behind hills, clothed in brown and green, in an endless undulating line. The carriage passed farms and villages that were remarkably neat and in good order and the inns that she and Constance rested at were comfortable and clean, staffed by courteous and obliging servants.

The stone walls and fields of Cornwall eventually gave way to the high hedges and deep rich soil of Devon. The country cottages were thatched in varying shades, ranging from the gold of ripe wheat, gray, taupe, russet, and rich brown, to the older, weatherbeaten, and smoke-stained roofs of darkest brown. Miranda knew from her cousin's letters that Willowswood was located outside one of these small villages. Through the months Anne's correspondence had contained several lively descriptions of the quiet Devon district in which she lived, so that as the carriage neared its destination Miranda began to recognize landmarks. She pointed out the window. "There is Willoughby Hall, Constance. My cousin described it perfectly," she said. She smiled as she recalled all that Anne had brought to such vivid life with her pen.

Three respectable manor houses distinguished the outer

reaches of the village, Anne had written. The first, Willoughby Hall, stood about two miles before the village, stood. The Hall had once been the site of many entertainments but now rarely saw visitors since the last scion of the house was a reclusive gentleman who preferred puttering in his garden among his rosebeds and his dove cote.

It was not that Mr. Willoughby rejected the society of his fellows; if someone called to extend an invitation, he usually accepted in a vague sort of way. But the moment that his visitor was out of sight, he promptly forgot the point of their conversation. However, there was always the hope among his more persistent neighbors that Mr. Willoughby would take the notion, as he occasionally did, to attend the various amusements in the neighborhood. After all, Mr. Willoughby was a young man, not above thirty in any case, and judged to be fairly well-favored in countenance and build. He was also the owner of Willoughby Hall, a proud house established during good Queen Bess's reign, and that must be counted for something by the parents of marriageable daughters.

The village was typical of those that Miranda and Constance had seen during their journey. The carriage rattled over the cobbles in the streets and quickly left it behind.

The second manor house on the outer bounds of the village was Stonehollow, inhabited by Mr. Bertram Burton and his incredibly beautiful sister, Mary Alice. Mr. Burton's friends and acquaintances could not exclaim enough over Miss Burton's violet eyes, her red rosebud mouth, and her perfectly endowed figure; but they received only an indifferent shrug and cynical laugh from Mr. Burton. Better than anyone, he knew that his sister's uncommon beauty clothed a nature both restless and capricious. He had ducked too many hurled missiles and been the target of too many tirades to subscribe graciously to his cronies' reverent opinions.

Nevertheless, however much he decried his sister's temper, Mr. Burton did harbor some sympathy for her. She knew herself to be wasted on the gentlemen in the neighborhood and looked higher for her place in life. And well she might, had declared Mr. Burton more than once. Mary Alice Burton was the prettiest piece the county had ever seen. Given the right entrées she could easily snare herself an earl or even a duke. But titles of that sort were not likely to turn up in such a sleepy district.

As for Miss Burton, she ruled what was offered with a high hand. As far back as she could remember, gentlemen young and old had catered to her every whim, spoiling her and encouraging her to rely on her sweet beauty to gain whatever she desired. As a consequence, at the age of nineteen Miss Burton was a spoiled, haughty young lady, bestowing her smiles and frowns with capricious want of thought or compassion. She was inevitably surrounded by a court of admirers and if she felt the lack of female friends and companionship, none could have told it by her devastating progress through the district's society. Miss Burton easily overshadowed her peers and when her violet eyes beckoned, the other young ladies despaired of retaining their own admirers' fickle interest.

Miranda looked for the squire's house, but it was too closely hidden by trees for her to catch sight of it. But her greater curiosity in Willowswood soon overran this disappointment. She knew from Anne's letters that the squire was the Townsends' nearest neighbor and she pressed close to the window for her first glimpse of Willowswood.

Anne and her husband had come to Willowswood but ten months previously; having inherited the property from an eccentric relative. Anne had said nothing much was known of the redoubtable old woman to whom Willowswood had belonged except that she was a lady born who detested society of any sort. Miss Claridge had steadfastly refused every invitation extended to her by her neighbors. One of her more stout-minded neighbors had once dared to call on her and had been sent packing. Upon being questioned by the curious, he had aptly described Miss Claridge as "a crank, very starchy, and decided in her opinions." When the good lady died there was much speculation about what would be done with Willowswood and by whom. Some thought the estate would simply go to rack and ruin; others wondered if Miss Claridge could possibly have left the house to an animal society, for it was known that she had a fondness for cats. Eventually it was learned with astonishment that Miss Claridge had a distant relative, a young army officer by name of Richard Townsend.

When the Townsends took possession of Willowswood the entire neighborhood had held back to see if they were anything like Miss Claridge. But Richard and Anne Townsend were discovered to be a delightful couple and their young son was variously described as "a mischievous young devil," "quite intelligent, though perhaps a bit too indulged," and "a regular right-un."

Anne had confided in her correspondence that she had been appalled by her first tour of Willowswood. Miss Claridge had kept most of the proud one-hundred-year-old house closed up with only a minimal staff, since she did not entertain. As a result, the estate was somewhat tumbledown and in need of much improvement. Richard had an independence that could carry the expense of the house, but it was not great enough to allow him to make over the house all at once. But Anne had assured Miranda that when she did visit them at Willowswood she would find all the comforts of home, for though neither Anne nor Richard were familiar with the running of a large house and grounds, they were determined to make of Willowswood a veritable showplace.

It was late afternoon when the chaise drove up the winding drive to Willowswood. Miranda could scarcely contain her excitement and curiosity. She had not seen Anne since they were both girls and though the cousins had remained close through the years by letter, it was vastly different to be able at last to meet Anne's husband and her small son. "I don't know what I shall say, Constance," she exclaimed as she caught sight of the pleasant gray mansion ahead. Willowswood was a three-story manor house graced on either end by a tall chimney. Vines clung to the sides of the house and large oaks shaded the west windows. A half circle of steps rose welcomingly to the wide door.

"Oh, I shouldn't worry my head over that. I have never known you to be without a proper word or two," said the maid dryly. Her tart observation earned her a glance of outrage from her mistress and she chuckled.

The chaise drew up at the steps. The driver opened the carriage door and let down the iron step. Miranda accepted the man's hand in descending and then stood motionless on the gravel to look up at the house. There was no movement at the windows, nor did the door open at the arrival of the chaise. She frowned slightly. The maid also was struck by the odd lack of activity. "Perhaps we should ring the bell, Miss Miranda," she suggested.

"Of course." Miranda and her companion climbed the stone steps and Miranda firmly pulled on the bell. She could hear its echoes within and nodded with satisfaction. She addressed the chaise's driver. "Pray set down our trunks and bring them in," she said. The man nodded, touching his cap in deference. Miranda turned again to the door, only to wait futilely for it to open. She and Constance looked at one another, their eyes reflecting the same question. Miranda shook her head. "Nonsense, they cannot have left. We were expected." She took hold of the brass handle, not actually expecting it to turn. She was therefore surprised when the door eased open on well-oiled hinges. For a moment she stood indecisive. Then she shrugged slightly and pushed the door wide.

"Do you think we ought?" asked the maid doubtfully.

"Come, Constance. It is not as though we are breaking into the house. The door is unlocked and we are expected guests," said Miranda, as much to reassure herself as her companion. She stepped inside, followed a moment later by the reluctant maid. The women stood in a wide pleasant hall. A staircase rose on the right hand, doubling back on itself to form a partial balcony of the upper hall. Several closed doors marched down either side of the entrance hall. The walls were covered with a charming paper of small white roses and mirrors that reflected sunlight dancing with dust motes across the marble floor. But the arrangement of blooms in the bowl on the occasional table had long since withered and dropped petals to the surface of the table and the floor. A thin coating of dust covered the straight-backed chairs that were set about for visitors. There was utter quiet.

Four

"I do not care for the look of it, Miss Miranda," said Constance firmly.

"Nor I," admitted Miranda. She heard a step behind her and turned. The burdened chaise driver had paused in the doorway to look about him. "Pray leave the baggage here. We shall go directly to find someone to tell us where it is to go," said Miranda.

"I needs to be getting to the inn in the village for me next fare, ma'am," said the man, setting down the load of baggage.

"Yes, I understand. We shall not be long, I trust," said Miranda. She gestured to Constance and they walked down the hall, opening doors as they went. In room after room the curtains over the tall windows were drawn, creating an impression of gloomy abandonment. Some of the rooms were surprisingly untidy. Ashes that had been left in the fireplace grates had spilled out onto the floor and an occasional window had been left open to allow debris and rain to be blown inside. Gray cobwebs festooned every corner.

Miranda felt more and more dismayed. It was hardly the welcome that she had expected. It appeared that she and Constance had come to an empty house.

"If there is someone here, Miss Miranda, we shall find

signs in the kitchen," said Constance. Her mistress nodded and together they went in search of the kitchen.

Most of the inner regions of the house showed signs of the same neglect they'd seen in the rooms off the entrance hall. When they did find the kitchen they were almost startled to find it inhabited. They paused in the doorway, silent with their surprise.

The elderly woman who worked at the stove did not at first notice that she was being observed. She stirred a large pot from which savory steam arose and tossed in a handful of scallions. Her wrinkled face was red from the heat; a strand of her gray hair had fallen out of its pin and she brushed it up impatiently. Her expression was tired, resigned. She turned to the table to pick up a rack on which aired fresh loaves of bread and chanced then to see her audience. She started violently and the bread jumped out of her hands to the table and floor. She stood with one hand pressed on her ample breast and exclaimed, "Lor'!"

Miranda entered the kitchen. "I beg pardon! We did not mean to frighten you. I am Miss Miranda Wainwright and this is my companion and maid, Mrs. Constance Graves." Miranda bent to retrieve a loaf of the bread. She sniffed appreciatively before setting it onto the plank table. With a friendly smile, she said, "How good fresh-baked bread smells. I take it that you are Mrs. Townsend's cook?"

The plump woman had regained her color and the look of fright faded from her eyes. She reached up to tuck the rebellious lock of hair firmly into its pin. "Aye, I am Mrs. Crumpet. I was that surprised to see you, miss. We—that is Mr. Crumpet and I—we had forgotten that you would be coming, but now that you have it might be the very thing. Mr. Crumpet wrote his lordship this two weeks past but never a word have we heard, and there be the mistress sick

27

in her bed and the boy running wild and us with no help—"
Tears started to the cook's faded blue eyes and she had re-
course to her apron. She wiped her cheeks quickly and gave
a watery sniff. "Forgive me, miss, but it has been a bit of a
burden as you may imagine."

Constance had quietly picked up the rest of the bread
and placed it neatly on the table. While the cook regained
control of herself, she exchanged bewildered glances with
her mistress. Miranda was alarmed by the cook's partial
revelations. "But what has happened? Where is Richard?
Surely if Anne is fallen ill, he would not leave! And what is
this about having no help? There must be others responsible for tending the house, surely!" said Miranda.

The cook shook her head. "When the mistress was
struck down with her illness, the others deserted her for fear
of the pox. Of those in the house, only myself and Mr.
Crumpet, who is the butler, stayed. And Master Richard—"

"Pox!" Miranda could not keep the mingled dismay and
fear out of her voice, and she knew that her expression must
mirror the same horror as was in Constance's face.

"No, no, miss! It is as I tried to tell those fools, who
would not stay to listen. The mistress had the chicken pox,
not the dreaded small pox. But there was true pox in the
countryside hereabouts not long ago and the fear was that it
had come again. And seeing as how the houseservants were
but a gaggle of silly geese who had no loyalty to a new mistress and master, they all left us without a thought of mercy
in their hearts," said Mrs. Crumpet bitterly.

"Then my cousin is lying somewhere in the house unat-
tended except for you and Mr. Crumpet? But where are
Richard and the boy?" asked Miranda sharply.

"Begging your pardon, miss, but Master Richard was
called back to the Army more than two months since. Mr.

Crumpet wrote him, too, but there is that fierce of fighting and running about on the Continent that Mr. Crumpet fears the letter went astray." The cook paused and shook her head. "As for the boy, Mr. Crumpet is looking about for him now. The little one is that wild and headstrong and lonely, what with his father being gone and his mother down in bed and no one to watch him. It is not enough, but Mr. Crumpet and I do our best."

"I am certain that you do. And I thank you most heartily for it. Well, Constance! It appears that we have found employment," said Miranda with an attempt at lightness.

"Indeed we have, Miss Miranda," said Constance with a slight smile. She removed her bonnet and her gloves to place them on an out-of-the-way chair. "I shall aid Mrs. Crumpet with the tea and perhaps a tray for Mrs. Townsend would not be amiss."

"An excellent thought, Constance. I shall wish to see my cousin as soon as possible. In the meantime, I suppose I should have our driver carry up our bags and then pay him off. We shall not be returning to the village as I had earlier half-suspected might be necessary from the state of the house," said Miranda. She turned to the cook, who was listening with every appearance of rising hope. "Mrs. Crumpet, if you would show me to the rooms most suitable for my companion and myself I would be most grateful. I should also like to see Mrs. Townsend."

"Of course, miss! I would be most happy to, I am sure!" said Mrs. Crumpet, and with hardly a glance for the stranger who was making herself familiar with her kitchen, she led Miranda back through the house.

The bedrooms that Mrs. Crumpet showed her into were covered in dust covers just as many of the rooms downstairs were. In the room that was to be Miranda's, Mrs. Crumpet crossed to the windows and vigorously pulled on the curtain ropes. The drapes flew open and sunlight streamed into the bedroom. "It will look better once I have them covers off, miss," she said, and set to with a will.

"Thank you, Mrs. Crumpet. I shall ask the driver to bring up our trunks now," said Miranda, who had disposed of her bonnet, gloves, and pelisse on the canopied bed. Before she laid her reticule beside her other belongings, she removed her purse and slipped it into her pocket so that she could pay off the driver.

The chaise driver was not best pleased to learn that he was expected to carry the heavy trunks upstairs. When he had set down the baggage in the middle of the bedroom, he looked around with a judicial gaze. "I ain't never seen such a house. No one about and everything covered like it was a morgue," he declared.

"We haven't time for your insults, my good man, so be gone with you," said Mrs. Crumpet, affronted by the man's gall. She whisked the last cover from the dresser and energetically bundled it up.

Miranda led the grumbling driver back downstairs and handed him the fare that she owed as well as a few extra pounds. When he saw the amount, his dour expression lightened. He touched his cap in deference. "I thanks you very well, ma'am."

Miranda shut the door and stood against it a moment in thought. She could yet scarcely believe the circumstances that she had found at Willowswood. With paying off the chaise, she had burned her bridges behind her. She was here for good and all. It was time to see her cousin and discover just how bad the situation truly was. Her imagination had already conjured up a grim picture. But it was not in her nature to quail in the face of adversity. Miranda went back upstairs to find Mrs. Crumpet and have the good woman show her to her cousin's rooms.

Anne Townsend appeared very fragile in the great canopied bed. Her fair hair spread damply over the down pillow. Her face was pale and her eyes were deep pools of blue underscored by dark shadows that testified to her sleeplessness. She looked faintly puzzled when she noticed Miranda standing behind Mrs. Crumpet. "Who is it, Mrs. Crumpet?" she asked, her voice faint.

"Anne," said Miranda, approaching the bed.

Her cousin's face registered happy astonishment. "Miranda! I can scarcely believe my eyes, but it must be you. You are much prettier than the cameo that you once sent to me."

Miranda laughed and took the slender hand that her cousin held out to her. "Yes, it is I. I am only sorry that I have come at such a miserable time. Mrs. Crumpet tells me that you have had the chicken pox."

Anne grimaced. She turned her head to cough hollowly behind her hand. "Such a childish disease to catch! I am well over it now. But I am still confined to my bed because I contracted pneumonia on top of it all. The excellent physician in the village informed me in his ponderous fashion that I was too weak to fight off the new infection. So here I am, still abed."

Miranda seated herself in the chair beside the bed. "Anne, if it does not tire you overmuch, I should like to have tea with you here. There is so much I wish to say."

"And I also! As for tiring me, your very presence is a breath of fresh air. I have been pitying myself a bit, you see. Mrs. Crumpet, if you will be so good as to arrange for our tea," said Anne, speaking in stronger accents than she had before.

"Aye, madame. The tea will be brought directly," said Mrs. Crumpet, beaming to see her mistress so much livelier. She turned to leave the room, only to be stopped by her mistress's query concerning the whereabouts of her son. Mrs. Crumpet frowned slightly. "Mr. Crumpet be looking for him now, madame. He has gone down to the wood again, I am sure."

"Thank you, Mrs. Crumpet. I know that you and Mr. Crumpet do your best," said Anne. As the door closed softly, she sighed and smiled over at Miranda. "I fret constantly over Robert. As you will soon discover, my son is a graceless scamp with a will of his own. Robert has never taken direction easily, but once I fell ill and the servants left, there was no one at all to curb him. I wish that Richard had not been called away so soon. There would then have been no question of our son's running wild or of the servants' desertion."

"Forgive me, Anne, but it strikes me as peculiar that every servant in the place chose to leave. Surely there were a few level heads among them!" said Miranda.

"There were precious few. Besides Mrs. Crumpet and her husband, who were in our service before we took possession of Willowswood ten months ago. Miss Claridge's old gardener and groom have also remained, though I think they stayed more because Willowswood was their home than for any other reason. Besides them, Miss Claridge had only her personal maid and a cook, and they both retired upon their mistress's death. So the household staff was newly appointed and had not yet learned loyalty to Richard and me," said Anne, coughing again. "But I do not blame the servants for panicking, Miranda. It was such a short time ago that pox passed through the countryside."

"I see." Miranda's lips tightened slightly. She did not

know if she could have been so magnanimous in the same situation. "But the doctor has been to see you. Surely he must have reassured the ignorant that Willowswood is not tainted by pox."

"I have thought on it and I think that perhaps the servants have not returned because they are ashamed," said Anne.

"Your household sounds a group of morons," said Miranda roundly. Her cousin laughed weakly, bringing on an extended bout of coughing. At this point, Mrs. Crumpet returned bearing a tea tray, and Miranda rose to assist her in moving an occasional table nearer the bed. Then she sat down and began to pour out the steaming tea.

"Mr. Crumpet has returned with Master Robert, madame. They are belowstairs now having their tea with Miss Wainwright's maid," said Mrs. Crumpet.

Anne nodded her thanks and the woman left the two cousins alone once more. Miranda helped arrange Anne's pillows so that she could sit up comfortably and then handed her a cup of tea. "I can see that you have not been sleeping well, Anne. I shall try to discover if there are any herbs in the medicinal cabinet or the garden that I can make into a soothing tea for you. In the meantime, I wish you to eat at least one of these biscuits. You appear sadly wasted," said Miranda.

"So Mrs. Crumpet has scolded me for more than once. But there is very little that appeals," said Anne, accepting a biscuit with reluctance.

"Never you mind about what appeals. Mrs. Crumpet was right to scold and I shall add my voice to hers. You must eat to regain your strength again, cousin, and I intend to see to it that you do so," said Miranda.

Anne laughed up at her. "I see that you are a tyrant,

cousin. I warn you, when I am up and about again I shall not allow you to easily browbeat me so you should take every advantage now."

"Fair enough. I hope that you do not take me amiss, Anne, but I think that there is much about the house that I and my maid, Constance Graves, can turn our hands to. It appalls me to see the place so neglected," said Miranda, thinking of the unlocked front door and the utter gloom of the shrouded rooms.

"I am not at all offended, Miranda. I feel already such familiarity between us that I can leave it in your hands without a pang. But it would ease my mind far more to know that you were keeping an eye on Robert for me. He is a dear, sweet little boy really," said Anne.

"Of course I shall, Anne. You may rest easy. Between myself and Constance, who comes of a large family and may be expected to understand small children, I am certain that we can redirect Robert's energies," said Miranda.

Anne touched her cousin's arm. "Thank you, Miranda. I am so pleased that you have come. I am only contrite that I cannot offer you the entertainment that you deserve. When I am fully recovered we shall have a much nicer visit, I promise you," she said.

"Pray do not give it a thought. I do not, you know. Now, I think it would be best if I clear away this tray and allow you to rest a little while. I shall return later this evening," said Miranda, suiting action to words.

Five

When Miranda appeared, Mrs. Crumpet hurried to take the tray from her and Miranda turned her attention to the other occupants of the kitchen. Mr. Crumpet was a tall, stooped man who perpetually wore a sad expression that was accentuated by his drooping brown eyes and long nose. The boy sat at the plank table eating his bread and jam with quick, nervous bites. His foot swung back and forth, monotonously kicking the table leg at each swing. His clothes were crumpled as though he had not bothered to change them from the day before and a ring of dirt could be seen around his young neck where his wrinkled collar gaped.

Miranda looked keenly at the boy's face, which appeared somewhat cleaner than the rest of him, undoubtedly due to Mrs. Crumpet's insistence on a scrubbing. Her small cousin appeared intelligent enough, she thought. His eyes expressed interest in all that went on about him and he met Miranda's gaze steadily but with wary curiosity. Miranda judged him to be about seven years old.

Miranda glanced at Constance, who smiled slightly. Taking heart from this sign of encouragement, Miranda said, "You must be Robert. I am Miss Miranda Wainwright, your mother's cousin. I hope that we shall learn to be good friends."

"How do I know that you are Mama's cousin? You may be a gypsy in disguise," said Robert through the crumbs in his mouth.

"Master Robert, you will not speak in such a fashion." After delivering his warning, which hardly seemed to have been effective, Mr. Crumpet turned to Miranda. "Forgive the boy, miss. He has run wild these last weeks without a hand to guide him. He was not so pert before Mrs. Townsend was taken so ill."

Miranda smiled at the butler. "You are Mr. Crumpet, of course. I am most happy to make your acquaintance. I understand that you are the butler at Willowswood."

Mr. Crumpet was startled by the lady's unaffected friendliness. "Aye, miss. The master and the mistress were good enough to bring me and Mrs. Crumpet to Willowswood when the house became theirs. It was quite a promotion in duties for myself."

"Yes, I can well imagine. And especially in the last few weeks," said Miranda dryly, with a glance toward the boy. Mr. Crumpet could not suppress a heartfelt sigh. Miranda decided it was time to set him at ease on his future responsibilities. "Mr. Crumpet, I have spoken to my cousin concerning the odd situation here at Willowswood and she has agreed that I might institute a few changes. First of all, Mrs. Graves and I shall shoulder some of the responsibility for Robert. I imagine that will enable you to go about your regular duties with a bit more freedom. Also, there was some mention of a gardener and a groom still being about the place. I should like to meet them, with the thought that they might also be trusted to watch over our adventurous young man whenever he is out of doors."

"Aye, miss." Mr. Crumpet began to look decidedly more cheerful.

But the same could not be said for the young man in question. Robert's expression clouded ominously. "I'll not be hedged about by a gaggle of women and servants," he announced with an arrogance that would have been comical if it had not been so irritating.

Miranda stared sternly at the boy. "It is not for you to decide, young man. Your mother has made the decision and it is I who will enforce it. We shall begin directly as we mean to go on. I see that you have finished tea. Very well. The first order of business shall be a bath. I find you appallingly filthy for a civilized young man. Constance, I place you in charge of the proceedings. Pray feel free to call upon Mrs. Crumpet and the gardener if you deem it necessary."

"It will be my pleasure, Miss Miranda," said Constance, glancing at the boy with a smile. The boy cast a swift glance about him, then bolted up from the table to make a beeline for the doorway. But he was not swift enough to elude Constance, who had been alert for just such a move. She held on to the squirming, yelling boy with the ease of long practice. "You remind me very much of my youngest brother, young sir. He was a fractious brother until he learned a few manners. Mrs. Crumpet, if you please, I should like some water heated while I skin this young person of his clothing."

"I would be most happy to oblige," said Mrs. Crumpet, a note of satisfaction in her voice. Master Robert had been a constant trial to herself and Mr. Crumpet. It was only proper that he should have his just desserts. She put on a kettle of water over the fire. Then she bustled off with Mrs. Graves and her struggling charge to the nursery to pull out the brass tub.

Miranda turned to the butler with a smile. "I think that we may safely leave Master Robert in Constance's capable hands, Crumpet. If you would be so good to act as my guide, I should like to see the house in its entirety so that I might judge what matters need to be addressed next."

"Certainly, Miss Wainwright," said Mr. Crumpet, a note of respect in his voice. He led her out of the kitchen on an extended tour of the house.

It was worse than Miranda had suspected from the quick glance she had given the shrouded rooms when she and Constance had first arrived. The house suffered badly from neglect. Windows were streaked with dirt. The rooms needed dusting and the covers removed. Linens upstairs and downstairs needed to be aired. The furniture and banisters were dulled by old beeswax. The marble floor in the hall required scrubbing. Upstairs, the beds needed to be changed and aired and ashes needed to be cleaned out of fireplace grates. In many areas it was clear that the servant had left hurriedly, not bothering to neatly fold the linens or gather the wash or finish polishing the silver.

As Miranda and the butler progressed through the house, Crumpet became increasingly apologetic, as though he alone was responsible for the slovenliness that was apparent everywhere. "I think that you and Mrs. Crumpet have done what was most important by taking care of Mrs. Townsend and the boy," said Miranda reassuringly. But privately her heart sank at the task she had set for herself. She had expected a mess, but what she saw called out for a small army if the house was to be brought back to the state that it deserved.

Miranda was appalled in particular at the damage that more than one rain had done to a rear gallery. A window had been left open and water and wind had contributed debris. Cobwebs hung thick and gray with dust in the musty room. At one corner the roof overhead was rotted and there was water damage on the walls and floor. It was obvious that the care that had until recently been given the front part of the house had never found its way here. Surely such chaos had not happened in the short month and a half that Anne had been ill, thought Miranda in dismay.

The butler seemed to read her expression. "The house was in a state of great disrepair when we—that is, the family—first arrived, ma'am. Miss Claridge kept all but her own apartments shut up and had only a maid and cook to serve her. Quite eccentric, if I may say so."

"So she let the house go to rack and ruin," said Miranda, staring about her with sick regret.

"Aye, miss. Mr. Townsend set to work directly to make the front section livable, and with remarkable result if I may say so. He means to begin restoring this part of the house when he returns from the Continent," said Crumpet.

Miranda sent a last comprehensive glance about the sad state of the gallery. "I think that we shall concentrate on the refurbished wing, Mr. Crumpet, and leave Mr. Townsend's project for his attention," she said. The butler agreed that would probably be best and they made their way back to the other end of the house.

When they had reached the kitchen once more, Miranda requested that Mrs. Crumpet fill her in on the needs of that domain. The good lady proceeded to do just that, listing everything from mutton and poultry to soap. "For I have no need to tell you, Miss Miranda, that we have not had the time to go into the village to do the shopping in ever so long. And we are not likely to get a delivery out of the blue when there are them who still thinks the mistress is a victim of the pox and speculating that we are all dead," said Mrs. Crumpet.

"I understand completely. The shopping must be the first order of business then, Mrs. Crumpet. Does Mrs.

Townsend advance you a household fund for the purpose?" asked Miranda.

"Aye, ma'am. But I have hesitated to ask the mistress for it since she has been so ill. I do have a good bit left from last month, seeing as how I did not get out for everything before the mistress first took ill and those worthless beings made off in hopes of saving their own skins," said the cook.

"May I suggest, then, that you and Constance make a trip to the village tomorrow afternoon for whatever items that you feel we are most in need of. Constance will wish to familiarize herself with the shops, I am sure, and with your guidance she will soon learn which to patronize. And I wish you to take Master Robert with you. It will be good for everyone to see that neither you nor Master Robert have been struck down with illness," said Miranda. She paused a moment. "Do I dare to ask where the boy is now?"

Mrs. Crumpet allowed herself a smile. "Mrs. Graves had Master Robert well in hand the last I saw of them. Master Robert was engaged in bringing order to his belongings abovestairs."

Miranda's eyes began to dance. "How singularly appropriate. I really must congratulate Constance on her fortitude."

"Aye, miss," said Mrs. Crumpet, her smile broadening.

"What time shall you wish to serve dinner, Mrs. Crumpet?" asked Miranda.

Mrs. Crumpet pursed her mouth, calculating. "I should think that it must be set back at least an half hour. I have yet the vegetables and the pie to do. It will be seven of the clock at least, Miss Wainwright."

Miranda nodded. "That will do nicely." Miranda turned to address the butler, who had stood silently listening to the exchange. "Crumpet, I shall need to call upon you to do more than your fair share of duties yet awhile. The house calls out for attention. If you would be so good as to address those matters usually best handled by yourself or a footman, I would be most grateful. Meanwhile, Mrs. Graves and I shall concentrate on bringing a bit of order to the rooms and alternate the care of the boy between us."

"Aye, Miss Wainwright," said Crumpet.

Miranda took a breath. "I cannot think of anything else at the moment. I shall be happy for any suggestions that may occur to either of you. After all, I am a stranger at Willowswood and hardly familiar with the way things should be done."

"I am only happy that you have come, Miss Wainwright. Mrs. Townsend, poor lady, must already rest easier knowing that you mean to handle the house for her," said Mrs. Crumpet.

"Thank you, Mrs. Crumpet." Miranda smiled at the couple and left the kitchen. She made her way upstairs to her bedroom, where she proceeded to unpack her belongings and to change her travel dress for a plain stuff gown.

It had already grown dark since Miranda and Crumpet had finished touring the house and she laid aside her immediate inclination to inspect the gardens. She would save that treat for the morning.

Miranda had noticed earlier that the dining room was in a better state than many of the other rooms. As she made her way downstairs she thought that she could probably make the dining room presentable in time for the evening meal. With a light heart she set herself to dealing with the general disarray. She removed the dust covers and sheets shrouding the long walnut table and high-backed chairs. With zeal and a feather duster she swept away the film that had gathered on the sideboard and its accoutrements, straightening as she went.

When she had finished she rang the bell rope to summon Crumpet, who surveyed the dining room with obvious astonishment. Miranda laughed at his expression. "I wish to have dinner served in here tonight, if you please, Crumpet. Master Robert and Constance will join me."

"Aye, Miss Wainwright. I shall inform Mrs. Crumpet," said the butler, permitting himself a smile. It did his spirits good to see this small evidence that the fortune of Willowswood was on the mend.

Miranda ran lightly upstairs to change and to inform Constance of the treat in store for them.

Dinner was not a protracted event. The boy was nodding toward the end of the meal and Miranda waved aside Crumpet's offer of coffee. "Thank you, but no. I daresay we are all of us exhausted this evening, what with all the unexpected happenings of the day. I myself am contemplating an early bedtime."

"And I also, Miss Miranda," said Constance. She glanced down at the snoring boy. "As for the young gentleman, I do not think we shall hear much objection."

Miranda laughed, her eyes warm in expression as she gazed at her small cousin. "Indeed, Constance. Wake him and I shall help you get him safely into bed." As she left the dining room, Miranda bade Crumpet a good night, which he returned with a bow. She and Constance left the dining room with Robert staggering between them.

Crumpet proceeded to clear the table and snuff the candles. He was vastly content. Order had once more come to Willowswood.

Six

The morning began early for Miranda. She took charge of Robert directly after breakfast to enable Constance to undertake some of the household duties with Mrs. Crumpet. Though Robert seemed willing enough to go with her, Miranda could easily measure the defiance in the boy's eyes. She decided her best course would be to enlist his help in familiarizing herself with the environs of Willowswood.

She and Robert spent the entire morning out of doors, which seemed to defuse the boy's latent anger. They inspected the stables, where Miranda met the laconic groom and learned that there were two horses broken to harness as well as a mount for riding. The horses were restless, suffering from lack of proper exercise. With the groom's qualified approval, Miranda suggested to Robert that he might like to become something of an apprentice trainer under the groom's supervision and exercise the horses on a daily basis.

The boy's eyes lit up. "Oh, may I indeed?"

Miranda nodded gravely. "Mind now, you are to listen to Jenkins. He knows just how to get along with horses and probably can show you all sorts of tricks," she said. The groom gruffly confirmed this and Robert promised quickly that he would be a model apprentice. It was agreed that he would begin his apprenticeship that very afternoon. And that ought to direct his energies for at least part of each day, thought Miranda with satisfaction.

When she and Robert left the stables, the boy was skipping with excitement. Miranda smiled down into his glowing eyes and listened to his eager tumbled words. It was difficult to believe that this was the same boy who had so dragged his feet when he learned that he was to be in her company that morning. She thought that she could learn to like this small cousin of hers well whenever he was in so bright a mood.

Robert guided her next to the gardens. Miranda was amazed and delighted to discover no hint of the awful neglect that afflicted the house. The ordered beds of roses, pinks, lavender, violets, and other familiar flowering plants considerably lifted her spirits.

The old gnarled gardener proved to be a sardonic, stubborn individual who cared for little else outside his own domain. He was occupied in trimming back the box hedges and had little inclination to even acknowledge his visitors' presence. He accepted Miranda's compliments on the care he lavished on the garden with a snort. "Miss Claridge was always one to insist on order," he said shortly. The only time he paused in his task was to point out the herb garden when Miranda expressed an interest.

"What a fusty old gaffer," said Robert judiciously. Miranda had to agree with him, but she was willing also to give the gardener his due. As she and Robert made their way in the direction of the herb garden, she had begun to realize from the curve of the carefully tended walkways and the layout of the flowers and shrubbery that they traversed an old-fashioned knot garden.

The herb garden was also set out in a knot but not in so intricate a design. Miranda soon discovered several old friends among the herbs. The medicinal herbs were separated from those with culinary uses. She showed Robert how to crush a leaf between his fingers or to brush his hands over the camomile, sage, rosemary, and various other herbs to release their heady scents. His face expressed open astonishment and pleasure. "I thought it was only flowers that smelled good," he exclaimed. Eagerly he plunged his hands again into the bright green mints. Miranda laughed at him and ruffled his dark hair.

By luncheon time she had the satisfaction of knowing that she had firmly established the foundation for friendship with the boy. However, her gratification was somewhat impaired when she was reminded by Mrs. Crumpet of the overdue shopping expedition and Robert learned that he was to go along.

"I shan't! I am to ride horses," he said willfully.

"When you return from the village you may go to the stables and spend as much time as you like," said Miranda. She won the ensuing contest of wills, but the victory was hollow when she saw that the happy light in Robert's eyes had died and was replaced by his former belligerent expression. But she did not retreat from her position and the boy was taken off by Constance to be made ready for the trip.

Miranda paid a visit to Anne, only to find her tired after an indifferent morning. Anne hid another of several yawns with an apologetic glance. "I am so sorry, Miranda. I cannot seem to help myself," she said.

"Pray do not regard it. You will do better for an afternoon nap instead of listening to me rattling on," said Miranda, smiling.

"Thank you, Miranda," said Anne gratefully.

When Miranda returned downstairs she found Constance, Mrs. Crumpet and Robert preparing to step out the door for their shopping expedition. Constance had a firm grasp on Roberts who stood beside her with a mutinous expression. Miranda glanced thoughtfully at the rebellious set of the boy's firm chin and the martial light in his eyes, then addressed her companion. "Constance, pray look about the village for a sweet shop, won't you? Perhaps Robert would like a treat; that is, if you deem that his behavior warrants it."

The boy stared up at her, suspicion and desire warring in his face. Miranda coolly returned his gaze. "I imagine that you can act the gentleman when you wish," she said.

"Of course I can," said Robert, puffing out his chest a little.

Miranda nodded. "I am happy to hear it. I have every confidence, then, that you will be a proper escort for Mrs. Crumpet and Mrs. Graves."

"We shall return with all speed, Miss Miranda," said Constance, smiling. She no longer held onto Robert with as firm a grip since the boy walked quite willingly out the door with her. Mrs. Crumpet came behind, shaking her head in marvel.

When the party had left, Miranda made her way to the broom closet. She had decided to open a few more rooms off the entrance hall so that morning callers could be comfortably entertained and the drawing room could be used in the evenings. She chose her tools and returned to the main hall, where her eyes were caught first by the bowl of wasted flowers that still drooped dismally over the occasional table. "This will not do," she said to herself. After dusting the table and gathering up the fallen petals, she took the bowl away and made a quick trip into the garden for fresh blooms. She had returned with bowl and roses and begun to arrange the flowers, humming as she worked when the front door bell rang, startling her so that she nearly dropped the stems in her hands. She stood indecisive a moment, not knowing whether she should answer it. Crumpet would have told her if anyone was expected.

The bell rang again, this time with a distinct touch of impatience. Miranda made up her mind. She set down the roses and went to the door.

Miranda opened the door only enough to enable her to see who had rung the bell with such force. She was startled at the sight of the elegant gentleman on the steps. He was tall and wore a gray multicaped greatcoat and dark beaver. His boots were polished to a fine mirror finish. Hearing the creak of the door, the gentleman turned quickly. His heavy brows were dark, as were his eyes. His features were handsome, but uncommonly lean and sharply chiseled. He wore an impatient frown, which did not dissipate upon seeing Miranda. If anything, his expression of disapprobation deepened as he swept her with a glance. "Well? Do you mean to keep me standing about all day?" he asked unpleasantly. With one gloved hand he unceremoniously pushed wide the door and entered the hall.

Miranda stumbled back before the gentleman to avoid his quick steps. She stared at him, shocked to speechlessness by his presumptuous air. Her wits seemed to have scattered. She watched dumbly while a valet carried in some trunks and a couple of portmanteaus.

The gentleman started to pull off his leather gloves, glancing about him as he did so. His frown became more pronounced at the dust and general untidiness of the hall. He stepped quickly to one of the doors off the hall and opened it to stare in at one of the shrouded rooms. He apparently did not care for what he saw since he closed the door with a snap and slapped his bunched gloves against one muscular thigh. He turned an angry gaze on Miranda. "I take it that your mistress has not been downstairs in some time, for I assure you that the slack management I see exhibited would not otherwise be tolerated. I do not know your name, nor do I care to. You are relieved of your duties from this moment. I expect you to be out of Willowswood within the hour," he said harshly.

"What!"

The gentleman had started to turn away, but at Miranda's startled and indignant exclamation he paused. There was an unpleasant curl about his mouth as he stared down his nose at her. "Did I not make myself perfectly clear, miss? I shall not have a slattern taking advantage of Mrs. Townsend's illness. If it is a reference you want, perish the thought. You will receive nothing from me and may count yourself fortunate that I do not throw you out on your ear this moment." After sweeping Miranda with a last indifferent glance, he set his foot to the stairs.

Miranda found her voice and her wits in the same instant. "One moment, sir! I shall take leave to inform you that I am not the housekeeper. And further, I take exception both to your manner and your tone. I should also like to know by what right you barge into this house and so familiarly start up the stairs to the family's private apartments."

The gentleman looked down at her from the advantage of the added height of the step. His brows were raised in haughty surprise. "My dear woman, I am Andrew Charles Townsend, the Viscount of Wythe, Mrs. Townsend's brother-in-law. I have a perfect right to be here, which is more than I know of you. By your accents I perceive that you are not English-bred, but you do have some education. Perhaps you will enlighten me as to your identity."

Miranda advanced until she stood at the banister, upon which he had rested his hand when he turned to confront her. Her blue eyes were darkened almost to black with sparkling anger. "I am Miss Miranda Wainwright, Mrs. Townsend's cousin. I arrived yesterday on a visit from America to find my cousin abed ill, her son untended and uncivilized, and the house as you see it. The house is deserted of servants. Of the household staff only the Crumpets have remained and they are quite unequal to the task of maintaining the household as it should be."

"And you, being an exceptionally practical young woman, have decided to turn a hand to the housekeeping," said the viscount with a faintly derisive tone to his voice.

"Do you know, you are a singularly unpleasant, arrogant, and rude man," said Miranda with studied thoughtfulness. She had the satisfaction of seeing a flash of anger in the viscount's brown eyes. She swept a brief curtsy. "Pray excuse me if I do not seem overly eager to remain in your company, my lord!" Miranda turned on her heel and left the hall, aware that the gentleman remained on the stair watching her until she had put a door between them.

Once out of the viscount's disturbing presence, Miranda gave vent to her furious annoyance with a few choice words. She was still seething when she found the butler, who was in the room off the kitchen polishing the silver. "Mr. Crumpet, the Viscount of Wythe has arrived. He will be upstairs by now visiting with my cousin."

"His lordship! Why, that is wonderful news, Miss Miranda. We—that is, Mrs. Crumpet and I—had quite despaired of his answering my letter of appeal. I will go up at once and discover what his lordship's wishes might be," said Crumpet, hurriedly laying aside the platter he was doing and throwing off his apron.

Miranda saw that Mrs. Crumpet was up to her elbows in flour, working with the day's fresh bread dough. "I expect that Lord Townsend will wish some tea. I will see to that," said Miranda, breathing slowly through her nose.

Mrs. Crumpet's mouth dropped open a little and she glanced at her husband. The butler hesitated, made uncertain both by Miranda's offer and the unusual agitation in her demeanor. "Miss Wainwright, I am not certain that it is at all the thing for a lady such as yourself . . ."

"Nonsense, Crumpet. I have been taken for a housekeeper and of a sudden it is a role that I fancy. Pray be so good as to direct me to the tea urn and biscuits," said Miranda with a firmness not to be denied. The butler reluctantly did so, then left her to it. Miranda nosed about the kitchen and pantry, as much to familiarize herself with the location of things as to discover something more filling than biscuits for a gentleman's tea. However much she had disliked the Viscount of Wythe on the first acquaintance, she would not allow it to interfere with her sense of what was proper. She found some slivers of cold pork left over from a previous meal and added the meat to the tea tray along with some thick slices of fresh bread.

Miranda carried the heavy tea tray into the dining room. She was pouring the tea when the Viscount of Wythe was shown in by the butler. Lord Townsend had somewhere shed his beaver and greatcoat. He was dressed in an admirably fitted fawn coat and tight buckskins. His startlingly white cravat, intricately tied and held with a sapphire stickpin, was in pleasing contrast to his browned countenance and dark curly hair. But Miranda was in no mood to appreciate the gentleman's physical appeal. He advanced across the room to place his hands on the back of one of the dining chairs. "I fancy that I owe you an apology, ma'am. My sister-in-law seems quite grateful for your presence," he drawled.

Miranda measured him with a cool glance. "Indeed, sir? I am naturally gratified by the intelligence." She gestured at the meager tea spread on the table. "Your tea, my lord. Pray excuse me now, for I have several tasks to attend to." She picked up the empty tray.

"Pray will you not keep me company, Miss Wainwright? I believe that there is much that we should perhaps discuss concerning Willowswood," said Lord Townsend.

His tone was not conciliatory. On the contrary, Miranda detected almost a note of command in his request and she bristled at it. However, what the viscount had said was undoubtedly true. The situation at Willowswood was an unusual one, to say the least. "Very well, my lord." Miranda set down the tray and accepted the chair that the viscount pulled out for her with a murmur of thanks. She folded her hands and waited while he went around the corner of the table to seat himself before the tea and food.

Lord Townsend did not speak until after he had made himself a sandwich and washed down the first few bites with some tea. Then he said, "Miss Wainwright, I did not realize until arriving how dire the situation is at Willowswood. Crumpet's letter naturally alluded to the exodus of the servants but I had put that down to the sort of exaggeration meant to impress. When I saw the state of the place I was appalled. You may then imagine my fears that my sister-in-law had been equally neglected."

"Fortunately that has not been the case. The Crumpets have been quite conscientious in that regard. They have also done their best in regards to the boy, but I fear with far less success," said Miranda.

The viscount shot her a frowning stare. "I seem to recall your mentioning my nephew before in rather disparaging terms. Pray elaborate, Miss Wainwright."

"When I arrived, your nephew was nowhere to be found and Crumpet was out scouring the estate for him. I gathered from Mrs. Crumpet that it was not an unusual occurrence and indeed, upon meeting Robert later, I ascertained that he has been quite a handful. He was unkempt and obviously wearing the same clothing that he had the day before. He was also rather surly in manner, quite unlike what I imagined a child of my cousin's to be," said Miranda. "However, I believe that there has already been some progress made. I let Master Robert know that his mother had given over some responsibility for him to me and proceeded to demonstrate what that would mean. At my behest, my maid and Mrs. Crumpet placed Master Robert in the bath. This afternoon they have taken him to the village and he was made aware before they left that if he minded his manners, he should be bought a treat. I fancy that that, as well as the time I spent with him this morning, will influence him somewhat."

"I perceive that you are a lady of resolute character, Miss Wainwright," said Lord Townsend.

Miranda was not certain that his tone conveyed commendation, but nevertheless she inclined her head slightly, "So I should hope, my lord."

The viscount had finished his sandwich and now poured himself a second cup of tea. He leaned back in his chair. "I must tell you, Miss Wainwright, that however grateful my sister-in-law may be to you, I myself find it appalling that the care of my family should fall into the hands of a stranger, however well-intentioned she may be," he said.

There was a short silence while Miranda digested his statement. She bit back the impulse to retort that she was certainly no stranger to Anne. "I can understand your reservations, my lord. Indeed, your sentiments do you credit," she said magnanimously.

"Then you will also understand why I have decided to remain at Willowswood until my sister-in-law is quite recovered," said Lord Townsend.

Miranda was disconcerted. It was the last thing she expected to hear. Thoughtfully, she swept the gentleman across from her with a slow glance. The Viscount of Wythe, who appeared every inch the elegant gentleman, did not strike her as the sort who would willingly spend even a weekend on a country estate. "Of course you must do as you wish," she said.

Lord Townsend laughed at that. "I always do, Miss Wainwright. I assure you. Now as for yourself, I understand from my sister-in-law that your brother was also expected, but I do not recall seeing him about."

"My brother, Jeremy, was detained in port. His ship was unfairly seized for being in violation of your government's Orders in Council and he has set in motion an official protest," said Miranda shortly. She was unwilling to discuss the matter in any great detail with this cynically smiling gentleman.

"I see. I must naturally wish Mr. Wainwright all success in his endeavor. However, it seems to me that we cannot expect his appearance at any time in the foreseeable future," said Lord Townsend in a dismissing tone.

"Perhaps not. I shall excuse myself now, my lord. As I mentioned earlier, there are a few matters that I wish to attend to," said Miranda, rising from the table.

The viscount flipped his hand at her in acquiescence and

showed her the barest courtesy by only half-rising from his chair. Miranda's eyes narrowed at this slight, but she said nothing. As she gathered up the tea tray and left the dining room, she thought that the arrogant, superior Viscount of Wythe would quickly learn that she was not to be dismissed so lightly.

Seven

Despite the Viscount of Wythe's unexpected appearance, Miranda continued with her plan to tidy the rooms on the ground floor, sweeping them of dust and taking away the sheets that shrouded the furniture. She had her first inkling that the shopping party had returned when she heard Robert's shrill voice.

"Uncle Andrew! Uncle Andrew!" There was a man's deep laughter and the sound of running footsteps. Miranda emerged into the hall just in time to see her young cousin fling himself into the viscount's arms and be swung about in a wide circle. She was astonished by the warmth in Lord Townsend's laughing expression as he spoke to his nephew. During their interview earlier she had decided that his lordship was a rather cynical, cold gentleman but the viscount's obvious attachment to his nephew tempered the negative opinion that she had formed of him.

Under cover of their laughter and the boy's excited talk, she addressed her maid. "How did it go with the young ruffian?" she asked quietly.

Constance chuckled. "Very well, Miss Miranda. Oh, there were a couple of incidents, to be sure. But overall Master Robert minded himself very well."

"I am happy to hear it. I trust also that the appearance of

Master Robert and Mrs. Crumpet in the village excited the proper attention," said Miranda with a glance at the cook.

"Aye, it did that. We'll have no more talk of plague and pox, I'll warrant," said Mrs. Crumpet with satisfaction.

The enthusiasm of the fond meeting between uncle and nephew had dissipated a little, enabling the viscount to overhear what had been said. "What is that, Mrs. Crumpet?" he asked sharply.

Mrs. Crumpet dropped a hasty curtsy. "Begging your lordship's pardon, I am sure. It was Miss Wainwright's thought, and a good one it was, for I and Master Robert to make an excursion into the village so that those who ought to know better would still their tongues about us here at Willowswood."

Miranda thought she could interpret the viscount's sudden frown. "It seems that my cousin's illness was rumored to be the pox, my lord. That is why the servants fled so precipitously."

"Good God, what ignorant fools," said Lord Townsend impatiently.

"Quite, my lord," said Miranda with a faint smile.

He eyed her for a moment. "I must bow to your ingenuity, ma'am. It was a masterful stroke." He held out his hand to his nephew. "Come, Robert. We shall go out to the stables, you and I. I drove down my gray team, you know."

"Oh, did you, uncle? How famous!" said Robert. With the boy skipping alongside, the viscount left the hall.

"His lordship seems a nice gentleman," said Constance.

"Does he? I suppose so," said Miranda with a marked lack of enthusiasm. Her companion threw her a wondering glance which Miranda chose to ignore. She turned to the cook. "I have made the drawing room habitable, Mrs.

Crumpet, so that we may have our coffee in there this evening."

"Oh, miss! You shouldn't have bothered. Why, it isn't fitting," said Mrs. Crumpet, somewhat distressed.

Miranda laughed, her blue eyes dancing a little. "I do not think that a little dusting will harm me, Mrs. Crumpet. It was so badly needed, there and in the other rooms as well. However, I shall want a bath before dinner is served, Constance. I have gotten myself quite untidy this afternoon."

"Of course, Miss Miranda. I shall attend to it at once," said Constance, preceding her mistress up the stairs.

After making ready for dinner, Miranda looked in on her cousin. Anne had just been served a tray by Mrs. Crumpet and seemed much more cheerful than she had previously. "Miranda!" She stretched out a hand to her cousin and urged her to sit beside her bed. "I am so glad you have come to see me. I have been dying to hear your opinion of my brother-in-law, Lord Townsend. Is he not a superb example of a true gentleman?"

Miranda was hesitant to disagree when Anne appeared so eager, so she hedged a little. "I think his lordship could be said to have an imposing personality."

Anne laughed at her. "What a quaint way you have, Miranda! If I did not know Andrew better I would suspect that he had set your back up in some way. But I know that cannot be true. He can make himself so very agreeable. Now tell me how you have spent your day. I am anxious to hear all about it." She settled herself more comfortably against her pillows and looked at Miranda expectantly.

Miranda obliged with a humorous account of her dealings with the Crumpets and Robert and her endeavors as a housekeeper. She also gave Anne a highly colored version of her meeting with the viscount. Anne laughed until tears rolled down her cheeks. "Oh do stop, Miranda! I shall die laughing at another word," she gasped. "To think that Andrew could make such a mistake. It is appall—appalling!" And she fell into a fresh peal of laughter.

"Well! I had thought to have my insult treated with more respect than this," said Miranda with mock affront. She frowned lugubriously at her cousin, who attempted and failed to sober her expression.

"I am sorry, Miranda. It is too—too bad of me," said Anne, wiping her face and still chuckling. Mrs. Crumpet had come in to take Anne's tray and nodded approvingly at how much had been consumed. She also beamed to see her mistress in such good spirits.

"I am only happy that I have been able to make you laugh," said Miranda. She leaned over to place her cool cheek against her cousin's in a tender display of affection. "I must go down to dinner now. I do not think that I shall visit you again this evening; but Robert will come up afterward, I am certain."

Anne nodded. She was still smiling as Miranda left her bedroom in company with Mrs. Crumpet. "The mistress has been done a wonder of good by your attention, Miss Wainwright," said the cook. "She has eaten two full meals since you have come and is livelier than she's been since the household servants deserted Willowswood. At this rate she'll be up and about in no time."

"I do hope you are right, Mrs. Crumpet," said Miranda, entering the dining room.

As a treat, Robert had been allowed to have dinner downstairs in the dining room with his uncle and Miranda. Constance also graced the table, though she appeared somewhat uncomfortable to be doing so whenever the viscount's glance happened to fall on her. When dinner was done, Constance took Robert back upstairs to visit his mother before going to bed.

"You are fortunate in Mrs. Graves. She is a woman of many talents, not the least of which is a firm hand with young boys," said Lord Townsend in an idle voice.

"Indeed, I do not know how I would go on without her. She has been the greatest support to me, especially during this visit," said Miranda. She watched as Crumpet brought a bottle to the table. "I see that it is time for your wine, my lord, so I shall make my exit and leave you alone to enjoy it."

"Pray do not go, Miss Wainwright. I detest drinking alone. Your presence will be a boon to me," said Lord Townsend.

Miranda hesitated, then acquiesced. She shook her head when he offered to pour a glass of the amber liquid for her. "Thank you, my lord, but I do not care overmuch for wine. I much prefer tea or coffee."

"Then you shall have it. Crumpet, a pot of coffee on the instant," said the viscount. The butler took the pot from the sideboard and placed it on the table before he bowed and left the dining room.

Miranda served herself a cup of the hot, fragrant brew, aware all the while that Lord Townsend was studying her face. A slight flush rose in her face under his scrutiny.

"You are an unusual young woman, Miss Wainwright. I have already seen the results of your efforts in the house and I speak not only of the housekeeping. I have spoken with the Crumpets and they have nothing but your praises to sing. Mrs. Crumpet in particular was determined to make me aware that Mrs. Townsend has shown improvement since your arrival," said the viscount.

"If that is the case I am heartily glad of it," said

Miranda. "Anne is very dear to me, though we have not seen one another since we were girls, and in the intervening years have remained close through our letters." She coolly met the viscount's eyes. "You seem to be quite a favorite of my cousin's, my lord."

Lord Townsend smiled slightly, aware of the reserve in her tone. "And does that surprise you, Miss Wainwright?"

"Not at all. I think that you are too clever to expose Anne to a taste of your bad temper when she is ill," said Miranda promptly.

The viscount threw back his head and laughed. "I see that I shall never live down my error in thinking you a slatternly housekeeper! I apologize again for my gross misjudgment, Miss Wainwright. There! Is that not done handsomely enough to allow us to be friends?"

"Perhaps, my lord. Your manners are very agreeable when you wish it," said Miranda, smiling.

Lord Townsend stared at her. He was reluctantly impressed with the dancing look in her extraordinarily blue eyes. It was not often that he found himself on the receiving end of such teasing. It was a new experience from a woman and he was not certain that he particularly enjoyed it, but certainly he had not been bored for a single moment in Miss Wainwright's company. "Allow me to return the compliment, ma'am. I was quite taken aback at what I shall term your graceless colonial manners. I am not at all used to receiving an upbraiding from a lady," he said with a bow from the waist.

"I can well imagine," murmured Miranda.

The viscount gave her a wounded look and threw up his hand. "Truce, ma'am! Let us agree on a truce, I implore you. I do not know if my sense of self-worth can withstand much more."

Miranda laughed outright. "Very well, my lord. I shall agree to such, if only to allow you to lick your wounds."

Lord Townsend bowed once more, thinking as he looked at her that he had never met a more infuriating female. But there was something about Miss Wainwright that went beyond the annoyance that she engendered in him with her spirited remarks. He had already taken note of the heavy, glistening chestnut hair done up at the back of her head. The chignon was unusual when short curled hair was the fashion, but it suited Miss Wainwright admirably. He had appreciated as well her deep blue eyes and creamy skin, her slender, swift hands that handled all that she touched with competence, and her trim, attractive figure. But it was her personality that most intrigued him. She was different from other ladies of his acquaintance. Her and completely lacking in the come-hither look to which he was accustomed when a woman's eyes dwelled on his person. It struck him suddenly that Miss Miranda Wainwright had not exhibited one iota of interest in him or his social status. And if that irks me, then I am sadly wanting in character that I must have a colonial nobody's admiration, he thought with something like chagrin.

"I am touched by your devotion to your family, my lord. Crumpet said that he had written to you of Anne's illness and the situation at Willowswood. It says much that you left your own pursuits to come down here," said Miranda.

"I was due for a rustication in any event," said Lord Townsend with a shrug. "I am presently out of grace with the Prince Regent and it is better that my face not be seen about London to remind his highness of his irritation." He leaned forward to pour himself another glass of wine and thus missed the expression of outrage and aversion that crossed Miranda's face.

"I will say good night now, my lord," said Miranda, rising from the table. She allowed no sign of the anger she felt to show in her expression at Lord Townsend's offhand confession that it was as much convenience that brought him to Willowswood as it was consideration for the well-being of his sister-in-law and nephew. But she could not control the darkened color of her eyes.

Lord Townsend was startled by the coolness of her tone and the abruptness of her move to depart. "But it is early, Miss Wainwright. Surely you do not wish to end the evening so quickly."

"I have had a rather fatiguing day and the coffee has had time to cool to indifference. From that standpoint alone, I think it a good moment to take my leave," said Miranda. She made a slight curtsy and had left the dining room almost before the viscount had collected himself enough to rise in courtesy from his chair.

He thought he saw a flash in Miss Wainwright's amazingly dark blue eyes as she swept out of the room. For a moment only he wondered what he had done to irritate her, then he shrugged indifferently. It was none of his concern, after all. He settled back into his chair to finish his wine.

Eight

The following morning Miranda rose and dressed with an eye to utility. She wore a stuff gown of indifferent color and fit and from somewhere produced an apron. Looking at herself in the mirror she was satisfied that she presented the very picture of an upstairs parlor maid. Constance stared hard at her mistress's outfit but she knew better than to comment when Miss Miranda held such a challenging look in her eyes. Instead she meekly accepted Miranda's suggestion that they clean the upper rooms after breakfast.

"An excellent idea, Miss Miranda. I shall join you directly after I have seen to the boy," said Constance.

"Of course. I had forgotten Robert," said Miranda with a small frown. "Do you take him in to see Mrs. Townsend this morning?"

"Oh no, not until luncheon. I expect Mrs. Townsend will appreciate a peaceful morning and after a few hours exercising the horses under Jenkins's strict eye, Master Robert will not be quite so feisty," said Constance wryly.

"I understand completely. You have it well in hand, Constance. I admit that I had my reservations in turning Robert over to the groom, but if he is able to curb my small cousin's exuberance he is an excellent man indeed," said Miranda with a laugh.

"Indeed he is, ma'am," said Constance.

Miranda went downstairs to the dining room. Crumpet was serving breakfast and his bow was all that was correct. However, there was a slightly shocked look in his eyes at Miranda's chosen form of dress. He recovered quickly and nothing could have exceeded his civility as he asked her what her preference would be from the sideboard.

Miranda requested poached eggs and toast. There was a dancing fun in her eyes when she glanced at the butler. "I am disappointed, Crumpet! Do I not sufficiently look the part of a housemaid for you to scold me for my presumption in coming to breakfast?"

"No one could ever mistake you for a housemaid, Miss Miranda," said Crumpet staunchly. But there had been the briefest hesitation before he replied that spoke volumes.

"Thank you, Crumpet," said Miranda, her lips quivering. She knew at least one person who would say otherwise. At the thought of Lord Townsend, she wondered whether she had already missed him. That would be a pity because she had anticipated that her outfit would provoke that gentleman to comment and she had a particular reason for wanting him to do so. She picked up the coffee pot to pour a cup of the hot brew. "Has his lordship come down yet?"

"No, Miss Miranda. His lordship was up very late and indicated that he would not be requiring breakfast," said Crumpet. His countenance and his voice were wooden.

The butler's statement combined with his style of delivery convinced Miranda that Lord Townsend had put his request a bit more strongly than Crumpet had intimated. She rather thought it probable that the viscount had finished off the bottle of wine on the dining table after she had left and then had subsequently made it clear that he had no desire for social pleasantries in the morning. "I understand, of course. Have you known the Viscount of Wythe long, Crumpet?"

"Indeed I have, Miss Miranda. For some years now," said Crumpet, preparing to leave her alone to enjoy her meal.

Miranda shot a level glance at him. "Is Lord Townsend often in his cups?"

The butler was startled by the clear intentness of her gaze. "Why, I really couldn't say, miss. That is, his lordship enjoys his wine like any other gentleman. He is the sort of rollicking gentleman one expects of a London beau. His visits to his brother have always been accompanied by high spirits and great fun. I have never seen his lordship moody or in a fit of the doldrums."

"Thank you, Crumpet," said Miranda with a nod.

As he left the dining room the butler was discomfited by the suspicion that he had perhaps said too much, but he cheered himself with the reflection that Miss Wainwright was a colonial, after all, and could not be expected to understand all the nuances of what he had left unuttered.

In that Crumpet was mistaken. Miranda was not at all behind in reading between the lines. Her eyes narrowed as she thought over the information that she had gleaned from the loyal butler. The Viscount of Wythe was a self-indulgent man who imbibed freely. He liked entertainments and was restless unless he could be on the go. He probably did not care for serious reflection or conversation. Crumpet's disclosure, coupled with Lord Townsend's own statement that he had left London because he was in disgrace with the Prince Regent, who from all accounts was a frivolous fop surrounded by a circle of acquaintances who were mad pleasure-seekers like himself, was fast-persuading Miranda that the Viscount of Wythe was a gentleman with no more substance or proper feeling than a cut-out paperdoll.

"How revolting," she said aloud. She felt an acute sense of disappointment. When she had first laid eyes on Lord Townsend, after those first few seconds when his frowning eyes had swept her with disdain, she had been startled by an incredible attraction to him. It was annoying to discover that once again she had been fooled by a handsome manly exterior that hid the shallowest of bases.

Miranda shook her head to rid herself of all thoughts of her former fiancé. That engagement had been a mistake never to be repeated. Though her thoughts had not carried her so far as to contemplate herself becoming affianced for a second time, the Viscount of Wythe was firmly shut out by her defenses. His lordship might be one of the handsomest gentlemen that Miranda had ever seen, but he was definitely not for her. Finished with breakfast and her reflections on Lord Townsend alike, she rose from the table and left the dining room to go in search of a feather duster.

Miranda spent the greater part of the morning in cleaning. When Constance appeared to assist her, Miranda had removed the last of the dust sheets from the furniture in several of the bedrooms and their adjoining sitting rooms. With an ongoing lively banter, Miranda and Constance cleaned grates and polished furniture to a shining mirror finish with an energetic application of beeswax.

Once Mrs. Crumpet popped in her head to inquire of Miss Wainwright whether she would prefer a boiled chicken or pot pie for the noonday meal. When she returned to the kitchen she expressed her astonishment to Mr. Crumpet at the sight of Miss Wainwright making herself so useful. "It's not decent, Mr. Crumpet, for a gently bred lady to put herself out so. My eyes fair started from my head to see Miss

Wainwright waving a polish cloth and to hear her joke of the ash from the grate marking her skirts," said Mrs. Crumpet, greatly distressed. She uncovered a large bowl and turned out the doubled bread dough onto a floured board. She gave the dough an unwarranted hard thump and it collapsed, giving off a fresh smell of yeast. "And you may be sure that Mrs. Townsend knows nothing about it, for when I took up her dry toast and gruel and the camomile tea that Miss Wainwright fixed for her this morning, she asked if her cousin was finding enough to entertain her. Entertain her! Why, the poor lady is in a fair way to working her fingers to the bone. Mark me, I did not say a word to the mistress, seeing as how Miss Wainwright has not. But it goes against the grain with me, Mr. Crumpet, and so I tell you."

Mr. Crumpet was frowning as he peered into the emerging shine of the piece of silver that he was polishing. "I shall discreetly mention the matter to the viscount. Though his lordship does not express an interest in such matters as housekeeping, I am certain that he would want to be informed of Miss Wainwright's activities."

His wife nodded her head, satisfied. Her large, capable hands methodically kneaded the bread dough. "Aye, you do that, Mr. Crumpet. His lordship will know what to do."

Crumpet chose the first opportunity that presented itself of informing Lord Townsend of the strange set of affairs. Crossing the hall to the dining room he chanced to meet the viscount, who was on his way to inspect the stables. His lordship was attired in buckskins and topboots and a well-cut somber brown coat and brass buttons that admirably set off his broad shoulders. "My lord! If I may have a word with you . . ."

"Well, Crumpet?" asked Lord Townsend, pausing to

pull on his kid leather gloves.

The butler threw a glance around the hall before indicating that he wished the viscount to step into the dining room. Lord Townsend did so, made curious by the butler's odd behavior. Crumpet turned to him and cleared his throat. "I beg forgiveness for the inconvenience, your lordship. However, there is a matter of some importance I wished to appraise your lordship of in privacy."

"What is it, Crumpet? Has my nephew once again escaped his keepers?" asked the viscount with a smile.

"No, my lord. At least not yet," said Crumpet, amending his assurance. "I wished to speak to you of Miss Wainwright, my lord."

Lord Townsend suddenly frowned. He thought he understood. The colonial was upsetting the traditional style of doing things and the Crumpets were naturally offended. "I take it that Miss Wainwright presents a problem to you and Mrs. Crumpet?"

"Yes, my lord. That is to say, not personally to us. But Miss Wainwright is quite unlike any other lady that I have had occasion to become acquainted with," said Crumpet, wallowing.

"Indeed, I too find her different," said Lord Townsend. He nodded to the butler. "Very well, I shall speak with Miss Wainwright. I shall not have her upsetting you and Mrs. Crumpet with her American way of doing things. You may be assured that she will not interfere with you in future."

Crumpet saw that he had not conveyed what he had intended. "Oh no, my lord! It is nothing of the sort. Miss Wainwright is no trouble to myself and Mrs. Crumpet. Quite the contrary! But she is not behaving as a lady should and—"

"What?" The viscount's tone was thunderous. His mind

leaped to one scenario after another, none of which reflected well on Miss Miranda Wainwright.

Crumpet whitened a little and he hurriedly finished what he wanted to say. "Miss Wainwright is *cleaning*, sir! Mrs. Crumpet and myself, we do not consider it to be proper employment for a lady to be polishing the furniture and sweeping out the grates."

"Sweeping out the grates?" repeated Lord Townsend, stupified by the utter banality.

Crumpet nodded. "Aye, my lord. And polishing the furniture. It isn't seemly, sir."

The viscount recovered himself. "Certainly it is not. I shall attend to the matter at once, Crumpet. I take it Miss Wainwright is at this moment occupied with her odd hobby?" The butler nodded as he opened the dining room door. As the viscount stepped into the main hall, the butler pointed up at the partial balcony where a door stood open.

Miranda looked at the clock on the mantel with a groan. Constance had left some minutes before to collect Robert and make certain that he was suitably cleaned and attired to take the noonday meal with his mother. Miranda had elected to finish polishing the last piece of furniture in the sitting room before she went to freshen up and change for luncheon. But the time had gotten away from her and the advanced hour caught her by surprise. "Well, I shall just be late to the table," she said. Exhausted as she was by her exertions, she had the satisfaction of being able to look about her and see that the room looked itself again.

Catching a glimpse of herself in the gilded mirror above the mantel, Miranda grimaced. A streak of dirt marked her forehead where she had brushed the back of her hand. Her hair, once neatly braided and pinned at the crown of her head, had come loose and wispy tendrils floated free about her face. She was perspiring and her gown was crumpled to a thousand wrinkles. Miranda wrinkled her nose. "I present a fine picture."

"Indeed, Miss Wainwright," said a male voice devoid of expression.

Miranda whirled and met the eyes of the Viscount of Wythe. He stood there in the doorway and coolly his gaze went over her. Miranda colored hotly. It was one thing to have planned to make a point with his lordship, but it was another to have him discover her in such untidy and soiled disarray. As Miranda took in the viscount's immaculate and nicely fitted riding clothes, she felt at a distinct disadvantage.

Lord Townsend closed the door. "I should like to speak privately to you, Miss Wainwright."

Miranda felt a flutter of nervousness. She walked over to a graceful settee covered in faded blue taffeta and seated herself. She laced her fingers together in her lap, at pains to project calm. "This is unexpected indeed, my lord. I am all curiosity."

Lord Townsend did not move from his place by the door. His hand remained on the brass handle. His gaze was somewhat frowning. "Miss Wainwright, I address you with the utmost reluctance, believe me."

Miranda put up her well-marked brows. "This becomes more curious by the moment, I swear."

"Miss Wainwright, it has come to my attention that you have taken upon yourself the burden of refurbishing Willowswood. It is a noble ambition but quite an improper one for my sister-in-law's guest to undertake," said the viscount.

Miranda was startled into laughter. Her eyes held a hint of derision. "My dear sir, I am not so poor a creature that I can see what needs to be done and not do it. If it is your fear that I overstep myself, I have spoken to my cousin on the matter. Anne does not object, I assure you."

"Come, Miss Wainwright, surely you are not telling me that my sister-in-law has been put in full knowledge of your activities!" He saw that she had the grace to appear a little guilty and he pressed his advantage. "Miss Wainwright, I should be loathe to acquaint Mrs. Townsend with the fact that her cousin is acting as her housekeeper. It would naturally upset her to learn that you were not enjoying your stay at Willowswood as you should. Pray leave the cleaning to others more suited for it, Miss Wainwright." Lord Townsend bowed to her and turned the knob.

"Oh? And who might those others be, my lord?" asked Miranda. Her dark eyes were suddenly serious in expression. "I suppose you expect my companion to take on the task. I must disillusion you, sir. Constance is already committed to me and to caring for your nephew. Or perhaps you envision poor Mrs. Crumpet on her knees scrubbing the floors between preparing of the meals?"

The viscount's brows drew together in a deep frown as he stared at her. He had not given thought to the matter other than to agree with Crumpet that Miss Wainwright was delving into what should not concern her. Blast Miss Wainwright and her sensible Yankee mind, he thought disagreeably. She was right, of course. There was no one else. He was beginning to see that this visit to Willowswood was not destined to be quite like any other. With reluctance he realized that the responsibility of the estate was placed squarely on his shoulders. Anne Townsend was certainly not in any condition to attend to her duties and he had virtually ordered Miss Wainwright to mind her own business. "I suppose the thing to do is to hire a proper housekeeper and a maid or two," he said lamely.

"A laudable thought, my lord. And perhaps a footman or two would also be in line. I should ask Crumpet's advice, but of course you have already thought of that. Who is to interview the applicants and make the decisions?" asked Miranda. She was aware that she was pushing him against the wall and she enjoyed the sensation.

There was a flare of irritation in the viscount's eyes. He looked at Miranda with dislike. "I shall attend to the matter myself."

"Indeed. I see that you are a gentleman of unusual talents, my lord. I would not have suspected that a London beau would be familiar with the hiring and outfitting of a household," said Miranda in a bland tone.

Lord Townsend stared at her a moment longer. "I find your manners atrocious, ma'am."

"I believe that your previous observation was 'graceless colonial manners,' was it not, my lord?" asked Miranda. She bestowed an amiable smile on him.

The viscount audibly ground his teeth. He yanked open the sitting room door and strode to the stairs. Upon descending, he found Crumpet hovering in the hall. "My lord? Will you be wanting luncheon?" the butler asked timidly.

The viscount did not bother to pause in his swift progress. "I am going riding, Crumpet. I do not know how long it will be before I return."

The door that gave access to the back of the house was closed sharply behind him. At hearing a peal of soft laughter, Crumpet turned a bewildered gaze up to Miss Wainwright, who stood at the balustrade above. She shook her head at him. "Pray do not be so concerned, Crumpet. His lordship has merely taken a pet because I pointed out to him that someone will need to hire a housekeeping staff. I somehow do not think Lord Townsend is looking forward to the task." She glanced down at herself. "I believe that I shall go freshen up before I set foot in the dining room. This guise has suited its purpose admirably." Blithely ignoring Crumpet's appalled expression, Miranda tripped away to her bedroom, humming to herself.

"And that," as Crumpet very soon related to his spellbound wife, "is just the way she said it. I very much think that Miss Wainwright meant to give his lordship a nudge, what with her working so diligent-like at the cleaning and whatnot."

"I can't say that I approve of the way Miss Wainwright went about it, but there is no gainsaying that his lordship would hardly have thought of doing anything on his own. What proper gentleman would, and especially one cut from London cloth as is his lordship!" said Mrs. Crumpet. She pursed her lips as she stirred the broth for that evening's side dish. "It will be interesting to watch, Mr. Crumpet, mark my words."

He did not quite follow his wife's thoughts. "What will, Mrs. Crumpet?"

But she only shook her head. "It will be interesting indeed. Only wait, Mr. Crumpet." He shrugged, dismissing the remark as one of Mrs. Crumpet's indecipherable musings, and turned to his duties.

Nine

Miranda ate luncheon in solitary splendor. Crumpet served her with all the punctilio that he would bring to a party of twelve and Miranda enjoyed the novelty. Though she and Jeremy had come from a family well versed in observing the social amenities, Miranda could only marvel at the formalness of the English way. She was perfectly prepared to serve herself and more than once it was on the tip of her tongue to dismiss Crumpet, but she sensed that if she did so it would gravely offend the butler. When she was finished, she thanked him for his attentiveness. Crumpet was gratified by her appreciation and bowed deeply as she left the dining room. "A fine lady is Miss Wainwright," he said to himself.

Miranda made her way upstairs to visit with her cousin. It had become her custom to sit with Anne for an hour or two during the early afternoon and it was a time that they both enjoyed. On this particular day Miranda found her cousin sitting up on a blue satin-covered settee by the bedroom window where she could look down on the knot garden below. Dappled sunlight gently warmed her face so that she did not appear as pale as before. Anne stretched out her hand in welcome. "Miranda! I have been looking for you these several minutes. Have you been enjoying your morning?"

"Indeed, my expectations for the morning were far exceeded," said Miranda. She bent to lightly kiss her cousin's soft cheek. She saw the immediate inquiry in Anne's eyes and laughed as she seated herself in the rosewood chair opposite the chaise. "I fear that you shall think me the greatest beast in nature, Anne, but I have actually extracted a promise from Lord Townsend that he will see about gathering together a household staff. Now do not eat me! It was his own decision, after all. I merely pointed out the need."

Anne settled back against her cushions. "Somehow I cannot picture Andrew in the role of agent. He is such a—a *laughing* sort, if you catch my meaning. One could never think of him as being serious more than a moment or two at best."

Recalling the viscount's irritated expression, Miranda said, "Oh, I rather think Lord Townsend was quite serious about the matter. And it will surely be a relief to you, dear Anne, to know that Willowswood will soon have the attention it deserves."

"Yes, of course. But Andrew! He knows nothing about servants except to notice when they are absent if he needs them. Miranda, you must promise me that you shall quietly advise him," said Anne.

"I! Why, I hardly know the gentleman, and frankly, his lordship hardly strikes me as one who would take kindly to advice, however well intended," said Miranda.

Anne waved aside her objections. "I am certain that you shall get along famously with him, Miranda. You have such a friendly way about you that one cannot help but respond. Do say that you will do it, Miranda. It will so ease my mind to know that I shall not end with some awful woman in charge of my home."

"Oh my dear, of course, I shall help in any way that I

can," said Miranda, keeping private her conviction that
Lord Townsend would rather consign her to the devil than
to take any advice from her. She and the viscount had
gotten off to such a rousing beginning and the dissention
between them had certainly not abated. But she would not
willingly erase the grateful and unsuspecting smile from
Anne's face. "Tell me how you are feeling today. You appear far more rested than previously."

"Indeed, I am sleeping easier now. I think your teas have
much to do with that. Oh, Miranda, I feel so much better.
This morning Robert expressed his surprise and pleasure to
see his mama sitting up. He is such a sensitive child. My illness has weighed heavily on him, I think. I am so pleased
that you have taken my boy under your wing. He appears
more content than he did before your arrival," said Anne.

"I think that it is Constance's influence more than mine.
She is quite used to children, you know. Also, Robert feels
usefully employed now that he is helping with the horses.
And he seems very attached to his uncle," said Miranda.

"Oh yes. Andrew has always been marvelous with him.
One would not think it to look at him, but Andrew actually
likes children. So many gentlemen do not, you know. They
cannot stand to have the small ones fussing about them.
But Andrew has never minded it when Robert nosed into
his things or mussed up his cravat. It is really very odd since
the Viscount of Wythe is known in London for such a
smart. Richard is forever teasing Andrew for what he calls
his brother's dandyism, but for myself I hold a sneaking admiration for a gentleman who carries himself so well," said
Anne.

Miranda made a decided effort to change the subject.
She thought she had heard enough about the viscount's
sterling qualities when she knew that his lordship was at

heart a mere seeker of self-gratification. "But tell me, Anne, when does the doctor next visit?"

"Oh, such a boring topic. Very well! I can see that you will not leave it until I satisfy you. He is to come next week. My strength is still not quite up to what it should be, but each day I can feel myself gaining in vigor. It will be soon, I think, that the good doctor will allow me to return downstairs and begin resuming a normal existence. I shall ask him about it when he comes, believe me," said Anne, laughing. She waved an encompassing hand at her bedroom. "I am so tired of these four walls. I think that I shall change the color as soon as I am up and about. In the past weeks I have learned to detest this particular shade of blue."

"I can well imagine. Have you given any thought to what color you shall replace it with?" asked Miranda. The conversation turned to a lively discussion of shades of rose and damask draperies and upholstery.

When Miranda left her cousin some two hours later she was satisfied that Anne was truly on the mend. She had not tired so quickly during the visit and there was a definite glow in her face. As Miranda walked down the stairs, sliding her hand along the sleek banister, she heard a quick step on the marble tiles of the hall and the viscount came into view. "Good afternoon, my lord," she called cheerfully.

Lord Townsend bowed. He stood waiting for her to finish her descent, his unfathomable gaze following her progress. When Miranda reached the bottom stair, she paused with her hand on the newel post to look at him with a cool air. With the advantage of the stair her eyes were nearly at a level with his. "Is there something the matter, my lord?" she asked.

"Not at all, Miss Wainwright. I have but this moment returned from a ride around the estate. I was not before aware of the extent of neglect that Willowswood has suffered. I have seen enough to suspect that my brother's bailiff was either an incompetent fool or a scoundrel. I wish to thank you for reminding me so graphically this morning that in my brother's absence the responsibility of the estate lies with myself," said Lord Townsend gravely.

Miranda was thrown off guard. For some reason she had assumed the viscount would never acknowledge anything that might point to an error in his own judgment. But here he was offering her both apology and gratitude at one and the same time. For lack of anything to say, she inclined her head.

"I wish also to ask a favor of you, Miss Wainwright. I am lacking in experience in hiring a proper household, whereas I gather you are not," said Lord Townsend, his brow rising in quizzical inquiry.

"I managed my father's household after my mother's death," said Miranda in reply to his unspoken question.

The viscount nodded, satisfied. "Then may I call on your advice in this matter? It would be of immense help to me."

"If that is what you wish, my lord, I shall be most happy to offer you whatever aid I can," said Miranda, disconcerted further. It seemed that Lord Townsend was actually concerned about the state of Willowswood. That did not fit into her picture of him as a sybarite, a man too selfish to please anyone but himself. She wondered if she had misjudged him.

Lord Townsend smiled. "Thank you, Miss Wainwright. And I hope that you will not take it amiss if I observe that your appearance is vastly improved over what it was this morning," he said.

Miranda colored faintly. She shook her head. "I am not at all offended, my lord. I own quite freely that I looked a perfect quiz. You must be famished after your ride. Shall I ring for Crumpet to serve you a late luncheon?"

"Thank you, Miss Wainwright. A plate of sandwiches in the study will be all that I require. I wish to begin going over the papers dealing with the estate this afternoon," said Lord Townsend. He excused himself and started upstairs to change out of his riding attire.

Miranda watched his broad back for a few seconds before she went in search of Crumpet. After speaking to the butler, she made her way out of the house to the gardens. She thought it would be pleasant to stroll slowly among the beds and breathe the fresh spring air after playing all morning at parlor maid.

At dinner the viscount announced to Miranda that he had spoken with his sister-in-law about the neglect he had seen during his ride about Willowswood and in the house itself. "I found also that my brother's records are in a shambles. It will take weeks to make sense of them. In the meantime, Anne has given me carte blanche to hire a household staff and groundskeepers. I have already sent to my solicitor in London to begin screening appropriate persons for all positions except cook and butler. I am naturally more familiar with the duties of groundskeepers and such, so I must rely on you, Miss Wainwright, to guide me with the household staff," said the viscount.

"Of course, my lord. After our conversation on this topic I mentioned the matter to Crumpet, hoping that we might draw on his experience. He gave me good advice about how large a staff to engage and I've made a list of the number of footmen, and so on, so that you may pass it on to your solicitor," said Miranda. She took a neatly folded sheet of paper out of her pocket and handed it to Lord Townsend.

The viscount looked at her as he unfolded the sheet. He perused it quickly, then put it inside his coat pocket. "Quite comprehensive, Miss Wainwright," he said. His tone was not markedly congratulatory. He was not certain that he cared for Miss Wainwright's independence of action. He was bothered she had not waited for his guidance, but he was irritated more that he had not thought to speak to Crumpet himself before he had written his solicitor.

Miranda was quick to hear the reservation in his voice. She put up her brows. "I believe that you are not best pleased, my lord. Why is this?"

Lord Townsend smiled but his eyes remained somewhat cool. "I do not fault you, Miss Wainwright. Quite the contrary, your talk with Crumpet has yielded a goldmine of specific requirements."

"But you disapprove that I should have acted on my own cognizance," said Miranda with a flash of insight. She knew that she was right when she saw the slight stiffening in the viscount's easy posture.

"Not at all. I wish only in future to be informed of your inspirations so that we do not duplicate our efforts," said Lord Townsend.

"Certainly, my lord. Just as I shall wish to be informed of your notions," said Miranda smoothly. She smiled when the viscount's brows contracted. His gaze was frowning and she met it with friendly eyes.

"You are a devilish headstrong young woman," said Lord Townsend irritably.

"So my brother often tells me. I consider it the highest compliment," said Miranda, nodding agreeably. She laid aside her napkin and rose from the table, smiling again at the viscount. "Pray excuse me, my lord, I have several notions that I wish to put into commission. And certainly I shall keep you informed of my progress." With that she swept out of the dining room.

As the days passed, Lord Townsend discovered that his irritation with Miss Wainwright only increased. He could not seem to put her out of his mind and when he thought of her, he almost audibly ground his teeth. It was not that she was openly defiant or antagonistic toward him. On the contrary, Miss Wainwright was always polite and cheerful, solicitously requesting his opinion on whatever matter she had in hand.

And that was the crux of the matter, he thought. Even as she spoke to him so civilly, laughter lurked in the depths of her eyes as though she was offering a sop to his ego. That was what galled him so, thought Lord Townsend. But still he could not put aside those feelings that he condemned as childish and unworthy of him. There was something about Miss Wainwright that at once put him off and yet drew him to her. She was a colonial nobody with little grace of manner toward her social superior.

Oh yes, Miss Wainwright, I have been made acutely aware that you are not impressed with me or my social status, thought the viscount, his gaze resting on Miss Wainwright's profile as she pointed out to him the particulars of a list that she had drawn up. The sunlight coming in the study window highlighted the purity of her skin, the smooth curve of her cheek, the fullness of her rose lips. Lord Townsend's gaze lingered on the sensuousness of her soft mouth. He wondered if she would be so indifferent to him if he were to take her in his arms. The stray thought startled him. Then the faintest of smiles crossed his face.

Miranda chanced to glance up at that moment. The pleasantness of his expression surprised her. When she had

first come into the study, she had not thought Lord
Townsend was in a particularly benevolent mood. "Do you
not agree, my lord? Mrs. Crumpet assures me that these particular items are essential if we are to have a well-run house."

"I bow to your judgment, Miss Wainwright. My only
consideration would be to consult with Anne. She will have
her own notions of what a well-run household should provide," said Lord Townsend.

"Naturally I shall talk to my cousin. Do you know, I
have a slight suspicion that Anne is actually relieved that
someone other than herself is organizing her house. It is an
attitude I cannot understand," said Miranda.

"But my sister-in-law is not so self-sufficient as yourself,
Miss Wainwright. She relies on my brother to guide and advise her," said Lord Townsend.

Miranda wondered if the viscount was subtly pointing up
what he considered a flaw in her feminine character. She
was well aware of his arrogant assumption that he was enti-
tled to preferential treatment, especially from any female
who happened to cross his path. Certainly the way he carried himself made one instinctively defer to him. The faintly
derisive light in his brown eyes and the mobility of his stern
mouth but added to his dark good looks. Miranda was
honest enough to admit to herself that she was intrigued by
Lord Townsend, but she thought she had managed to resist
succumbing to his attraction. She studied his face to see if
he was throwing down yet another gauntlet, but his expression revealed nothing more than friendliness. "If Anne has
no objections, I shall inform Mrs. Crumpet that she may
purchase these necessary items when next she goes shopping in the village," said Miranda, picking up her list.

As a result of the earlier shopping trip undertaken by

Mrs. Crumpet with Constance Graves and Robert, word had swiftly spread through the countryside that there was no danger of pox at Willowswood. The village doctor had been saying the same for weeks and he enjoyed needling those who had condemned him for treating Mrs. Townsend. At his suggestion, and much to his satisfaction, a very worthy woman of his acquaintance, named Grace Buffin, applied for the post of lady's maid to Mrs. Townsend and was taken on.

When the doctor paid his looked-for visit to Willowswood, he was in the greatest of spirits as he told of the turn-around of opinion in the village and surrounding countryside. His ginger-colored brows wagged with his enthusiastic talk. "Aye, you should see their faces now, Mrs. Townsend. Your neighbors are shamefaced to have neglected you in the past weeks. Do not be surprised if you should receive a flurry of morning calls," he said as he finished his examination.

"But shall I be up to receive visitors?" asked Anne.

"Indeed you shall, Mrs. Townsend. I perceive no reason why you cannot begin going downstairs again this very evening," said the doctor expansively.

"There, Anne! We shall have you presiding at the dinner table at last," said Miranda, pleased.

After a few more minutes, the doctor took leave of his patient and Miranda accompanied him downstairs to the door. She held out her hand to him. "I am so very glad for the news you have given my cousin, sir. She has been somewhat restless these last few days with just thinking about the possibility of leaving her room."

The doctor bowed over Miranda's hand. "I am happy to have been of service, Miss Wainwright. It always gratifies me to be able to relate good news. And may I say that I am most pleased to have made your acquaintance. Before you came upstairs, Mrs. Townsend was telling me how your presence had brought her greater peace of mind than she had at any other time during her illness. I believe that factor alone may have contributed a powerful positive influence and accelerated her recovery."

"You flatter me, doctor, but I thank you," said Miranda, smiling.

The doctor hitched himself up into his gig and shook out the reins. The horse between the traces started off docilely and the gig rolled smoothly away down the drive.

Miranda turned back into the house and Crumpet closed the door. She found that the viscount was regarding her from the doorway of the study.

"The sawbones seems a pleasant enough fellow," he remarked.

"Quite. I was pleased both with his professional manner and his good nature. I can well understand the faith that Mrs. Townsend has in him," said Miranda.

"I detected in his manner a strong hint of partiality for you, Miss Wainwright," drawled the viscount.

"What utter nonsense. The doctor is merely kind to a stranger," said Miranda.

"I bow to your superior judgment, Miss Wainwright," said Townsend. He was smiling as he reentered the study and softly closed the door.

"That is the most infuriating gentleman," said Miranda under her breath.

"Beg your pardon, miss?"

She turned to the butler. With a shake of her head and a smile she dismissed Lord Townsend. "Crumpet, I know that you must have gathered that Mrs. Townsend will be able to leave her room now. I should like to celebrate at dinner tonight. Do you think that Mrs. Crumpet might whip up something special?"

"Of course, Miss Wainwright. I know that Mrs. Crumpet will be most pleased by the request. Is there anything else?" said Crumpet.

"Yes. We shall have Master Robert join us for dinner. I think it would be most appropriate and it will please his mother very much to think that her adored son has grown so in manners," said Miranda with a chuckle. "I must warn Constance of the treat in store so that she may prepare my young cousin for his role of the tidy gentleman. And I shall do my best to awe the young rascal into dignity."

Crumpet allowed himself a smile. "Yes, miss. I shall be certain to treat Master Robert with all the deference at my command."

"That alone might serve to convince Master Robert of the importance of the moment. At least, I devoutly hope so," said Miranda.

Ten

That evening was a particularly nice one. Anne Townsend came downstairs leaning heavily on her brother-in-law's arm, looking beautiful and frail in a soft rose satin gown ruffed about the neck with Belgian lace. She was seated at the head of the candlelit table, flanked by her son and Miranda. Constance sat beside Robert in case he should begin to fidget. The viscount not unhappily found himself seated next to Miranda. Anne looked about the table with content. The only face missing was Richard's, but even that could not dim her pleasure in being able to come downstairs and join her family, she thought.

Robert was thrilled to sit at dinner downstairs rather than being brought a tray in the nursery. Hoping that this evening would mark the end of his nursery days, he was mindful of both his manners and his deportment. His thick unruly hair was carefully combed and his attire clean and sharply pressed. He fairly glowed when his mother and his uncle complimented him for his gentlemanly conduct.

Miranda was pleased for the boy and she signaled her approval to him with a conspiratorial wink. She little knew that someone at the table noted her sparkling eyes and soft beauty with admiration. Miranda had chosen a deep blue gown that brought out the dark shade of her eyes and highlighted her fair skin. The square bodice was cut low across the bosom, to reveal a glimmer of shadow between her well-formed breasts. She wore her shining hair in a plaited chignon that set off her slender neck, adorned with a double string of pearls that matched the pearls gleaming in her ears.

Lord Townsend's eyes often strayed to the tantalizing glimpse of Miss Wainwright's shapely bosom and he was acutely aware of the warm feminine scent of her perfume. He found her vivacious speech pleasing to his ears. Idly, he contemplated her soft full lips, his thoughts wandering pleasantly from the conversation.

"And Andrew, I wish to see you enjoying yourself more as well."

Lord Townsend dragged his attention back. "What, Anne?"

"Oh Andrew! Surely you are not woolgathering tonight over business. Miranda has told me how hard you are working with the estate and though I appreciate it, I do not want you to bury yourself in the study. It cannot be how you planned to entertain yourself at Willowswood," said Anne.

"Anne, you know me better than that. If I did not enjoy it I should not do it," said Lord Townsend. He intercepted a swift glance from Miss Wainwright and wondered at her expression. Surely he had not seen annoyance in her eyes. He looked at her more closely, but she had lowered her lashes and he could no longer read her expression. "Perhaps Miss Wainwright feels that entertainment is scarce at Willowswood, but I do not," he said quietly.

Miranda glanced at him, startled. Surely he did not expect her to believe that he wasn't pining away for London and all its attractions. He met her gaze steadily and

Miranda was the first to look away. The viscount had
shown remarkable concentration in pulling the estate together. According to what she had gathered from Crumpet,
he rarely sat long over his wine, preferring instead to work
into the night. Perhaps she did him an injustice, she
thought reluctantly.

"That is just my point, Andrew! Both you and Miranda
are sitting here bored to tears, and I shall believe neither of
your claims to the contrary. *I* know what it is like to spend
week upon week with idle time on my hands. So not another word of protest from either of you. Once it is learned
that I am well, I expect to have invitations from about the
neighborhood. Miranda, I insist that you accompany me to
whatever functions we are invited to, and as for you, Andrew, I expect that we may rely upon you for escort," said
Anne.

"In short, you insist that we are to be civilly entertained," said Lord Townsend. There was a smile lurking in
his eyes.

"Yes, Andrew, I do so insist," said Anne, laughing at
him.

The viscount sighed and with a shrug turned to
Miranda. "Our fate is sealed, Miss Wainwright. It is of no
use to beg off, for our captor is heartless and will no doubt
lock us in our rooms and feed us thin gruel until we capitu-
late."

His nephew's eyes rounded. "Really, Uncle Andrew?
Will Mama really do that?"

That brought laughter from around the table. Still grin-
ning, Lord Townsend nodded at his nephew. "I am sorry to
say so, but yes. Your mother can be a very stern lady when
she chooses."

Anne leaned forward to put an arm about her son's

shoulders and hugged him. "Your bad uncle is funning again, Robert. Not that I won't feed him thin gruel if he doesn't learn to behave himself. Now I think it time for you to go up to bed, young man. Your eyes are nearly closing. Mrs. Graves, if you will be so kind as to accompany him?"

Constance nodded and rose. Robert dutifully kissed his mother and went out of the dining room with the maid. Anne looked after them a moment, then turned to Lord Townsend. "There is one other detail that you may look into for me, Andrew. I should like a regular governess or tutor to be engaged for Robert. It is not right that Constance should be obliged to look after him when she has her own duties to attend to."

"I can assure you that Constance does not mind it in the least," said Miranda. "And between her and Crumpet, as well as myself and his lordship, Robert is far less likely to fall into mischief than before."

"Yes, I know. You are all marvelous with Robert. But Constance is also your companion and maid, Miranda, and Crumpet also has a position to maintain. It is not fair to expect such double duty from them," said Anne.

"I agree. I shall look into it immediately and see if I cannot scare up a proper bearleader for Robert," said Lord Townsend.

"What a thing to say! Bearleader indeed! Of course, Robert can be—nevertheless, Andrew, I take exception to your term," said Anne, half-laughing and half-serious.

The viscount chuckled, his eyes dancing wickedly. "I bow to a mother's blind eyes, Anne."

Anne had the grace to blush. "I suppose I do think of Robert as being more saintly than he is."

"Robert is hardly saintly, Anne. I would say he is a normal, spirited, and lovable child," said Miranda.

Her cousin flashed her a beatific smile. "Thank you, Miranda," said Anne.

"How admirably you have smoothed the maternal feathers," murmured Lord Townsend in Miranda's ear.

Miranda pretended not to have heard him. She rose from the table saying, "Anne, why do we not leave his lordship to enjoy his wine?" Anne agreed and the ladies shortly made their way into the drawing room.

Anne settled herself in a deep armchair with a deep sigh. Miranda looked at her with concern. "Are you all right, Anne? Shall I call for Crumpet?"

Anne shook her head. "No, no. I am fine, truly. I am only a little fatigued by my first excursion. I shall be better presently."

"Very well. If you do not mind it, I shall play a little on the pianoforte," said Miranda.

"Oh, I should like it above all things. Music is so soothing to the ear after sitting at table, do you not think?" said Anne.

Miranda sat down at the pianoforte. Playing softly, she soon became engrossed in the music and her thoughts floated with it. Without being conscious of it, she began to sing in a low rich voice.

She was not aware of it when Lord Townsend entered the room and paused, his expression registering surprise. Quietly, he crossed the carpet and seated himself behind her to listen. A few moments later Crumpet came in with the tea urn. The viscount silently gestured for him to leave the service on the sideboard. Crumpet did so and departed, softly closing the drawing room door behind him.

Miranda had played for some time before she chanced to look up at the clock mantel. She was startled to see that it was ten o'clock. She had played uninterrupted for an hour and a half. She was dismayed she had neglected her cousin for so long. Immediately she stopped and turned on the bench. "Anne—" She was startled to meet the Viscount of Wythe's somber gaze.

"You are quite accomplished, Miss Wainwright. It has been a long time since I have enjoyed a musical evening half so well," said Lord Townsend quietly.

Miranda felt warmth rise in her face. It was disconcerting to realize that he had been listening. "Thank you, my lord. Anne—" Her glance went to her cousin and she saw that Anne was fast asleep in the chair.

"She was asleep when I came in and I did not wish to disturb her. I suspect that your lovely voice acted as a soothing soporific," said Lord Townsend.

Miranda blushed again at his compliment. She wondered why he honored her so extravagantly when there were probably many musical events that filled the viscount's usual social schedule. "I knew that Anne was more exhausted than she let on. She wouldn't allow me to call Crumpet," said Miranda.

"I do not think that Anne will take any harm from falling asleep in a chair. We will rouse her in a few minutes," said Lord Townsend. He indicated the tea urn. "Do you care for tea?"

"Yes, I would." Miranda rose from the pianoforte bench and followed the viscount over to the sideboard. She was surprised when he insisted upon serving her.

Lord Townsend gestured to the settee in front of the fireplace. Miranda accepted his invitation and gracefully seated herself. The viscount sat at the other end of the green damask-covered settee and balanced his cup and saucer on crossed knees. "You are a singularly unusual female, Miss Wainwright. Have I told you?"

"Not in so many words, no. I believe that you have touched only on my abominable manners and headstrong tendencies," said Miranda dryly.

"And I swear that every word I uttered was true. You and I are so often at loggerheads that I have been behind in noticing that you are also a lady of wit and talent," said Lord Townsend.

"Thank you, my lord. I am sure that is a high compliment, coming from you. I could almost suspect you of setting up a flirt with me," said Miranda with a smile. She picked up her cup to put it to her lips.

Lord Townsend set aside his tea on an occasional table before he stretched one arm across the back of the settee. His fingers brushed Miranda's shoulder. His gaze dropped briefly to her deep décolletage before he spoke. "I believe that I am, Miss Wainwright."

Miranda's cup rattled loudly in the saucer. She stared at him, disconcerted. There was an intensity in his brown eyes that made her heart begin to race. With a wavering laugh she tried to pass over the moment. "I am flattered indeed, my lord. But really!"

Lord Townsend seemed to take no notice of her interjection. He brought up his hand to gently touch her silken cheek. For a long moment Miranda was transfixed by his expression. Then a vision of her former fiancé rose before her mind's eye. Abruptly she leaped up, her nervous hands letting go of the cup and saucer. The china shattered across the Oriental carpet.

The noise awakened Anne, who roused slowly. "Oh, have I been asleep? So rude of me, I am sure." She blinked at her cousin, who stood motionless with an odd expression on her face. "Why, Miranda, you have spilled your tea! And your skirt is stained."

Miranda recovered herself. "It is of no consequence. I am sorry for the cup and saucer, Anne. I do not know how I came to be so clumsy. Pray excuse me." She quickly left the drawing room, passing Crumpet in the doorway. The butler had heard the sound of breakage and had come in to sweep away the pieces.

Anne was a bit startled by her cousin's hasty departure. "What on earth? It was only a bit of china."

Lord Townsend endeavored to turn her attention. "Anne, allow me to escort you upstairs to your room. I am on the way to bed myself. It has been a singularly pleasant evening, but I believe that we are all a little fatigued," he said, bending over his sister-in-law and offering her the support of his arm. Anne accepted his aid with a smile. The viscount chatted companionably to his sister-in-law as they climbed slowly up the stairs and made their way to her door. He handed her into the care of her maid before going on to his own apartments.

As he passed the rooms given over to Miss Wainwright, a faint smile crossed his face. Miss Wainwright had bolted like a startled doe. He found that curious. Perhaps the lady was not as immune to him as she would like him to think. As he entered his rooms Lord Townsend was whistling to himself.

The following day Miranda avoided the Viscount of Wythe as best she could. When she did chance to meet him, she was aware that he seemed amused at her expense and that brought an unbidden blush to her face. She managed to ignore the satiric look in his eyes and speak quite calmly to him.

Lord Townsend's startling announcement had thrown her into a mild state of confusion. She was astonished to discover within herself regret that she had rejected his advances so conclusively. But she could not so easily set aside the wariness that her last experience with a gentleman's professed regard had engendered in her.

Miranda thought it best to keep Lord Townsend at arm's length. He was a London beau and obviously an accomplished flirt. She could not shake the conviction that he was toying with her.

Late in the afternoon Crumpet came into the sitting room where Miranda was darning some sheets. He had gotten the post and there was the usual letter from her brother, Jeremy. Miranda immediately tore it open and perused it quickly. Jeremy wrote that he had done all he could with the port authorities and must now go to London to plead his case. He asked Miranda how she was getting along with their cousins and reminded her that she was certainly being better amused than if she had stayed in Falmouth. Miranda laughed a little at that when she thought of the difficulties of the neglected household and her dealings with a lively seven-year-old boy. But it was the often prickly relationship between herself and the Viscount of Wythe that she shook her head most over.

Jeremy concluded with the London address at which he would be staying. Miranda toyed with the idea of writing her brother with the latest particulars of the situation she had discovered at Willowswood, thinking that she could make it sound fairly amusing. But in the end she decided to say nothing that could possibly create anxiety in Jeremy about herself. He was burdened enough with the fight for the *Larabelle*, thought Miranda. But she did miss him horribly. His was such a level head and she could have confided to him her confusion over Lord Townsend's incredible declaration.

Eleven

The doctor's prediction came true. Almost at once, morning callers began to come to Willowswood. One of the first was the reverend and his wife. Anne very graciously accepted their profuse apologies that they had not been to see her while she was ill.

During the course of the conversation, the reverend made a passing mention of the former owner of Willowswood, and Miranda curiously asked if he had been well acquainted with Miss Claridge.

"We knew Miss Claridge as well as she would allow anyone to know her. Miss Claridge did not encourage visitors. I suspect that she preferred the company of her cats over people," said the reverend with a laugh.

"I had heard that Miss Claridge was a recluse and a bit of an eccentric. Indeed, Richard only vaguely recalled her from a visit as a boy. He was quite surprised to have figured in her will," said Anne.

"I am not at all surprised, Mrs. Townsend. Miss Claridge had her odd ways, but she was of an excellent mind. No doubt there was something about Mr. Townsend as a boy that impressed her those many years ago. Besides, one could not expect her to leave an estate such as Willowswood to her cats!" said Mrs. Averidge with a grave smile.

"That would have been eccentricity indeed," said her husband. He turned to Miranda. "I am glad to see that Mrs. Townsend has family to support her. It is a trial to be ill at any one time, but so much easier to bear when one is surrounded by loved ones."

Miranda threw her cousin a glance. "Indeed, Reverend Averidge, how true. Of course, it is pleasant also to know that one has the support of neighbors and friends during one's black days. I am certain that you and Mrs. Averidge must be pillars of strength for those in the community who are less fortunate. I harbor the greatest respect for those who aid their fellow man no matter what circumstances may prevail."

The reverend's feelings were mixed. He was not quite certain how to take Miss Wainwright's statement, whether she had just gently rebuked him for not earlier demonstrating his concern for Mrs. Townsend or paid him a compliment for carrying out his duties in a conscientious manner. Mrs. Averidge, who was not of as agile a mind as her husband, nodded graciously to Miranda. "Thank you, my dear. It is not always easy to carry the burden, of course. But Reverend Averidge and I do try to discharge our duties with a cheerful countenance."

"Indeed," murmured Miranda, with a glance at the reverend's frowning expression.

Hastily, Anne offered the biscuit tray to the reverend and his wife. "Pray do take another biscuit. Or perhaps you would care for another cup of tea?"

Mrs. Averidge had taken another biscuit and was about to nod her acceptance of a second cup of tea when the reverend firmly refused both. She looked at him with a bit of surprise and then regretfully turned down the refill of tea. The reverend leaned forward, his expression earnest. "Mrs.

Townsend, Mrs. Averidge and I must be going. But before we take our leave of you, I wish to assure you that you may call upon me for whatever needs you may have. I shall hold myself available at all times."

"Actually there is a service that you might do my cousin better than any other, Reverend," said Miranda. She smiled at the sudden wary look in the reverend's eyes. "I was quite shocked to discover when I arrived that my cousin and her son had been deserted by her household staff. There was fear of the pox, I understand, but surely that is now long since past."

"The good doctor informed most of us that the fear of the pox was a mistaken assumption, yes. But you must not blame the servants overmuch for their desertion, Miss Wainwright. The pox swept through this area only a few years ago and there are still vivid and painful memories of loved ones lost," said the reverend gently.

"I quite sympathize," said Miranda, nodding. "But apparently not all took the good doctor at his word. Reverend, it would be so helpful if *you* could reassure the neighborhood that Willowswood is not contaminated, so to speak, and that Mrs. Townsend will be happy to receive applications from those seeking a post in the house."

The reverend's frown lightened. "I understand, Miss Wainwright. It is a good thought. I know of several who now regret leaving Willowswood's employment. Yes, yes, I will be glad to be of service in this matter." He rose and his wife rose with him to proffer their gracious excuses for leaving. Anne, who leaned lightly on Miranda's arm for support, exchanged pleasantries with her departing guests as they walked to the door.

When the Averidges had stepped up into their gig and started away and Crumpet had closed the door, Anne looked at Miranda with a pained expression. "My dear cousin, did you have to prick the poor man so?"

"Come, Anne! He well deserved it. Where was he a few weeks ago when you were confined to bed, I should like to know? He admitted that the doctor reported there was no pox. If his conscience bothers him now, so much the better," said Miranda.

"You have such a combative spirit, Miranda! I almost envy you that. I think that I should have weathered this so much better if I was more like you," said Anne with a laugh.

"But then we should not get along half so well. Jeremy says when he becomes quite frustrated with me that I am nothing less than a hedgehog," said Miranda on a laugh.

"What in the world is a hedgehog?" asked Anne. She saw that Miranda was going to tell her and held up her hand. "No, do not tell me. It must be a horrid beast. Shame on Jeremy for teasing you. I think you the finest creature alive to care so for Robert and me."

"As if I could do less! Anne, we really must discuss what you want done with the household staff. The viscount has hired an undergardener and a gamesman and I have interviewed three women for the position of housekeeper. I am not certain which would be most suitable. Or would you prefer to invite back your former housekeeper, who I gather from Mrs. Crumpet, was from the village?" said Miranda.

"That woman I shall not have again in my house," said Anne with decision. "She was among the first to leave, spouting wildly of doom for us all, which did nothing to soothe the fears of the others. I was quite disappointed in her too as a housekeeper. She was rather more lax than I should have liked. I was on the point of letting her go when I was taken ill."

"Then I shall not call her back. The other three ladies all

appear most qualified. It is simply a matter of which you prefer. Shall I ask each of them in this afternoon so that you may talk with them? I requested that they all remain at Willowswood another day for a decision to be made," asked Miranda.

"Of course I shall talk with them," said Anne. "I do appreciate that you are handling the greater share of this, Miranda. I am so much stronger, but I do not think that my nerves would support such drudgery just yet. I am especially grateful to the doctor for sending Grace to me. She is a jewel and knows just what to do."

"I am glad to hear it. Since you have been up and about, you have needed your own maid," said Miranda.

She kept to herself the heartfelt comments of her companion, who had acted as lady's maid to both Miranda and Anne while at the same time endeavoring to keep an eye on the lively Robert.

"I am that happy to have another woman in the house, Miss Miranda. I was beginning to feel all at sixes and sevens what with Mrs. Townsend's requirements and watching the boy," Constance had said one evening while brushing Miranda's hair before bed.

Miranda had looked at her in the mirror. "And I am such a trial as well."

Constance shrugged and gave a small half-smile. "You are as you have always been, miss. Though you have been thoughtful and do tend to yourself more than some other ladies would. I won't deny that has been of help to me."

Miranda turned on the bench and caught the older woman's hands. "Constance, you are more appreciated than I can possibly tell you. You and I have been together a long time. And in the last months I do not know what I should have done without your support and advice. That fix I found myself in with Harrison Gregory . . . Well, we shan't dredge that up! But you have always been my companion and friend. You must know I value that about you," she said.

Constance Graves's eyes went a little misty. She gave a decisive sniff. "Now that is enough sentiment for one evening, Miss Miranda. You will have me crying like a baby if you do not leave off." She took up the brush again and vigorously put it through her mistress's thick hair.

There were a few moments of companionable silence. Then a thought occurred to Miranda. "Constance, I know that you have become very attached to Robert. Would you mind awfully if his lordship were to find a tutor or governess for him?"

The hairbrush paused in its action. "Why, I have not given it much thought," said Constance slowly. She brushed a few strokes, turning it over in her mind. "I am fond of the boy, true. But my feelings would not be hurt to have him given over to someone else, if that is what you are asking. Master Robert is a lively one and I am lazier than I used to be. He does need someone who is better able to enter into his flights of fancy."

"Flights of fancy," repeated Miranda. She sighed. "He manages to escape us all at times, does he not? Willful and brilliant and adventuresome is our Master Robert. I think that I shall advise his lordship to find a youthful tutor, one who has not quite forgotten what it is to be a child. Perhaps there is one who can channel Robert's energies into less harrowing occupations. Did I tell you that yesterday he managed to elude me, just for a moment, and I subsequently discovered him dangling from the third-story window ledge? He wished to see the sparrow's nest, he said.

My heart was in my mouth, I assure you. It took both Crumpet and myself to get him safely back inside."

"I will warrant that Crumpet's face was a picture," said Constance with cold-blooded amusement.

"He could have been no more white than I! And then Lord Townsend walked into the room. Robert danced over to him as happy as you please to recount his little adventure. Such a look Lord Townsend gave me! After he had sent Robert off with Crumpet, he very politely informed me that he was astonished that I allowed the boy such latitude. I was never in my life more mortified," said Miranda.

Constance gave a last swipe to her mistress's gleaming hair. "I should think his lordship would understand, seeing as how Master Robert has played off a few of his tricks with him as well."

"Yes, but somehow that is different, you know. That incident with the horses was quite unavoidable, whereas I should have kept Robert somehow chained to my side. I shall never understand a gentleman's logic," said Miranda with a touch of asperity, rising from the bench and slipping off her robe. She got into bed, yawning widely.

"I doubt the gentlemen have any more claim to logic than women, despite their claims to the contrary. Remember Mister Gregory's reasons for wishing to wed you? It was not only your ties to a shipping family that intrigued him, you will recall," said Constance, preparing to leave the bedroom and seek her own bed.

Miranda grimaced. "Truce, Constance. My independence posed a challenge to Gregory. He admitted it to me. But it was hardly logical for him to believe that once we were engaged, he could mold me into his ideal of womanhood!"

"Good night, Miss Miranda," said Constance, and softly

closed the door. Miranda reached over to blow out the candle on her bedside table and slid lower beneath the bedclothes. She was asleep almost instantly.

Twelve

Anne told Miranda that she and Richard were not too well known to their neighbors since they had taken possession of Willowswood only ten months previously. She was therefore looking forward to getting better acquainted. Miranda wondered that her cousin did not harbor any ill feeling toward her neighbors for their lack of concern when she was ill, but kindness was an integral part of Anne's nature. Anne Townsend rarely said a disparaging word about anyone, and when she did it was always tempered with a possible excuse for that person's behavior.

The first invitation that those at Willowswood received for an evening's entertainment came from the local squire and his wife. Mrs. Earlington and her daughters paid a morning call shortly after the Reverend Averidge and his wife, and extended a personal invitation to a dinner dance. Though Anne said that she did not think that she was yet up to dancing since the least exertion still tired her, she announced quite firmly that Miranda and Andrew were to enjoy themselves and not bother about her. She would sit quietly with the matrons and enjoy a comfortable coze while her cousin and brother-in-law took advantage of the dancing floor.

Miranda also looked forward to the evening. It had been

some time since she had whirled about on the dance floor. She knew herself to be a graceful dancer ånd so had never been anxious about her ability as so often was the case even with ladies considered beyond coming out.

Not wishing to stand out too obviously as a colonial, Miranda dressed carefully. She chose a gown with a demitrain that had been sewn for her by a talented seamstress who was not above making tiny adjustments to patterns gotten from England. Though recognizable as a current fashion, the gown had a fresh quality that was rare for a made-up pattern. Tucks of gossamer lace and satin ribbon adorned the low bosom, the sleeves were slim and reached over the hands from the wrist bands. The skirt was open in front to reveal a lavishly ornamental petticoat.

Constance fixed Miranda's hair high on the crown of her head, pulling forward wispy curls to soften her face. Miranda wore an amethyst set that had been her mother's. The lilac stones glowed softly in her dainty ears and in the necklace clasped about her neck. Placing a cloak over her shoulders, she took one last glance in the mirror, and with a friendly word to Constance, left the bedroom.

Lord Townsend was already downstairs waiting for the ladies. When he saw Miranda, his eyes took on an appreciative gleam. "Well, well. You look most lovely this evening, Miss Wainwright," he said.

"Thank you, my lord," said Miranda, feeling her heart beat faster when she looked at him. She thought that she had seldom seen a more handsome man. The viscount's hair was brushed into the fashionably disheveled look of *à la Titus*, which emphasized the planes of his lean face. His moderately high shirt points were starched to perfection, his stark white cravat was intricately tied and secured with a diamond stickpin that flashed under the light whenever he turned. His superb shoulders were set off by the close cut of his black evening coat. Beneath a dark gray satin waistcoat, he wore a ruffled shirt and fobs hung from black ribands at his trim waist. His black breeches outlined muscular thighs and calves. In short, Lord Townsend was splendid in evening gear. Miranda was irritated that she felt a constraint on her part as they spoke. He was still the same gentleman that she had learned to like, she reminded herself.

Anne came down soon after Miranda. The viscount handed the ladies into the carriage and got in himself for the short drive to the squire's place. Miranda inquired of Anne what she knew of the Earlingtons.

"It is generally known that Squire Earlington is a sporting gentleman. As for Mrs. Earlington and the daughters, you may judge for yourself from their visit. They are a healthy lot and genteel to boot," said Anne.

The squire's house stood on a small wooded hill above the village. George Earlington was a congenial gentleman who welcomed all to his hall with expansive goodwill. He was generous to a fault and treated his family with unusual latitude. His overwhelming interest was breeding the best hunting hounds and his reputation exceeded the limits of the district for several surrounding counties.

The squire was a hardy gentleman who believed strongly in the positive effects of good bloodlines and had chosen his wife accordingly. Mrs. Earlington was a good-natured well-built woman who had admirably proven the squire's theory. She had not been sick more than a handful of days in her life and she was capable of putting long hours into her responsibilities. As a consequence, the squire was a contented man. The manor's reputation as an oasis of comfort and ease reflected well on him and if he regretted at all Mrs. Earlington's tendency to produce daughters he was never heard to voice it.

However, Mrs. Earlington knew herself to have failed in this one area. Though she loved all three of her daughters with the same generous spirit as did her worthy spouse, she sighed from time to time with regret that there would not be an Earlington of Earlington to carry on the squire's torch. But she was nothing if not a practical woman. The squire's pronouncements and good fortune in breeding much sought-after hounds had not been lost on Mrs. Earlington. When she had thought about it, she concluded that her daughters came from some of the best blood around and she made up her mind that every one of the Earlington girls was worthy of a gentleman from good family and back-ground. Her ambition became to settle her three daughters in just such a happy situation as she had found with the squire so that she could look forward to the advent of healthy, strong grandchildren.

Accordingly, Mrs. Earlington's greeting to the ladies was cordial but her greeting to Lord Townsend was a bit more effusive. The Viscount of Wythe was handsome, eminently eligible, and from all accounts well-heeled. Whomever he bestowed his name on would never go about in rags, Mrs. Earlington was certain of that.

"My lord, how good of you to grace our small gathering. I told the squire but this morning how your attendance would be the capstone of what looks to be a fine evening. Pray do come with me. I should like to introduce you to the squire and my daughters," she said.

With her hand firmly attached to Lord Townsend's sleeve, Mrs. Earlington spared a glance for Anne and Miranda. "Mrs. Townsend, I am certain that you know quite a number of people. Mrs. Averidge, for instance, was just telling me of the most pleasant visit that she had with you last week. Here she comes now. I am happy to see you again, Miss Wainwright. I have always had an interest in the colonies. Perhaps we shall speak more later. This way, my lord."

Lord Townsend had been startled by the lady's degree of friendliness, but his expression smoothed to its usual urbanity as he accepted what was obviously his due as the highest socially ranking personage. "Certainly, Mrs. Earlington. I will be glad to make the acquaintance of my sister-in-law's distinguished neighbor," he said affably. He allowed himself to be whisked across the ballroom.

Anne and Miranda glanced at one another, matching mirth in their eyes. "I do not think Andrew quite appreciates the impact that he will have tonight," said Anne.

Miranda scanned the ballroom quickly. "No, indeed. There must be at least half a dozen more ladies in attendance than gentlemen. And unless I miss my guess, all have already spied the elegant stranger in their midst. The viscount will be busy all evening making the rounds," she said, laughing, and thinking it a grand joke on him.

Mrs. Averidge came up to them and spoke gently on general topics. She took upon herself the duty of making the Willowswood ladies known to several personages. Anne was soon ensconced with the matrons, who welcomed her to their midst not only for her own sake but also out of curiosity about her guests. As for Miranda, she was gratified to be asked almost at once onto the dance floor.

The viscount's bearing and smart evening dress was of an elegance seldom seen in the provincial neighborhood and the ladies in the ballroom were acutely aware of his presence. He was swiftly judged to be the most attractive gentleman in the room and not only from the standpoint of his refined dress. His very manner, at once arrogant and easy, proclaimed him a London smart. As for the gentlemen, who were the sort to be found at any country gathering talking of horses and hounds, they were not so quickly accepting of his lordship. Those attributes that most appealed to the ladies put the gentlemen off until it was discovered that the viscount was an enthusiastic hunter and spoke as knowledgeably about hounds and jumpers as the next man. Then the viscount's dandyism was forgiven him and the cut of his coat and the intricacy of his neckcloth ceased to be the objects of scorn among the elder horsy gentlemen.

The younger set, especially the aspiring dandies, from the first moment of laying eyes on the viscount, recognized him as a blade of the first water. His dress, his mode of speaking, his carriage were all avidly devoured by the younger gentlemen. One voiced the consensus of them all when he vowed that beginning on the morrow he meant to acquire those attributes that lent the London gentleman such distinction.

"Yes, but does he drive to an inch?" asked one young gentleman who was of a more questioning mind than his fellows.

"Of course he must. All the London beaux do," stated a childhood friend impatiently. "It is a requirement, you know." His companions nodded sagely. Still the one young gentleman looked dubious. But since this thin young man had little actual interest in sporting events and preferred to spend much of his time with his nose buried in the latest papers on agriculture, his opinion did not weigh overmuch with the others, who could be said to be sporting-mad.

The Viscount of Wythe was not unaware of the interest he generated and it amused him. He was used to the highest degree of regard, of course, but he was treated with almost a hint of reverence by some of the individuals that he came into contact with that evening. With good-humored contempt he dismissed them variously as toadeaters and social climbers. It did not occur to him that he would have felt astonished if he had not garnered such attention in a small district. It was merely his due.

Miranda had met many of the young ladies by that time. More often than not they were more interested in her acquaintance with Lord Townsend than they were in her. She could not help laughing to herself at the transparency of their questions and the direction of their conversations. She had difficulty in remembering their names since they all seemed alike in their interests.

One young lady, however, stood out from the rest. Mary Alice Burton was a brunette of astonishing beauty. Her eyes were violet, her mouth a perfect pink rosebud, her figure slender yet voluptuous. She approached with what Miranda was startled to realize was the wariness of a feline checking out a potential rival.

Miss Burton introduced herself to Miranda with an assurance born of her exalted position as the reigning neighborhood beauty. "I am Mary Alice Burton. I understand that you are Mrs. Townsend's cousin from America," she said. Her tone conveyed the impression that she held America to be a place of barbaric peoples and customs. She swept Miranda with a sharp glance, appraising the colonial's becoming hairstyle and well-made lilac gown.

Miranda smiled. "Yes, I am Miranda Wainwright. And I rather enjoy being an American."

There was a momentarily startled look in Miss Burton's eyes that gave way to a sharper examination of Miranda's face. "Quite, Miss Wainwright. I do apologize if I sounded condescending, but it has not been long since the states belonged to England, has it? One learns a certain attitude, of course."

"I am certain one does," said Miranda with a hint of amusement. She could see that she had irritated Miss Burton, and smiled with all the friendliness at her command. "I believe you and I need not spar further, Miss Burton. We have already taken one another's measure, do you not agree?"

"Indeed. And as such is the case, let us be completely frank with one another," said Miss Burton. Her beautiful eyes were chilly. "You are in a unique position as Mrs. Townsend's cousin and guest, Miss Wainwright. I think you know to what I refer."

"I believe I do. You are not the first lady this evening to inquire into the Viscount of Wythe's background and eligibility, Miss Burton," said Miranda dryly.

"But I am the only one of consequence," replied Miss Burton, smiling slightly. Her face was as pleasant to look at as a new-blown rose, until one chanced to register the hard expression in her eyes. "I already know Lord Townsend is a bachelor, and a wealthy one. I do wonder, however, about the extent of your relationship with his lordship."

"I beg your pardon?" said Miranda, stupefied.

"I don't think that your wits have gone begging of a sudden, Miss Wainwright! I wish to know if you fancy yourself a viscountess as do these others," said Miss Burton impatiently, with a dismissing gesture of her fan at the crowded ballroom.

Miranda felt the edges of her temper curl. "My dear Miss Burton, I shall not confide in you one particle of my thoughts. What I think of your impertinence can well be imagined, however."

Mary Alice smiled almost pityingly at her. "I understand

you, of course. And do understand me. I shall ride rough-shod over anyone who impedes me. From that standpoint alone you would do well to put a wide berth between your-self and the Viscount of Wythe." She inclined her head in a nod and took her leave of Miranda with all appearance of friendliness.

"What an unwholesome, arrogant little baggage," said Miranda indignantly.

"Who is it that you are castigating so heartily, Miss Wainwright?" asked an amused voice.

Miranda turned to find the viscount standing nearby. "Oh, it is you, my lord."

"Pray, must you sound so matter-of-fact? I must tell you that in the last hour I have gotten quite used to expressions of gratification at my mere existence," said Lord Townsend with a grin.

"How diverting for you, my lord!" said Miranda with a touch of asperity.

Lord Townsend was startled. He raised a well-marked brow. "Who could it have been that has so set up your back? Surely not the exquisite creature who just left your side. She is the only young lady who has not managed to present herself to me."

"That is Miss Burton. She informed me of her ambition to become a viscountess," said Miranda coolly.

The viscount threw back his head and laughed. When he had sobered, he said with dancing eyes, "Thank you, Miss Wainwright. You have put it quite neatly in perspective for me. I am a *cause célèbre* not for my wit or charm, but for my person and title. I do not think that thought has crossed only Miss Burton's mind. I am familiar with the chase and ever since I have set foot in this ballroom I have felt most uncomfortably like the fox."

"How silly of you, my lord. As though a knowledgeable, wily gentleman such as yourself could ever be so easily trapped. No, I believe that it will take much more than a few hungry houndish gazes," said Miranda. "I think that a long run is what will be required to snare such a prize as yourself and there are probably a few ladies here this evening who would be most willing to donate their efforts to the cause."

"I appreciate your succinct analysis of my situation, ma'am! I can see that I shall receive no pity from your hands. But perhaps you will indulge me in a turn about the floor? The squire's three marriageable daughters are bearing down on us, you see," said Lord Townsend. He swept Miranda onto the floor without waiting for her consent.

"That was quite cowardly of you, my lord," said Miranda with mock disapproval.

"But very expedient of the fox," said Lord Townsend with a disarming grin. Miranda was laughing as the movement of the country dance separated them. When they came together again, he said, "It occurs to me to wonder why Miss Burton would confide her ambitions to you, Miss Wainwright."

"Perhaps I struck her as a particularly sympathetic confidante," said Miranda with a flippant air.

Lord Townsend looked down at her with a speculative gleam in his dark eyes. "I do not think that is at all probable. More likely the beauty was testing her powers to intimidate. Were you intimidated, Miss Wainwright?"

"Not in the least," said Miranda promptly, and then regretted her hastiness when she saw the look of satisfaction in his eyes. She did not have long to wait before he struck.

"Then Miss Burton was satisfied that you are a rival for my affections," said the viscount calmly.

The dance parted them again before Miranda could react to his outrageous statement. When he took her hand once more, Miranda hissed, "You are the most horridly arrogant man! Let me take leave to tell you, sir, that I would not lower myself to—to *compete* for a gentleman. Especially one so—so . . ." Words failed her.

"Arrogant, conceited, full of myself?" suggested Lord Townsend helpfully.

Miranda sent him a daggered look. "Yes, yes and yes!" she snapped, and she made up her mind that for the remainder of the dance she would refuse to speak another word to him no matter how provoking he managed to be. She swiftly discovered that Lord Townsend could be very provoking. She could do nothing to stop his outrageous whispers. Nor could she show her displeasure, since there were several people who were taking note of Lord Townsend's attention toward her. She could only pin a smile to her face and appear to be enjoying herself. For the most part she kept her gaze lowered whenever the dance brought her together with the viscount, but occasionally her lashes flew upward to reveal the flash of impotent fury in her blue-black eyes.

Miranda was never more glad for a set to end. She returned to her seat with almost unseemly haste and she was not best pleased to find that Lord Townsend followed her. "Do go away," she begged. She was unaware that one or two of the matrons nearby heard her and that their faces expressed startled incredulity.

The viscount was aware of the ladies' riveted attention, however. As it was not his intent that he and Miss Wainwright become the subject of speculative gossip, he smoothed over the moment as best he could. "Certainly I shall. Thank you for informing me of Anne's request. I shall attend to it immediately," he said, and bowed. He smiled at Miranda's look of bewilderment and walked away.

One of the matrons leaned over in her chair toward Miranda. "My dear Miss Wainwright, his lordship is such a handsome gentleman, do you not agree? My heart palpitates in quite an unseemly manner whenever his glance chances my way," she said.

Miranda was startled. She knew the lady, but it took her several seconds to place her as one of those who had called at Willowswood not many days before. She had been amused at the time by the lady's frosty eyes and measuring questions and she had dealt with the starchy dame in her most gracious manner. Mrs. Heatherton had unbent enough to give her a sharp nod of approval as she was taking leave of her and Anne, and had promised them invitations to a small rout that she was planning for later in the season.

Miranda had stared at Mrs. Heatherton for such a long moment that the lady began to wonder if Miss Wainwright had gone into some sort of trance. Miranda collected herself and smiled. "Oh, you mean the Viscount of Wythe. Yes, I suppose that he is. Pray excuse me, ma'am. I should like a lemonade, I think." She rose and made her way sedately to the refreshment table.

Mrs. Heatherton turned to her companion to exchange an expressive glance. "These colonials. I had always heard that they were an odd lot. Now I understand what was meant. To think that the young woman did not realize that I was speaking of the viscount! As though any other gentleman here could hold a candle to him!" The ladies shook their heads and pitied Miss Wainwright for her lack of appreciation for the manly qualities.

Thirteen

Robert kicked a stone in the drive discontentedly. Ever since the sparrow incident and his uncle's quiet stricture on the matter, he had not really been able to find much to amuse him. At first it had been great fun to hang about the stables, but Uncle Andrew's groom had taken on some of the exercising of the horses so that his friend Jenkins had less time for him. In addition, Uncle Andrew had specifically forbidden such amusements as climbing out of windows, wandering the estate without permission, teasing the bull, or setting snares for Mrs. Crumpet's chickens. Uncle Andrew had also been very plain on what he considered other evils and reluctantly Robert saw that his days were to become grossly unexciting. It was really not fair. And though he would have felt no compunction about disobeying Crumpet or Constance or even his mother, there was something about the expression in the Viscount of Wythe's eyes that warned him to abide by his uncle's new set of rules.

As for Cousin Miranda, she was of no use to him. Robert had observed that Uncle Andrew often listened to Cousin Miranda, though he pretended not to. He had hoped that Cousin Miranda might intervene with his uncle on his behalf. But she, too, had read him a short lecture and her tone had been decisive. He could not look for leniency there.

Robert's restless eyes roved over the grove of trees alongside the drive. He had that terrible feeling of aloneness that he so often got. He did not know or understand why, but it drove him to do things that normally he might not conceive of, if only to escape that awful feeling for a time. It always came back, though, whenever he was alone but especially at night. At night was when he thought about his father, his jolly papa who played with him and quietly talked with him as though he was much older. One day Papa had put on his soldier's uniform and gone far away. He used to think about his mother at night, too, but she was getting better and better and he saw more of her. But though he loved his mother, it was not the same as being with his papa.

Robert's eyes blurred. He swiped away the tears with the back of his hand. That awful hollowness seized him and he began to run, heedless of direction or obstacles.

When at last he stopped, his lungs hurt with the great gulps of air that he pulled in and his legs trembled. He was sweaty and his face and hands were scratched and stinging from the whip of branches and grass. His short coat was ripped at the shoulder and his trousers were streaked with dirt, but he spared not a thought for his clothes.

Robert leaned against the rough bark of a wide oak, his chest heaving. The feeling was gone. As he blinked the perspiration out of his eyes, he became aware of the sound of water running over rocks. He stumbled forward to the edge of a tranquil and sun-dappled stream. Throwing himself to the ground he ducked his head into the cool water. When he raised his head he was spluttering. Droplets sprayed as he shook his wet hair. Robert cupped his hand and drank deeply before rolling over on his back. He rested on the bank for a time, staring up into the branches of oak and willow and birch. Through the leaves he could see the clouds moving majestically across the blue sky and his thoughts moved slowly with them.

He must have slept because when he next became aware of his surroundings the position of the sun had changed and his hair was dry. Robert sat up. He spied a squirrel and he watched as the small creature scurried up the trunk of a slender birch. Just as the squirrel's weight threatened to collapse the thin branches, it leaped across to a second tree, leaving the first tree dipping and swaying. Robert laughed. The squirrel, startled by the alien sound, chirruped agitatedly and whisked its golden-brown tail up and down.

Robert looked thoughtfully at the still swaying tree. His knowledgeable eyes measured the trunk. The tree would bear his weight up to a point. He rose, dusting off his hands, and shinnied up the tree. The higher he went the more he felt the trunk sway. His heart pounded with each dip of the trunk but he only climbed higher. The top of the supple tree suddenly dipped down in a dizzying fast arc. The boy's legs flew free but he still held tightly to the trunk with his hands. Just feet above the ground Robert lost his grip. The tree snapped upright and he tumbled to the grassy ground. He lay stunned a moment, his heart racing, as he caught his breath. Then he leaped up and raced again to the tree.

Time and again the boy climbed the tree to experience the crazy descent. He became ever bolder and climbed higher before letting go with his legs. Delighted laughter burst from him with each frightening ride. At first he did not hear and then he did not pay attention to the ominous groan that began to grow a bit louder with his continued play. He noticed only that the tree seemed to lean a little more than it had.

Suddenly the slender trunk snapped in two, the broken half of it gripped futilely between Robert's hands as he fell. His eyes flew open to their widest extent. His mouth opened in a soundless scream. The sky tipped madly, green rushed past him. The iron ground drove pain into him and Robert's world disappeared.

The sun was nearly set when the boy at last sighed and stirred. White-hot pain shot through his body with the slight movement. He cried out and became fully conscious. Slowly, carefully, Robert raised his head to look down at himself. His left leg lay at an awkward angle. Even as his mind coolly took note of the fact, he tested his arms one at a time. Bruised and shaken though he was, the boy gripped his lower lip between his teeth and raised himself to a sitting position. He already knew from the way his left leg felt that it was the center of the pain. But it was not until he could see his ripped, bloodied trousers and the bone jutting out of the stretched skin that the pain truly hit him. His face blanched. It hurt so badly that he could barely keep from crying out. His fingers clenched in the grass on either side of his thin shanks. He bit his lip hard, tasting blood. "Papa would not cry. He would not ever cry," he said manfully. A desolation washed over him. "Papa!" He choked on a sob and tears slipped down his dirty face. An owl called softly on the breeze as the sun slipped further behind the trees.

Miranda took a restless turn about the drawing room. She did not know how long she had paced. She threw another glance at the clock on the mantel and smacked her hands together. The drawing room door opened and she turned quickly. "There you are at last, my lord!" she exclaimed.

Lord Townsend caught her outheld hands in his. "My

dear Miss Wainwright, if I had but known of your strong attachment to me, I would never have absented myself from the estate," he said jestingly. Then her expression registered with him and his fingers tightened on hers. "What has happened, Miranda?"

She did not even notice his use of her Christian name. "It's Robert. He has been gone for hours and now it is growing dark. No one has seen him and he is not to be found anywhere about the house or stables. My lord, you know that I am not a female given to vague fears. I know that something dreadful has befallen him."

Lord Townsend stared down into her anxious eyes. He was too well used to Miss Wainwright's steady nature to believe other than that she spoke the truth. "Has the copse been scoured and the meadow across the hedgerows?"

"Yes, yes! I have been out myself with Crumpet and Constance. Your valet and the grooms have searched as well and have found no sign of him. I don't know what to tell Anne. She will have to know, but I have put it off until she comes down to dinner," said Miranda.

"No, there is no need for Anne to know just yet." The viscount's expression was hard. "The rascal has gone far afield, then. When I find him I will have something to say to him about it. Miranda, ring for Crumpet and request lanterns. And we need something of Robert's for the hounds."

"Hounds!?" exclaimed Miranda, staring at him. She pulled on the bell rope hanging beside the sofa.

The viscount favored her with a faint grin, though the amusement did not quite reach his eyes. "My groom and I brought back a few hounds from the squire's place. I wanted to try the hunter I bought two weeks ago from Bertram Burton to see how it would go with a pack," he said. "Now it seems that the hounds must be put to quite

another use. Damn the boy! I spoke to him about his esca-
pades only days ago."

"He is not a boy one can effectively hem in," said
Miranda.

Lord Townsend caught her gaze, recalling how grim he
had been with her over the sparrow incident, and he
laughed. "Your point is well-taken, Miss Wainwright. Ah,
Crumpet! I am informed that Master Robert has gotten
himself lost. We will require lanterns and one of the boy's
jackets or shirts at once. Bring them to the stables. I will be
readying the mounts and the hounds."

The butler's face did not change expression. "Very good,
my lord." He left on his errands.

The viscount was about to leave the drawing room when
Miranda caught his sleeve. "Pray have a horse saddled for
me, my lord. I shall be going with you," she said.

"The devil you say! You shall remain here and soothe
Anne," said Lord Townsend.

"That can be left far better to Anne's maid, who has a
way with her mistress than cannot be excelled. I shall inform Grace at once of the matter and then I shall join you
in the stables," said Miranda, sweeping past him through
the door. On the stairs she paused. "And I would take grave
exception to your going without me, my lord."

Lord Townsend looked startled, then he grinned. "You
know my mind too well, Miranda. Very well, I shall wait on
you. But only a few minutes, mind. I wish to begin the
search as swiftly as possible."

"That is all I ask," said Miranda. She had at last noticed
that he had taken liberty with her Christian name and her
face was warm with color. She found that his familiarity was
not at all offensive to her. Without another glance back at
him she ran lightly up the stairs.

The party that set out from Willowswood consisted of Lord Townsend, his groom, and Miss Wainwright. The hounds had quickly gotten the scent of the boy from one of his shirts and nosed about for the trail. One of the dogs bayed suddenly and loped off, the rest of the pack surging after it. The riders spurred after the hounds, their lanterns bobbing crazily over the ground.

It began to drizzle. The viscount cast a glance up at the dark sky, his face carved in grim lines. He knew that if the boy were too far afield the scent would be washed away in the rain before he was found. Fear rode him and he urged on the hounds with harsh shouts.

Robert was found closer than expected. He lay curled in an awkward ball in a small clearing. The hounds circled him excitedly. Lord Townsend jumped off his horse and waded through the dogs, cursing fluently. Miranda and the groom also dismounted and came quickly across the wet grass. The viscount set his lantern down beside the boy's head. Its light illuminated Robert's whitened cheek, streaked with dirt and tears. Lord Townsend knelt and gently turned his nephew over.

The boy was breathing shallowly, rapidly, and he shuddered convulsively with cold. His eyes remained closed. "Robert? Robert!" The boy's lashes fluttered but did not open. Lord Townsend bent to raise him from the ground.

"Wait, my lord!" The groom held his lantern high. "His leg is broke, my lord. Best tie it afore lifting him onto your brute."

Lord Townsend's mouth tightened as he gazed on the ugly wound, now swollen and black with bruising. He nodded abruptly. "Find some suitable branches, Hawkins." Gently he lowered his nephew's shoulders back onto the ground. The viscount unclasped the stickpin that secured his voluminous neckcloth and stripped off the length of silk.

Miranda knelt beside her small cousin, not heeding the water that soaked her riding skirt. Brushing aside his tumbled hair, she laid a cool hand against his forehead. "He is burning with fever," she said quietly.

Lord Townsend ruthlessly ripped his expensive neckcloth into lengths. "He will be fortunate if he does not die from exposure," he said grimly.

The groom returned with two long branches that he had trimmed clean. The viscount nodded to him and without a word exchanged the two men prepared to set the broken limb. Miranda took firm hold of Robert's shoulders, dreading the moment that the leg was straightened. It was as bad as she thought possible. The boy's body rose under her straining hands. He cried out in a succession of rising screams and his hands tore frantically at her restraining arms. At last it was done. The boy went limp, sobbing pitifully.

Miranda sat back on her heels, shaken in every nerve. Lord Townsend wrapped his nephew in his coat, throwing a glance at her as he did so. "Are you all right, Miss Wainwright?" She nodded and got to her feet, turning away toward her horse. The viscount jerked his head at his groom, who hurried to aid the lady into her saddle.

With the boy held against his chest, Lord Townsend walked to his mount. He waited for the groom and gave his nephew into the man's hold. Then he stepped into the saddle and reached down to once more take the boy. Lord Townsend settled Robert as comfortably as he could before him in the saddle before he started the horse into a walk.

The boy sighed. He knew that somehow he had been found and he was safe. He burrowed closer against the reassuring security of his uncle's body. "Uncle Andrew," he breathed. "I'm sorry. But you didn't say anything about trees."

Lord Townsend looked down at the top of his unruly head. The worry he felt sharpened his voice to anger. "My God, boy, what were you thinking of?"

The boy's eyes flew open and in a passing shaft of moonlight they were quite lucid. "Papa. I was thinking of Papa." His lashes drooped once more and his chin sank onto his chest.

Fourteen

When the search party returned to Willowswood the dinner
hour had already come and gone. The viscount carried his
nephew inside the house, leaving his mount to his groom's
care. Miranda followed him, pausing only long enough to
give instructions to Crumpet, who met them at the door.
The butler nodded and went at once to carry out his orders.

As Lord Townsend strode through the hall, Anne came
out of the drawing room at a rush. Her face was white and
her eyes were large pools of anxiety. She exclaimed incoher-
ently at sight of her son lying limp and unmoving in his uncle's arms. His head had fallen back over Lord Townsend's
arm and Anne realized that he was unconscious. The maid
who accompanied her laid a calming hand on her arm, but
Anne shook her off. She caught up with Lord Townsend at
the stairs. "Andrew! What has happened? Is he . . . Oh dear
God."

"No, he is not dead! Out of my way, Anne. He needs to
be put to bed," said the viscount impatiently. He brushed
past his sister-in-law and quickly took the stairs.

Miranda and the maid converged on Anne, who stood
immobile, staring after her son. Unheeded tears slipped
down her face. Miranda put an arm around her cousin's
fragile shoulders. "Robert has suffered a broken leg, Anne,

and he was horribly chilled by the night air. Once he is warm and comfortable he will be fine," she said soothingly.

Anne clutched her arm. "With Richard gone and wondering every day if he is safe, alive . . . Miranda, I could not bear it if anything should happen to Robert. He and I are all either of us have right now."

Miranda met the maid's eyes and the woman nodded slightly. "I understand, Anne. I think it best if you go with Grace now. It would not do for you to appear at Robert's bedside just yet. Your tears would frighten him."

Anne dashed her hands across her eyes. "You are right, of course. How incredibly silly of me. But Miranda—the doctor! He must be sent for."

"I have already requested Crumpet to send someone for the good doctor. Do go on, Anne. I shall look in on Robert myself and after I have seen him I shall come at once to you," said Miranda.

Anne nodded. "Very well, I shall do as you ask." She allowed the maid to lend her support for the climb up the stairs.

Miranda did not match her cousin's slower steps but went swiftly up to the nursery. She pushed open the door. Lord Townsend looked up at her entrance but he did not address her. He was holding his nephew while Constance Graves swiftly put a clean nightshirt on the boy. Robert was conscious. His lips were compressed and his small face tight. His limbs were nearly rigid and his body jumped at the least jar to his leg. At last the task was done and the viscount gently laid him down on the pillows. Robert sighed in relief and turned his head aside to the wall.

Miranda came up to the bed. As best she could without touching the leg she studied the wound. It was inflamed and filthy and swollen. Sight of the fractured bone was almost obliterated by the traumatized flesh around it, but it looked to have been cleanly set. When she retreated from the bedside, the viscount took her place, dragging a chair close so that he could sit beside his nephew. He took Robert's limp hand in his own.

Constance, who had observed her mistress's frown, moved a little away from the bed to join Miranda. "What think you, Miss Miranda?" asked Constance quietly.

Miranda turned to her. Her low voice was crisp. "It must be cleaned immediately. Already infection has set in. I shall have to gather some fresh herbs. The medicinal cabinet is woefully inadequate. Pray ask Mrs. Crumpet to heat some water, Constance. I shall need it to steep the comfrey and for the catnip tea," she said. The maid nodded and departed from the room.

Miranda was about to follow her when her arm was taken in a strong grip. She looked up, startled.

"What are you intending, Miss Wainwright? I warn you. I'll not have my nephew quacked," said Lord Townsend harshly.

Miranda raised her brows. "I do not intend quackery, my lord. That wound must be cleaned as soon as possible if we are to prevent blood poisoning. I intend to apply a poultice of comfrey, commonly known as knitbone. Comfrey has been used since the Middle Ages to promote the mending of bones and reduce the swelling of wounds. As for the catnip tea, it will aid in reducing the boy's fever. Believe me, Robert will be much more comfortable for it." She glanced down at the viscount's hand. "If you will release me, my lord, I shall be about my task."

Lord Townsend stared at her, frowning. Vaguely he recalled from his childhood his nurse extolling the virtues of knitbone and other herbs. He was not certain that he placed as much value in herbal remedies as others did, but there was no denying that the teas Miss Wainwright made up for Anne had been of benefit to his sister-in-law's nerves. And he also had recognized the insidious signs of infection in the flesh torn by the fractured bone. The very thought of blood poisoning left him cold, but he was helpless to do anything for his nephew except wait for the doctor to arrive. Miss Wainwright at least offered some sort of action. Slowly he let go of her arm. "Very well, Miss Wainwright. I bow to your superior experience."

"Thank you, my lord," said Miranda. After collecting a cloak from her bedroom, she went downstairs and let herself out into the herb garden. The rain was coming down harder, making it difficult to see. Miranda held her lantern high, peering through the drumming rain. When she found the beds she wanted, she knelt on the wet flagstones and placed the lantern beside her. Taking scissors out of the small basket she carried, she clipped good measures of each of the herbs she needed.

When she returned to the kitchen, she found that Mrs. Crumpet had hot water standing ready. Thin cotton strips were laid on the table near the pots. She stripped off her streaming cloak, saying, "Thank you, Mrs. Crumpet. It will take but a few minutes to make the poultice." She brushed back her damp hair. The cloak had not completely protected her from the weather, but Miranda ignored the unpleasant sensation of wet, dragging skirts. She washed the comfrey leaves quickly and pressed them dry between linen cloths so that it would be easier to chop them up.

"Aye, miss. Mrs. Graves tells me that you were wanting a catnip tea as well. My own mother always recommended a bit of camomile and peppermint be added, with a touch of honey for taste. That will relax the poor lad as well as work on his fever. I would be happy to make it up for you whilst you are busy," said Mrs. Crumpet.

"Of course, Mrs. Crumpet! I have brought in peppermint but I did not think of the camomile," said Miranda, gesturing with her knife at the basket of fresh herbs.

The cook picked up the lantern that Miranda had set on the table. "We'll have camomile in the medicinal cabinet. I won't be a moment, miss." She left the kitchen.

Constance smiled across the table at Miranda. She was getting together on a tray a basin containing soft clean cloths and a kettle of hot water. "Mrs. Crumpet approves of the old remedies, Miss Miranda. You have risen high in her esteem."

"Lord Townsend has far different feelings, however. He disapproves of what he terms my quackery. Actually, I am somewhat surprised that he did not refuse to allow me to treat the boy," said Miranda. She swept the chopped comfrey into boiling water and mixed the brew.

Constance picked up the tray. "His lordship is very attached to Master Robert. Perhaps he felt some help is better than none. I shall go up and clean the wound."

"Enlist the viscount's aid, Constance. It will give him something useful to do and you will need him to calm Robert, who I suspect will object strenuously to the entire process," said Miranda, not looking up as she took the pot of comfrey out of the heat.

"Yes, miss," said Constance with grim amusement as she left the kitchen.

Miranda tentatively tested the temperature of the boiled concoction. It was too hot and she sighed impatiently. She turned to the basket of herbs and took out the catnip and peppermint. The pungent scents wafted up as she stripped the leaves from the stems and prepared them for making of the tea.

Mrs. Crumpet returned. She set down the lantern with a clank on the table. "What with the mistress's camomile tea each night, the supply in the medicinal cabinet is low. We'll need to gather fresh very soon," she said. She dropped the camomile into a steaming kettle.

Miranda handed the chopped peppermint and catnip over to her. "Here you are, Mrs. Crumpet. The comfrey is cooled enough now for the poultice. I will take it up immediately. Whenever you have the tea ready, pray be so kind as to bring it up."

"Aye, Miss Wainwright."

Miranda returned to Robert's bedroom with the poultice, a sandwich of thin cloths containing the boiled comfrey leaves. She was not surprised by Lord Townsend's grim expression or the sound of whimpering from the bed. It could not have been a pleasant experience for Robert to have the tender wound cleaned, and certainly his uncle appeared the worse for wear from enduring the sight and sound of his nephew's torment.

Miranda went over to the bed. Without a word she positioned the poultice over the open wound and gently pressed it into place. Robert jumped and then lay tensed in every muscle, but when there was no additional pain and instead a soothing warmth, he slowly relaxed. "It is only a poultice, Robert, that will help take down the swelling," said Miranda quietly. With swift fingers she securely bandaged the poultice across the wound. The boy nodded and closed his eyes with a sigh.

The bedroom door opened and Mrs. Crumpet entered. The cup of tea she carried was greenish in color. "Here is Mrs. Crumpet, Master Robert, with a nice cup of warm tea with a bit of honey to sweeten it. Drink it up, there's a good lad," she said.

"I don't want any tea," protested Robert.

"You shall drink it, however. Mrs. Crumpet has gone to a great deal of trouble to prepare it and you are in need of fluids, my boy," said Lord Townsend sternly. He slipped his arm under the boy's shoulders to raise him up, then took the cup from Mrs. Crumpet with a nod of thanks. Placing the cup to his nephew's lips he encouraged him to drain the tea. When Robert had finished, coughing a little, the viscount laid him down gently again on the pillows. He looked up at the women. "Pray go about your usual schedules, ladies. I shall sit with Robert myself tonight."

Miranda hid her astonishment. "Very well, my lord. I shall look in again in an hour or so," she said. She would not have thought Lord Townsend capable of such an expression of concern. Certainly he was fond of the boy, but that was vastly different from taking on duty in a sickroom.

Miranda once again was struck that such compassion existed in a gentleman who had at first impressed her as more interested in his own concerns than those of his family. Lord Townsend had been going to a great deal of trouble to bring the estate under proper management and restore order, thought Miranda. Perhaps he had always had a stronger concern for the welfare of his family than he had led her to believe.

The women quietly left the bedroom. Lord Townsend did not look around, but remained sitting at his nephew's side. His large hand engulfed the boy's smaller one and his eyes never wavered from Robert's small, flushed face.

Miranda went at once to her cousin's apartment. Grace let her in and at the sight of her, Anne sprang up from her chair. "Miranda! I have grown positively distracted waiting for you. Tell me how Robert is, I beg you."

"He is much more comfortable than previously, Anne. The bone is cleanly set and I have put on a poultice to reduce the swelling. Mrs. Crumpet made up some camomile tea to soothe his nerves and he will probably sleep for some time. He was exhausted by the ordeal, poor little boy," said Miranda.

Relief eased Anne's tight expression. "I am so glad that he is all right. Has the doctor been in to see him yet?" she asked.

"I don't think that he has arrived yet or else Crumpet would have let us know," said Miranda.

"I know that between you and Andrew, all that can be done has been done. Miranda, do you think I may go in to see Robert?" asked Anne.

"Of course you may. His lordship is sitting with him now and will likely be glad of your company. Robert is not rattling along in his usual conversational style, you know," said Miranda dryly.

Anne gave her a swift hug of gratitude. "Oh, Miranda! I know that everything will be fine when you can joke about it," she said. She left the bedroom without a backward glance.

Miranda tiredly made her way to her own room. The discomfort of her damp clothing suddenly struck her and she started to rid herself of her riding dress and boots. It would be wonderful to slip into a warm bath and a comfortable well-worn dress. She pulled on the bell next to the bed and Constance answered its summons from her own quarters. "Constance, could you prevail upon Mrs. Crumpet to put on another pot of water? I should so like a bath," she said.

"I have already done so, Miss Miranda," said Constance with a lurking smile. She reached behind the door and pulled a brass hipbath into view.

"You anticipate me too well, Mrs. Graves. If I am not careful you will soon be reading my very thoughts," said Miranda, laughing.

Her companion positioned the hipbath in front of the fireplace and put up a screen that would protect Miranda from drafts. There was a brass pot of cool water standing beside the grate and Constance poured it into the hipbath before she left to go for the hot water.

Miranda finished undressing and drew on a dressing gown, belting it tightly about her neat waist. Seating herself on the bench in front of her mirror, she began to take the pins from her hair. The heavy braid that made up her usual neat chignon fell down her back. She drew the plait back over her shoulder to unravel the damp braid, then shook out her loosened hair so that it could dry.

Constance returned with a brass pot of steaming water and poured it into the hipbath. Mrs. Crumpet had followed her with an additional pot of water and put it on the fireplace grate where it would be in reach and could be added to rewarm the bathwater as it grew cool.

Then Miranda was left alone to slip into her bath. She twisted her damp hair and pinned it up on the top of her head before stepping in. She lay in the water, luxuriating in the steaming warmth and letting her tense muscles relax. She had not realized how strongly Robert's accident had affected her. It had very nearly taken all her strength to hold him down while his leg was set. Miranda thought she would never forget his agonized screams and how he had twisted to get away. "Anne is not the only one who goes to pieces over that child," said Miranda aloud. She had grown extremely fond of her little cousin. It would be difficult to leave him behind when she returned home, for it would likely be years before she saw him again.

Miranda stared across at the fire's yellow flames. She wondered why she should be thinking of leaving Willowswood. Confused feelings uncoiled from her subconscious. Lord Townsend's face arose vividly in her mind. Miranda was aghast at herself. Surely she could not actually be attracted to him. But the direction of her errant thoughts could not be denied; nor could the edge of fear that accompanied them.

"I could not fall in love with him! How could I ever entertain so preposterous an idea after what I endured for breaking my engagement?" she exclaimed. Even now it made her shudder to recall the scandal that had followed her difficult decision. She had become almost a social outcast. But the worst had been Harrison Gregory's alternating ravings and reproaches. It had been such a horrible experience that she had vowed to herself never to become entangled with anyone again.

But oddly enough the thought of herself and the Viscount of Wythe brought a faint smile to her lips and for a moment she dreamily regarded the warm fire. Then, abruptly, she sat up in the bath. The water surged around her breasts and splashed over the side of the hipbath. "I must be mad!" she exclaimed. She reached for the soap and vigorously scrubbed herself as though she could eradicate her treacherous thoughts.

Miranda knew in her heart that what she was beginning to feel for Lord Townsend was very different from anything she had ever experienced before. But it frightened her to think what result could come from succumbing to her new passion. For all she knew, he could have been flirting with her only to enliven his stay at Willowswood. She knew that the pursuit of such amusement was not beyond the fashionable young men of the *ton*. It was not until she had finished with her bath and dried herself with the large towel that Constance had left draped over the screen that it occurred to her that Jeremy was still in London. She could join him there and escape from the possible heartbreak of another entanglement so soon after her last disastrous infatuation.

Miranda was immediately disgusted with herself. "How cowardly, when I have always prided myself on a resolute character," she said. She would not flee Willowswood, she thought. Instead, she would remain to face her growing attraction for the Viscount of Wythe and discover whether he held any genuine matching regard for her.

Fifteen

Dressing in a comfortable stuff gown, Miranda rebraided her nearly dry hair and pinned it at the back of her head. She returned to Robert's bedroom to find that Anne had already left. Lord Townsend and the doctor were in consultation beside the bed. They looked around at her entrance.

"Ah, Miss Wainwright! It is a pleasure to renew our acquaintance," said the doctor jovially, coming forward to take her hand.

Miranda was surprised by the effusiveness of his greeting. She suddenly recalled Lord Townsend's observation that the doctor admired her. She glanced at the viscount and saw that his lordship was looking somewhat amused. She knew that he was enjoying himself at her expense. "Why, thank you, sir. I assume that you have been examining our patient," she said quietly, withdrawing her hand from the doctor's grasp.

The physician nodded. "I was just telling his lordship that between the lot of you, you have done an excellent job. I was particularly interested in the knitbone poultice. I have seen such rarely in the past few years, but that old remedy is naturally as effective as ever. I was informed that it was you, Miss Wainwright, who thought of it." He looked at her from behind his spectacles with approval.

Miranda inclined her head. "I hope that I may assume that Robert is on the mend."

The physician pushed out his lower lip in a thoughtful expression. "As to that, I do not like the infection that has set in. The boy would be far better off without it, but we must deal with what we find. I have told his lordship that is my main concern. I have left an antiseptic powder for the wound and I recommend the continued use of the knitbone. Also, I should like the boy dosed with garlic water at regular intervals to guard against blood poisoning. Sweeten it with a bit of honey if he objects too strongly to the taste."

Miranda and the doctor had come up to the bedside as they talked. Miranda looked down at the sleeping boy. She bent to lay her hand on Robert's pale brow. "He still has a fever," she said softly.

"Aye. That will be from the infection. The boy's temperature must be kept down as low as possible. I predict a crisis point will be reached in the next several hours. Then we will know if blood poisoning has set in or not," said the doctor.

"Mrs. Crumpet has given the boy a tea for the fever," said Lord Townsend.

Miranda answered the quizzical question in the doctor's eyes. "Catnip tea with a good amount of peppermint and camomile," she said quietly.

The doctor nodded. "Another good remedy, though perhaps in this case it will not be as efficacious as one could hope. I suspect the infection will give the boy a strong fight. Nevertheless, the tea will help to make him less restless."

"Is there anything more that we can do for my nephew?" asked Lord Townsend.

The doctor shook his head. He reached for his bag and closed it. "At this point we can only wait, my lord. I shall return in the morning to see how he is getting on."

The viscount offered his hand to the doctor. "I thank you for your efforts on my nephew's behalf, doctor."

"No trouble at all, my lord. No, no, do not exert yourself. After my several visits to Mrs. Townsend, I know my way out. Miss Claridge was a regular patient of mine, too, you know. Though I think that she liked the attention more than she actually heeded my medical advice," said the doctor with a laugh. He left the bedroom.

Lord Townsend looked at Miranda. "I must apologize, Miss Wainwright."

Miranda was bewildered. "Whatever for, my lord?"

"I recall quite distinctly accusing you of practicing quackery," said Lord Townsend. "I have been firmly set in my place for my ignorance."

Miranda chuckled. "Anyone who has not been exposed to herbs and their uses would certainly say the same, my lord. But it must be remembered that many of the powders and tonics prescribed by our doctors have come directly from such origins."

"I perceive that my education is strongly lacking in useful knowledge. Perhaps you will enlighten me in the days to come," said Lord Townsend with a grin, his eyes warm and friendly.

Miranda felt her heart turn over. The intimacy of his gaze struck at her defenses too soon after discovering her own heart's treachery. She could hardly bear his close proximity. Her senses tingled with sudden awareness of his maleness. With an effort she managed to speak with a teasing note in her voice. "Certainly, my lord. But it is said that one cannot teach an old dog new tricks."

"We shall see, Miss Wainwright. I should like to find out, in any event. Come, we must not delay dinner any further. Crumpet informed me some minutes ago that he would be serving a late supper within the quarter-hour," said Lord Townsend, taking Miranda's arm.

She glanced back at Robert. "But should someone not sit with him?"

"Robert is sleeping peacefully at the moment and Anne will return shortly. She went down to the dining room at the insistence of her maid, whom I perceive to be a woman of sterling quality and inflexible will. Anne consented to leave once she learned that her son was in no immediate danger. However, she announced that she means to sit with Robert tonight," said Lord Townsend. He drew Miranda out of the bedroom and down the hall toward the stairs.

"But Anne is still so easily fatigued," said Miranda.

The viscount shrugged. "My sister-in-law has steel hidden somewhere within that fragile exterior. I suspect that when it comes to the welfare of her husband and son, Anne's determination to do as she thinks best will overcome all our objections."

Miranda made no further objections, certain that the viscount's analysis of her cousin was correct. Anne would certainly do all in her power to protect those she so passionately loved. But Miranda decided privately that she would relieve her in the early morning hours. Her cousin did not need to run herself into the ground and invite a recurrence of her recent illness.

As it turned out, Robert's fight with the insidious infection lasted three full days. The doctor came frequently and his opinion was more guarded than his first assurances had been. It was obvious the feared blood poisoning had set in and that the boy's chance of recovery was uncertain. Miranda was infuriated by the resignation she sensed in the physician and she labored over Robert with all her energy and skill. She stayed with him more than anyone else so that she was immediately available to soothe his restlessness and treat his raging fever as best she knew how.

Anne, too, remained long hours at her son's bedside, defying any attempts to persuade her to rest. She became increasingly hollow-eyed and the cough that had continued to plague her became worse. When it became glaringly obvious that she was endangering her health, Lord Townsend forcibly removed her from the sickroom and placed her in the stern care of her devoted maid. Anne protested, but she had grown so weak that even she had to accept the necessity of bedrest. The doctor shook his head over her folly, saying that she had indeed incurred a relapse of the pneumonia. He told her that if she wanted to recover quickly, she had best leave Robert's nursing to those with stronger constitutions. Anne had broken down in tears, but she promised to follow the doctor's orders. She sent Grace almost hourly for a report on her son's progress, until Miranda with gentle firmness let her cousin know that she was only succeeding in irritating everyone involved in Robert's care. Miranda pledged herself to let Anne know the very moment something happened and Anne had to be content with that.

The crisis point that the doctor had predicted earlier came at last. Robert lay listless, no longer thrashing about as he had been doing while in the worst throes of the fever. Miranda recognized the signs and steeled herself for the battle ahead. Lord Townsend, who had insisted on taking his turns in the sickroom, had left but a short hour before and Miranda knew that it would be some time before she could expect Constance to relieve her. "It is only you and I, Robert. Fight hard, little one," she said softly, her hand automatically seeking the boy's brow. It was burning to the touch. Miranda took a fresh wet cloth from out of the basin sitting beside the bed and began to bathe Robert's hot skin. She pulled the bell rope for Mrs. Crumpet to bring more cold water when the basin of water she was using grew tepid.

It was hours later when Miranda straightened from her post beside the bed. She brushed aside a lock of hair that had fallen out of its pin and smiled wearily as she looked down at the boy's peaceful face. The fever had at last broken. Robert's brow felt cool to the touch for the first time in days. Even as she watched, the marked flush in his cheeks began to slowly fade.

The bedroom door opened and Constance quietly entered. "How is he, Miss Miranda?" she asked softly as she neared the bed.

"The fever broke but moments ago. He ought to sleep peacefully now," said Miranda, exhaustion hoarsening her voice.

"Praise be to God. I have felt that sorry for the little rascal. I shan't mind his wild moments half as much now," said Constance gruffly.

"Only give Robert time to recover and I warrant you shall change your tune, Constance! Anne sent Grace in some hours ago to extract a promise from me that I would wake her if there was any change. But I think that the news can wait until the morning. My cousin needs as much sleep as she can get," said Miranda, unable to stifle a wide yawn. She stretched her back until it popped.

"And so do you, Miss Miranda. You've been at it longer than any of us. Take yourself off to bed now. I shall stay with the boy for the remainder of the night," said Constance.

Miranda smiled her gratitude and nodded. She left the room, softly closing the door behind her, and walked down the hall toward her bedroom. There was a shaft of light across the hallway carpet and Miranda paused.

The door to the viscount's sitting room stood half open. Miranda could see him inside sitting before the fire. He obviously waited to hear news of his nephew and Miranda's heart was touched. Miranda softly pushed the door wider and walked in. Lord Townsend, staring at nothing, did not look around at hearing the rustle of her gown. Miranda halted beside his chair, made uneasy by his continued silence. She touched his shoulder. "My lord? My lord, Robert's fever has broken at last. He will recover."

The viscount's hand came up swiftly to catch her fingers. Miranda winced at his painful grip but she did not withdraw from it. She searched his hard, immobile profile. "Did you hear, my lord? Robert is on the mend."

Lord Townsend moved and for the first time she saw the letter clenched in his far hand. His voice was strangely flat. "Crumpet handed me the day's post at dinner. A friend with the army has written me. The boy's father has been killed."

Miranda was stunned. Her mind buckled at the enormity of his statement. "B-but the *London Gazette* said nothing. The name Richard Townsend was not listed. It cannot be for certain!"

Suddenly he towered over her. The letter fluttered to the carpet. His fingers flexed through the stuff of her gown to bruise her soft shoulders. Menace blazed in his dark eyes. "Can you not find suitable words, ma'am? The lady who prides herself on her quick wit! Is there nothing that you can utter to bring a laugh to this horror?" Miranda stared up at him, shocked. Her eyes dilated at the pallor and suppressed violence about his mouth. Then as abruptly as his anger had come on him, his face altered and the furious light in his eyes went out. "Forgive me, I had no right to blaze up at you. But my brother!" His voice cracked suddenly. "Miranda . . ." His eyes squeezed shut against the tears that suddenly washed his ravaged face. A tortured sob tore from his chest.

Miranda was appalled at the intensity and suddenness of his grief. Instinctively, she put her arms around him. He buried his face in her hair. His hands slid down her back to hold her tight against him as though he was in dire need of an anchor. She felt the shudders that shook him as he fought against his grief. With her cheek pressed against the hollow of his shoulder, Miranda closed her eyes. "Oh Andrew," she whispered. "My poor Andrew." She tightened her arms about his rigid frame. They stood unmoving clasped in one another's arms for what seemed an eternity of feeling.

At last Miranda felt him straighten, though his arms did not fall from around her. She lifted her head and her eyes met his pain-darkened gaze. "Andrew," she murmured softly. She reached up to smooth the lock of hair that had fallen across his brow. His expression altered and Miranda's heart suddenly thudded. She stared up into his unfathomable eyes.

Slowly he lowered his head and found her lips in a tentative, questioning kiss that left Miranda utterly shattered. She was barely conscious of it when the circle of his arms tightened. With his lips he traced her closed eyes and the smooth skin of her temple, before he fastened again on her lips. The pressure of his mouth became compelling, desperate.

Miranda's lips parted under the force of his and she tasted the salty traces of his tears. An inarticulate sound broke from her. A tidal wave of long-damned need flooded her, its wake leaving her spent, with all her inner barriers down. She clung to Andrew and arched hungrily into his kiss. He responded with fervent passion.

Shocks of emotion exploded through her nerves. She felt his hard frame against hers, his maddening, exploring lips, his hands caressing her body to fire wherever they roamed. Abruptly, Jeremy's parting words to her flitted through her mind: "Miranda, think before you leap!"

Suddenly, horrifyingly aware of what she was doing, Miranda wrenched herself free of the viscount's embrace. She backed away, staring at him from huge eyes.

"Miranda!" exclaimed Lord Townsend softly. He took a quick step toward her, one hand outstretched.

With a sob, Miranda whirled and fled from the room.

The following morning Lord Townsend was in the breakfast room before her. Miranda hesitated in the doorway at sight of him, but when he turned his eyes toward her an innate pride would not allow her to retreat. The viscount rose at her entrance and in his usual manner held her chair for her. With a swift-beating heart, Miranda took her customary place at the table. "Thank you, my lord," she said hoarsely through the constriction in her throat.

Lord Townsend bowed and reseated himself. There was no attempt on either of their parts to strike up their usual friendly, teasing conversation. Miranda knew that the viscount glanced her way several times as though he was on the point of speaking, but she studiously avoided his gaze. She dreaded what he might say. Her fast behavior must have given him a totally false impression of her character. A gentleman of Lord Townsend's sophistication could well assume that she was as worldly as himself. She was inordinately grateful that Crumpet came into the dining room twice to remove serving dishes, his presence being a deterrent to any private speech. It occurred to her of a sudden that she was fortunate the household staff was still so inadequate or otherwise her headlong flight from Lord Townsend's apartment last night would not have gone unobserved. She could just imagine the knowing and curious looks from the servants, who might well have assumed she had become Lord Townsend's mistress.

The thought left Miranda with little appetite. She was able to finish only a biscuit and even that threatened to choke her. She rose as soon as it was polite to do so and made for the door.

Lord Townsend was before her, his hand falling gentle on her arm. "Miss Wainwright, I must speak with you."

"There is no need, my lord," said Miranda, forcing herself to speak with calm. After a single fleeting glance up at his face, she could not raise her eyes again to meet his gaze. To her mind, she was sunk beyond reproach. At that moment Miranda would have given anything to have been able to reclaim this particular gentleman's respect.

When he touched her arm, Lord Townsend had seen the color drain from her face to leave her cheeks white. He was surprised by her intense reaction. It made his apology all the more necessary. He lowered his voice. "I believe there is, Miranda. What happened between us—"

With horrible, dreadful certainty she knew that he meant to propose an illicit *affaire d'amour*.

"Oh, pray do not!"

Pressing the back of one hand tightly against her mouth, Miranda rushed from the dining room.

The butler was preparing to enter the room to clear the dishes away. He stared after Miss Wainwright's precipitate flight with open mouth. He turned his head to look at the viscount. "My lord? Is there aught amiss?"

"Amiss?" Lord Townsend gave a savage laugh and strode out of the room. The butler shook his head over the vagaries of the Quality as he went about his task.

Lord Townsend's first thought was to pursue Miranda and force a confrontation between them. But by the time he reached the stairs his better sense prevailed. Instead of following Miranda upstairs he turned on his heel and strode out the front door. The early morning air was light and cool and he sucked in deep breaths as he walked. He had recognized the look of mistrust and fear in Miranda's eyes. She was understandably distraught, he thought. He blamed himself for what had taken place the night before. He had taken unpardonable liberties. His only excuse was that he had been beside himself with grief and had not known what he was doing.

Stopping short beneath a tree, Lord Townsend swore. But he *had* known what he was doing. That was the damnable part. The challenging sparkle in Miranda's dark blue eyes, her straightforward manners, the simple beauty of her glistening chestnut hair when it was struck by the sun . . . all had grown on him until he had thoughts of little else. When she had come to him, her eyes so full of feeling and compassion, he had sensed that she was vulnerable.

"God, what a fool I am!" he exclaimed, his voice sounding harsh on the soft morning. But even as he cursed himself he knew that he had not touched on the real issue. There had grown to be something special shared between himself and Miranda that he had not known for a long, long time with a woman. It was a quality new and tender, and horribly subject to destruction if it was not protected and nurtured. It was this fragile thread that he feared was broken. Yet even as he acknowledged the emotion for what it was, he thrust aside the knowledge. The thought of loving a woman in that way seemed perilous to him.

Sixteen

Anne was informed of the contents of the viscount's letter that morning. Miranda found that she was forced to put aside all thought of her own concerns for her cousin's sake. Anne was at once grief-stricken and disbelieving of the validity of the news. "There must be some mistake," she kept saying, before bursting into a fresh stream of tears. Her hands shook as if with palsy. By luncheon time she was white and listless and would not eat. She turned her face away when Miranda tried to talk with her. All the good progress she had made by resting and harboring her strength seemed to waste away with astonishing speed. By the end of the week, Anne was a shadow of her former self. She wanted nothing but to be allowed to stare out her bedroom window at the knot garden below.

Alarmed, Miranda summoned the doctor. He was shocked by Anne's condition. When they had left the bedroom, he asked sharply, "What has occurred, Miss Wainwright? It cannot be the boy, when he is recovering so nicely."

"Lord Townsend received a letter from a friend stating that Captain Townsend has been killed. His lordship thought it would be better to break the news to my cousin gently rather than wait, on the chance of her reading it in the *Gazette* with no warning," said Miranda.

The physician's eyes blazed. "Could it not have waited a few weeks, Miss Wainwright? Mrs. Townsend is of a frail constitution just now. Her worry over her son had already exhausted her. Now you can see what the shock has done!"

Miranda stood mute before the doctor's tirade. Suddenly she was crying. Her nerves had withstood so much in the last several weeks—she could not endure any more. Blindly, she turned to flee back up the stairs. She was caught by strong arms and instinctively she turned into them. Over her head the viscount's voice was furious. "Enough, sir! I will not have Miss Wainwright so abused. It was my decision to inform my sister-in-law of the probability of my brother's death. The responsibility lies solely with me."

The doctor bowed stiffly. "Very well, my lord! My apologies to Miss Wainwright. I shall return in a few days to see to my patients. Good day." He swung around and left the house. Crumpet closed the door after him and turned his appalled gaze back to Miss Wainwright, who was sobbing as though she were a baby. It shocked him that the cool imperturbability he had come to associate with Miss Wainwright had been broken.

Lord Townsend held Miranda close and murmured incoherent words to her. His sharp features were unusually softened. He became aware of scrutiny on him and raised his eyes to see Constance standing on the stairs. He nodded to the maid, who came down at once. "Constance, pray see to your mistress. She has had a trying time," he said quietly.

"Yes, my lord," said Constance. She put her arm around Miranda and drew her up the stairs.

Lord Townsend stood below, his expression brooding as he watched Miranda ascend. Then he turned on his heel, his riding boots rapping hard on the marble tiles as he left the hall.

The only person Anne was interested in seeing was her son and Robert could hardly stand to be around his mother. Even though Anne tried to hide her grief when Robert was with her, he was intelligent enough to sense it and question her about why she was so sad. His solicitation nearly set Anne off again and it was all she could do to underplay her emotions. "I am a little anxious about Papa is all," she said, trying to smile. "But I will get over it."

Still weakened from his ordeal, Robert emerged on his crutches from his mother's chambers both troubled and frightened. He knew that something was terribly wrong but no one had told him what it was. Strangely enough, no one considered Robert's fine perceptions. Anne had been thought to be strong enough to handle the news of her husband's probable death, but she and the viscount had agreed that until confirmation came it would be best to shelter Robert from the interim suspense.

But Robert noticed the long faces of Constance and his mother's maid. He knew that the Crumpets and the housekeeper abruptly stopped whispering whenever he came upon them unexpectedly. He tried to pump his stable friends, but the grooms would only shake their heads. When even the hardened gardener vouchsafed him a gruff word of friendliness, Robert's sense of dread was complete. His nightmares worsened and the persistent sense of aloneness overwhelmed him in its intensity.

Robert fled his loneliness the only way he knew how. He insisted upon spending considerable time with Miranda as she went about the house and garden. He seemed to appreciate that she spoke to him calmly and as though he was an adult. When he was not with Miranda, Robert shadowed his uncle, who had begun to set in motion the refurbishment of the estate and was in the process of hiring a new bailiff. Robert spent hours sitting quietly in the study while Lord Townsend interviewed various applicants or explained to him the intricacies of keeping up an estate like Willowswood.

Over the long days Lord Townsend thoughtfully studied his nephew. The boy was hollow-eyed and obviously bored to death by his forced inactivity. He would not otherwise dog a dull uncle's heels so attentively, thought Lord Townsend. It was certainly an appropriate time to begin Robert's formal education. The viscount posted a reminder to his London solicitor that he had requested screenings of possible tutors. He hoped that a youngish scholar would be found who could understand a seven-year-old boy's exuberance and restlessness and yet could curb his wilder tendencies.

As for Lord Townsend's own grief over his brother's probable death, he never again revealed his feelings in quite so naked a fashion as he had with Miranda. With Anne he felt obligated to place himself in the position of the proverbial shoulder to lean on. The stress was evident in his drawn mouth, however. His expression was grimmer, his eyes bleaker.

Miranda was unhappy that her lively exchanges with Lord Townsend seemed to be at a permanent end. The friendly intimacy that had grown up between them seemed to have died with the passion they had shared. It was partly her own fault. After the disastrous encounter in the breakfast room she had been at pains to erect a barrier between herself and Lord Townsend, but as time passed she discovered that the distance was painful. The viscount's obvious withdrawal into himself over his brother only added to the situation. Miranda was glad, however, to see that Lord Townsend did not show the same coldness of spirit toward Robert. The boy reminded her so much of a forlorn waif, drifting hither and thither with a perpetual anxiety deep in the depths of his blue eyes. Robert obviously needed attention and though she and Constance did their best with him, and his mother gave him as much as she seemed able to, Robert still needed something more. He apparently had that need satisfied through the viscount.

The only time that the viscount relaxed into a warmer attitude was when he was with his nephew. He recognized that the boy needed attention and he was conscientious in giving of himself and his time. He made a point of going up every evening to visit with Robert at bedtime. The boy appeared unnaturally grateful to him for the treat and was always reluctant to let him go.

One evening the viscount discovered Robert curled tensely on the windowseat, staring out at the darkened sky. Robert did not look around at his uncle's greeting. Abruptly he said, "Papa is dead, isn't he?"

For several seconds Lord Townsend stood silent. He said slowly, quietly, "Yes, Robert, I believe that he is."

The boy's shoulders slumped and his body visibly relaxed. He sighed deeply. When he turned his head there were tears in his eyes. "Thank you, Uncle Andrew," he said simply.

With a flash Lord Townsend understood his nephew's sudden bewildering dependence. Anne and he had done the boy a gross disservice. Robert had sensed his father's death all along and he had suffered from their misguided attempt to protect him. "Oh my God," murmured Lord Townsend. He gathered his nephew up against him. The boy's thin arms wound tight around his neck.

Robert's voice came muffled from against Lord Townsend's shoulder. "I knew Papa wasn't coming back. I knew it when I fell out of the tree. But no one would tell me! Everyone acted as though everything was all right." There was grief and rage in the boy's voice. He started to cry in great gulping sobs.

Lord Townsend tightened his arms about him and smoothed his unruly hair. "Forgive me, Robert," he said, his voice roughened.

It was a long time before the viscount emerged from the nursery.

Though he felt in his heart that his friend's information was correct, the viscount did not accept the letter without making inquiries of his own with friends in positions who might be expected to be able to verify the harsh truth. A few weeks later the official notice of Captain Richard Townsend's death was printed in the *London Gazette*.

When the lists came out, Miranda thought that the viscount showed exquisite consideration for Robert's feelings and her own sense of love and loss swelled with this fresh evidence of his lordship's true inner character. She shed tears in the privacy of her bedroom and began to appear a bit thinner and paler than before, but no one except Constance had the wit or inclination to notice.

Though Constance would never dream of betraying her mistress's confidence, she frowned and now and again tried to influence Miranda not to exert herself so much in the running of Willowswood. But someone had to respond to the condolence calls and the cards that began to be received and Anne was totally unequal to the task. She rarely left her bedroom and on the few occasions that she did so, it was only at Robert's pleading. At times the duties seemed overwhelming and Miranda felt incredible anger toward her cousin. But she had only to look at Anne's wan, saddened face to feel ashamed of her uncharitable thoughts. Anne had lost her husband. It would take time to heal the wound.

Miranda received the morning's letter from Jeremy and her low spirits immediately lightened. She was delighted to learn that the fight to regain possession of the *Larabelle* and its cargo was all but won. Edward Billingsley was pushing forward the inquiry into the fate of the missing American sailors, and he seemed confident that the men would shortly be reunited with their countrymen. Jeremy, obviously satisfied with how events were transpiring, promised to join her at Willowswood very soon. Staring at the words, Miranda had mixed feelings. She wanted so much to be reunited with her brother, but Jeremy knew her too well. She would not be able to disguise her unhappiness from him. She doubted that he would accept that Richard's death and the responsibilities of Willowswood were solely to blame for her emotional state. Jeremy's inevitable questions would eventually unearth her feelings for the Viscount of Wythe.

Miranda was not given much time for reflection on this new dilemma. At Lord Townsend's insistence, she began interviewing possible household servants. "I can screen these individuals but as for discerning their true worth, I must give that over to someone who is familiar with the running of a household," said Lord Townsend.

"And Anne is far too preoccupied to turn her mind to it," said Miranda with a tired nod.

Lord Townsend gave her a sharp glance. Not for the first time he saw that the fragile skin under her eyes appeared bruised and she had grown thin. It did not surprise him when he recalled how she had been the tower of strength for all of them for several weeks. His voice softening, he said,

"It is not proper that the burden of Willowswood should fall to you, Miss Wainwright. But I would count it a true service to the family if you would take on the hiring of the household staff."

Tears pricked at Miranda's eyes. She bent her head, ostensibly to better arrange the violets that she had brought into the study. He had spoken so gently and with such consideration. Though he had never been other than courteous and polite to her, there had been a distantness in his manner since the morning that she had rejected his attempt to talk about what had passed between them. She had prayed that he would never again refer to the shattering encounter. He had not, and she had been at once relieved and distressed. She was unable to rid herself of the notion that Lord Townsend, if he thought about that night at all, considered it but a mistake easily dismissed and forgotten. Somehow she would have preferred that he had been as shaken by the experience as she was herself.

"Of course, my lord. I would be happy to take on the task. I hope the candidates we have shall have better sense and a stronger loyalty than those first hired by Richard and Anne," said Miranda.

"We shall have little trouble there, I think. Already as I have talked with those who aspire to the outer posts of the estate, I have gathered the impression that the villagers are more than eager to make amends for deserting Willowswood," said Lord Townsend. He turned back to the papers on the desk with a sigh and Miranda thought that she was once more forgotten.

All in all, Miranda saw far less of Lord Townsend in those hard weeks than she had at any other time since their separate arrivals at Willowswood. The viscount spent his time with estate business and with his nephew. He also seemed to relish more the gamehunting that was to be had at the squire's place and Stonehollow. Once he politely asked Miranda if she would like to participate in the fox hunts, but she declined the treat. It was not a sport that she particularly enjoyed at any time, let alone when her spirits seemed to have sunk to a permanent low. That same week in church she overheard Miss Burton wax enthusiastic over the hunting that season and the viscount's prowess on the field. With a twinge of jealousy, Miranda rather thought that Lord Townsend was not missing feminine company in the least if the beauty's possessive glances and frothy laughter were anything to judge by.

On an evening when Anne felt well enough to stay downstairs after dinner, Lord Townsend mentioned that his brother's death had given him much sober thought. "I now realize how frivolous my life has been up to this point. Richard had an adequate independence which was enhanced by his inheriting of Willowswood, but still he chose to enter the army because he believed in what England is fighting for. I myself have done nothing but pursue my own pleasures and establish a tenuous friendship with the Prince Regent. I suddenly find that inadequate for myself," said Lord Townsend. He stood at the fireplace, one boot resting on the grate and his arm on the mantel as he stared into the fire. He looked up at his sister-in-law and Miranda who were seated on a settee nearby. "I have been thinking of joining the army myself."

Miranda pulled in her breath sharply. Her heart suddenly constricted and her expression reflected disbelief. But it was her cousin's reaction that drew Lord Townsend's eyes. "Andrew! But you cannot!" exclaimed Anne, exhibiting more spirit than she had in some time.

"I do not have a purpose in my life, Anne. The months

that I have spent bringing Willowswood around, I have had opportunity to reflect on it more than ever before in my life. I find that I can no longer live as I have done these past several years," said Lord Townsend.

Anne's face flushed. It was forcibly borne in on her that she could not rely on Lord Townsend, or Miranda, to remain at Willowswood forever. There would inevitably come a time when their lives must diverge from hers, and she must have the strength to carry on without them. But she did not want that time to come so soon. She still needed their support. "Then think of this, Andrew. My son is fatherless. He desperately needs someone who can in some ways replace his father, to guide him and act as his trusted confidante. The new tutor can hardly be expected to fill that role. I know of no one else who can so well accomplish that than his beloved uncle. Is that not purpose enough? Or is it more important for you to follow some quixotic notion of avenging Richard's death and possibly withholding from my son the support he needs by being killed yourself?"

There was a moment of silence while Lord Townsend studied his sister-in-law's face. Miranda held her breath, her eyes never straying from his stern expression. Finally the viscount shook is head. "You have asked me a difficult question, Anne. My first instinct is to deny that I seek to avenge Richard's death. But I am compelled to admit that it is unpleasantly close to the truth. As for my nephew, you know my affection for him. I would do nothing to deliberately harm him, but——"

"Then you will not enter the army, Andrew," said Anne with finality. "Robert knows that his papa went away to the army and he is not coming back. It would devastate him to wonder if you also would not be returning to him."

"You are dramatizing, Anne," said Lord Townsend shortly.

"Am I, Andrew? You know Robert's sensitivity and his intelligence. He is a child with a child's perception of the world. Can you honestly say that the fear of such would not touch him?" asked Anne.

Lord Townsend straightened with a sigh. He ran one hand over his face. "No, Anne. You are right about Robert. It is precisely what he would conclude."

"Then you will not join the army?" asked Anne. There was a pleading note in her voice. "For I, too, need you, Andrew. I am still quite lost without Richard. I do not think I could bear it if you went away also."

"I will make no promises, Anne. I will say only that I will give it more consideration," said Lord Townsend. He became aware of Miranda's fixed gaze and there was something in her eyes that gave him pause. "Have you thoughts on the matter as well, Miss Wainwright?" he asked quietly.

Miranda lowered her eyes to the mending in her lap. "Since you ask, my lord, I take leave to tell you that I feel much as my cousin. I believe your place to be more properly here at Willowswood. One day that will surely change, but for now I think that the boy must be of primary importance. But you must decide for yourself what is best," she said, her voice calm and almost neutral in tone. But inside she quivered so that she was nearly on the point of nausea.

Lord Townsend felt unaccountably disappointed. "Nevertheless, your opinions are always of interest to me, Miss Wainwright," he said shortly.

Miranda's eyes flew toward him, but he was already crossing the drawing room to the door, leaving the ladies alone by the fire. Miranda wondered exactly what he had meant by his last remark. Surely he could not really place such emphasis on what she thought.

"Andrew is not very patient these days. I fear that all this trouble has greatly vexed him, especially Richard's death," said Anne sorrowfully. "I only wish that he could discover a lady to share his life with. Then he wouldn't feel so overwhelmed."

The thought of Lord Townsend becoming wed to some unknown lady struck Miranda with strong revulsion. "I would not be overly anxious about his lordship if I were you, Anne! He seems a capable gentleman, well able to handle his own problems," she snapped. She spoke more sharply than she intended, earning a look of astonishment from her cousin. She ignored Anne's surprise and calmly continued to darn the garment she held. But she thought she would do better to watch her tongue. It would not do to give Anne the impression that she cared for the viscount as anything more than a cousin. She had difficulty enough in persuading herself of that.

Seventeen

A visitor arrived in the neighborhood. There was a buzz of speculation and comfortable anticipation, for the guest at Willoughby Hall was a young naval officer. He was said to be the commander of a sloop-of-war, which seemed a thoroughly romantic occupation in the minds of the young ladies and unquestionably exciting to the young gentlemen who had visions of derring-do on the high seas. He was also said to be well-favored in face and person and, what was most important, unattached. Those with marriageable daughters geared up for a round of entertainments in honor of the new arrival.

Captain William Daggett, not long since severely reprimanded and temporarily relieved of his duties for seizing an American vessel under false charges, was extremely gratified by the flattery and honeyed words that he was served. When he had sought out an old school acquaintance, Angus Willoughby, it had been only with the thought of burying himself somewhere where he was not known for the period of his disgrace. He had not actually anticipated any enjoyment from his forced exile even though his host went out of his way to make him welcome.

Mr. Willoughby was known to be somewhat of an eccentric. He was a bit vague at times and his relationships with

159

people reflected an appalling forgetfulness and lack of insight. But he did remember a William Daggett from the old public school and he thought it vastly kind of this obviously successful career naval officer to descend upon him. If he wondered at all at the fact that William Daggett had never before shown him much notice or was bothered at the strangeness of the officer's sudden appearance on his doorstep, he dismissed it with the vague reflection that he was not one himself for the intricate formalities that society expected of one. Therefore Mr. Willoughby accepted both Daggett's unexpected presence and his glib explanation of being given holiday leave and wishing to spend it renewing his acquaintance with an old friend. Though Mr. Willoughby knew himself to be entirely unsuited for polite society, he nevertheless made an extraordinary effort to introduce his guest into neighborhood society. Once that task was successfully accomplished, he happily returned to his usual routine and left his guest to his own devices.

Captain Daggett was hardly disappointed by Mr. Willoughby's eventual desertion. He regarded Willoughby with all the remembered contempt of their school days. But nothing of that showed in his manner when he spoke of a thoroughly fictitious friendship of long standing between himself and Willoughby to those who were curious enough to wonder at the connection between the reclusive eccentric and the dashing naval officer. The neighborhood was favorably impressed with Captain Daggett and he began to receive invitations which he was not behind in accepting once he realized the pleasantness of his situation. His wounded pride and embittered hatred of one Jeremy Wainwright, Esquire, answered well to the soothing balm of social prominence in a small district.

The older personages offered him warm welcome and

courteous deference in view of his patriotic calling. If his manner seemed at times somewhat arrogant and his glance a little cold, it was put down to an admirable reserve for a gentleman still in his thirties. The young gentlemen fawned over him and lapped up any farrago about the sea life that he chose to spin for them. At first taken by surprise by the younger set's interest, Daggett adjusted quickly to the unfamiliar role of hero. It amused him to see how far he could lead on those he thought of as stupid, thick-headed bumpkins with the most outrageous tales that he could possibly contrive.

As for the young ladies, they gazed upon him with adulation and shy invitation. Looking about him with the cold calculating eyes of a bird of prey, Daggett speculated that he could easily manage to bed a goodly number of the ripe little creatures before his exile was done. The very thought was mildly erotic and he tightened his arm about the neat waist of the maiden he danced with. She gasped faintly in surprise. Her eyes swiftly met his, then dropped as soft color rose in her face. Daggett smiled. It might be that he would begin tasting the fruits of the district that very evening, he thought. He began to calculate how he could maneuver his timid little dove into the garden for what he intended to be a very pleasant interlude.

Then he chanced to glance across the dance floor and all thought of seduction was driven from his head. "My God!" he breathed. The young lady that he partnered looked around to discover the cause of the gentleman's violent exclamation. Her pretty face lengthened when she saw that the neighborhood's acknowledged beauty had arrived, late as usual.

Miss Burton paused just inside the doorway of the ballroom and allowed her glance to slowly scan the company.

For a second only her eyes paused on Captain Daggett, then her gaze swept on. She was looking for the Viscount of Wythe's unmistakable figure, but he was not to be found. A frisson of irritation ruffled her composure. How dare his lordship not be present when she made her entrance. It did not immediately occur to her that it would have been unseemly for Lord Townsend to attend a full-fledged ball so soon after his brother's death.

Miss Burton knew that she had created a sensation and accepted it as her due. She acknowledged the profuse greetings of her court and deigned to accept the invitation of one of the gentlemen who rushed toward her as though they were of one mind.

"Who is that exquisite creature?" asked Daggett of his partner, his eyes still on the incredible beauty.

The young lady gazed miserably at one of the large shining brass buttons on his coat. "That is Miss Mary Alice Burton. She is reputed to be our local beauty," she said.

Daggett gave a short bark of laughter. "I should say instead that she is a diamond of the first water!"

"Should—should you like to meet her?" asked the young lady. Civility demanded that she make the offer, but she felt as though she would really rather cut her heart out instead. It was so very frustrating to have all one's chances with the eligible gentlemen fly out the window whenever Mary Alice Burton happened to float into view. It was the burning hope in the breast of every young lady in the district that Miss Burton would soon be discovered by some old earl or other and be whisked off, leaving her rivals from childhood to at last enjoy their own small triumphs.

Daggett hesitated. All his inclinations urged him to go at once to the beauty's side and discover himself to her. But the way Miss Burton had made her entrance, her haughty carriage, the arrogant expression in her eyes when they had briefly met his own, told him that to introduce himself now would be fatal. In that single glance he had perceived far more about Miss Burton than she would have liked anyone to know. Daggett had immediately recognized the total self-assurance of a young woman who had never been refused. Miss Burton had but to crook her little finger for a score of gentlemen to kneel at her feet, panting to satisfy her least whim.

Daggett thought it would suit his purposes far better if he were to hold himself aloof. Such a one as Miss Burton would not be able to resist any hint of disregard. She would come to him, as surely as the moth flies to the candleflame. Daggett wanted her. And he meant to have her. Daggett could hardly bare the ache in him at the thought of the pleasure to come. But he made the massive effort necessary to control his instinctive desire to go to the beauteous Miss Burton's side. Deliberately, he smiled down into the young lady's eyes. "It would be vastly rude of me to rush away just upon the entrance of another lady, do you not think?"

The young lady's soft pink mouth formed a soundless "oh." Her drooping expression lightened magically. "I should like a lemonade, Captain Daggett, if you would be so kind," she said happily.

"Of course." Captain Daggett leisurely escorted his partner across to the refreshment table. He glanced down at her, his eyes now critical where before he had seen only fresh loveliness waiting to be harvested. The girl's figure was still slight, her small rounded bosom yet immature. Her bubbling giggle, before so charmingly virginal, now fell on his ear with irritating childishness. He found that he no longer had a desire to take her into the garden. His desire was directed at quite another target, one of lush and smoldering passions, if he did not mistake the matter. His thoughts dwelled on Miss Burton and his thin lips curled. Miss Burton would be well worth the effort, he thought.

That evening became something of an occasion. After Captain Daggett had escorted her back to the protection of her beaming mama, the young lady lost little time in recounting the extraordinary event that had just taken place. A gentleman had actually declined the honor of an introduction to Miss Mary Alice Burton. Instead, he had finished out his set with one of Miss Burton's rivals and from thence had gone on to request the honor of leading out still another young lady. The story swiftly made the rounds and soon the room was filled with low exclamations of wonder and amazement.

It was not long before the tale reached Miss Burton's exquisite ears. At first she was inclined to dismiss it as so much nonsense. No gentleman would dare behave in such a cavalier manner as that toward herself. But as the evening wore on and Captain Daggett never did present himself to her, she was forced to realize that a gentleman had so dared. Her temper was not of the best and it was further exacerbated by the glances of malicious amusement that were thrown her way. Miss Burton was vexed to discover that she had actually dug furrows in her palms with her long shapely nails.

One of the squire's daughters, a squint-eyed freckled creature whom Miss Burton had always contemptuously brushed aside as no rival at all, had the audacity to approach her. "Isn't it a marvelous evening, Mary Alice? Captain Daggett is such a handsome gentleman and so chivalrous, too! Why, he has stood up with me three times this evening. And I am not the only lady so honored. I am in a positive whirl, I assure you, and so is every other lady here who has had the pleasure of his company," said Tabitha, enjoying herself hugely. She had longed for ages for the chance to set down the odious Mary Alice and at last her dreamed-of opportunity had come. Her voice, never at any time fashionably low, carried quite clearly and her comments were widely heard.

There was a laugh, quickly changed to a cough, but Miss Burton's hearing was acute. She trembled with rage. Her lovely mouth stretched into a gracious smile. "Indeed, Tabitha. One must certainly wonder at it. There are not many gentlemen who have such a high tolerance for self-inflicted boredom," she said.

Tabitha's green eyes narrowed and the temper bespoken by her carroty hair flashed out with devastating accuracy. "It has not gone unnoticed that Captain Daggett has yet to lead out yourself, Miss High-and-Mighty! Perhaps he draws the line at selfish, haughty butterflies." She swept away with a giddy feeling of sublime and long-anticipated retribution.

Miss Burton stood alone. She was aware that the exchange between herself and Tabitha Earlington had been listened to with avid and malicious interest. Even the gentlemen who counted themselves honored members of her loyal court were not above enjoying her discomfiture. She had ruled too haughtily and too capriciously for it to be otherwise. Of course the incident would soon be forgotten by the gentlemen and there would be no change in their adoration. But for Miss Burton, there would always be a raw memory of public humiliation.

Her eyes stared daggers at Tabitha Earlington's back and she vowed revenge, but she found that the majority of her anger was directed at Captain William Daggett. He had been the engineer of her humiliation. He had dared to ignore her, Mary Alice Burton, the toasted beauty of the district. He would soon learn an excruciating lesson in manners. Before I am done he will crawl on his knees and beg for my favor, she thought vengefully.

Captain Daggett's avoidance of the beauty grew too marked to be ignored. When she could not bear any longer the titters and the cattish glances directed her way, Miss Burton made an abrupt exit from the dance, citing a migraine. But even the most devoted of her beaux was not behind in giving his opinion that she was in a towering rage.

Miss Burton went home to throw a spectacular tantrum that reduced the household staff to abject misery. Her brother Bertram toed the broken crockery that he had ducked but moments before Mary Alice fled in tears to her bedroom. He said bitterly, "I will be the happiest fellow alive when she marries away from Stonehollow." He was glumly aware that he himself could not look about for a bride until his sister was out of the manor. Any wife of his would be no match for Mary Alice when she was at her worst.

Eighteen

Lord Townsend learned of the incident that had taken place at the ball when he was at the squire's place returning the pack of hounds. He was vastly amused by the squire and his wife's lively recounting of the tale. Mrs. Earlington was particularly proud of her youngest daughter's triumphant sortie against the beauty. She had long looked upon Mary Alice Burton as the nemesis of every mother who harbored the least ambitions for a daughter's future happiness. It had done her heart good, she confided to her husband privately, to see the haughty baggage properly rolled up. The squire, who like every other older gentleman in the neighborhood held a soft spot for such a beauteous example of womanhood, was inclined to pity Miss Burton even as he admitted that she had deserved a lesson in humility.

Lord Townsend was quite able to pick up on these undercurrents, which only added to his amusement. He too admired Miss Burton's beauty and had been aware the moment that she had set her cap for him. But he was too experienced in sophisticated drawing room games of seduction to fall for Miss Burton's obvious wiles. Even as he paid her easy compliments and favored her whims when they chanced to meet socially, he was careful to spread his attention to whatever other ladies happened also to be present.

His manners were thought to be very good and his ease of familiarity with ladies young and old to be unexceptionable.

Miss Burton had nothing of which to complain in Lord Townsend's attentiveness or his obvious admiration of her beauty. But there was a certain amusement in his eyes when his gaze rested on her face, an elusive quality about him, that bothered her. It was as though he was privately laughing at her. Miss Burton was torn between aggravation and fascination. She did not know what to think of her chances with the Viscount of Wythe and so was careful to treat him to far less caprice than she was wont to do with her other suitors.

Her feelings about Miss Miranda Wainwright were clearly defined, however. She had frequently observed a degree of easy communication between Lord Townsend and Miss Wainwright that infuriated her. She had warned Miss Wainwright not to position herself as a rival for the viscount's interest, but the colonial had not seen fit to heed her friendly advice, so she had decided to see to it that Miss Wainwright fervently regretted her presumption.

Miss Burton delivered every snub and insult she could devise to Miss Wainwright, all under the guise of social friendliness. She had been confident that Miss Wainwright would be at once too embarrassed and impotent to retaliate in kind, but such had not been the case. Miss Wainwright had proven rarely at a loss for a stinging riposte.

As a consequence of the public skirmishes, Miss Wainwright had very quickly been taken up in the neighborhood's social circles and was to be found everywhere. This circumstance could not but bring great dissatisfaction to Miss Burton, but she was powerless to counter it. Her only consolation was that Miss Wainwright appeared incurious regarding the gentlemen of the district. But that hardly reconciled Mary Alice to Miss Wainwright. On the contrary, she saw Miranda's aloofness as a sign that her true interest lay in Lord Townsend. It was for this that Miss Burton thoroughly detested the American woman and she treated her with disdainful hauteur whenever they chanced to meet.

When Lord Townsend was done recounting the latest gossip, Anne turned to Miranda with a laughing expression. "There now, Miranda! Does that not convince you that justice is yet to be found in this world?"

Miranda was vividly recalling her own public humiliation, the snubs that she had endured at the hands of supposedly well-meaning matrons, and the near segregation from polite society. Miss Burton had not been subjected to such thorough mortification, but Miranda discovered that she could readily sympathize with her. "Actually, I rather pity Miss Burton," she said.

Anne regarded her with astonishment. "Miranda! After all the insult that young woman has heaped upon you, how can you say that you *pity* her? I certainly do not."

"Miss Wainwright's position does her credit, Anne. She proves herself the better woman, you see," said Lord Townsend lazily. He was rewarded by a dark flash from Miss Wainwright's eyes. It was not often these days that he was able to break through her reserve and he had discovered an ever-increasing desire to do so. There was a quality about their former relationship that he very much regretted losing. He was determined to recapture it if he could possibly do so.

"This dashing naval officer sounds quite an exceptional gentleman," said Miranda. "I shall be most curious to meet him. Did you happen to catch his name, my lord?"

Lord Townsend frowned slightly. "I am certain that the squire and Mrs. Earlington must have mentioned it a score of times, but I was far too amused by the tale to pay particular attention to it."

"I too am all agog to make his acquaintance. Perhaps we shall pay a call on Mr. Willoughby. I have for some time had a desire to inspect his roses," said Anne, funning.

"Yes, and I suppose you are a devout dove lover as well," retorted Miranda. When her cousin stoutly maintained with a somewhat sheepish air that she was, Miranda began laughing and could not stop. It was left to Lord Townsend to tease his sister-in-law unmercifully over her heretofore unsuspected passions.

As Miranda listened to their lively banter she marveled not for the first time over her cousin's resiliency. Anne had been prostrate with grief only weeks before, her condition compounded by her indifferent health. But there had lately been a significant change in her. Anne had begun to make an effort to sit at dinner with the rest of the family and to spend part of her days outside her bedroom. She had also conveyed to Miranda an interest in the hiring of the staff.

For Miranda, the most telling point of all had been Anne's eventual willingness to accept the expressions of sympathy that she received from her neighbors. She was also astonished when Anne had sent a request for the village seamstress to wait on her at Willowswood and ordered several gowns done in mourning colors. Within days, Anne was attired in the somber dark grays and black, which suited her pale coloring. Those who called on her took away impressions of fragile, brave beauty.

The Viscount of Wythe and Robert had also taken to full mourning. Miranda, who was not of the immediate family, settled for shades of soft gray, blue, and mauve. She retrimmed her less frivolous gowns and bonnets in black satin and velvet ribbons and filled in those gowns that were cut low across the bodice with ruchings of fine lace.

The number of invitations received at Willowswood declined sharply once it was known that the Townsends were in mourning. There were a few functions that Miranda deemed unexceptionable, but Anne would attend none of them, preferring instead to remain secluded at Willowswood except for attending Sunday chapel. She did, however, pay a handful of morning calls on those acquaintances who were exceptionally kind in their expressions of condolence.

Miranda was pleased that Anne had come down out of her bedroom and it was very good to hear her cousin laughing as she was this evening. Perhaps Lord Townsend had been right in informing Anne so early of Richard's death. It seemed to have given her time to adjust to the idea before having to face it publicly. She was certainly making the effort to resume her place as mistress of Willowswood, which could only be beneficial both for herself and for Robert. Robert was obviously pleased by the change in his mother. His nightmares had begun to abate and though the boy grieved for his father in his own quiet way, Miranda thought the boy was adjusting better than could have been expected.

As for herself, Miranda found that she was coming to terms with her feelings for Lord Townsend. She knew that she could never expect a declaration from him. He was far superior to her socially and could choose a bride wherever he liked. She only hoped that she would be long gone before he did so. In the meantime, she was grateful for the gradual narrowing of the once-impossible distance that had separated her from Lord Townsend. It meant that they had regained a good measure of their former easy companionability and conversation. Miranda did not consider herself happy, but neither was she particularly unhappy. Content was perhaps the best word to describe her feelings. She did not recognize her state of mind for the emotional limbo that it was. But it would soon become all too clear to her.

One Sunday morning as the ladies were leaving church and Lord Townsend was handing them up into their carriage, a horseman coming down the lane reined in at the hall of an acquaintance.

Mr. Olive counted himself one of Captain Daggett's best friends in the district and it puffed up his consequence when the naval officer stopped to speak with him. "Eh, Daggett, had an early ride, have you? I wouldn't have thought to see you up after your late night at the alehouse, and especially when you had such a delectable piece for company," he said convivially. He snorted laughter.

Captain Daggett was somewhat irritated. He was not ashamed of his vices but it was another thing to have some idiot trumpet them aloud for the sharp ears of all the starchy matrons. It did not suit him to garner disapproval. His social situation was presently satisfying to him and he wanted nothing to change that. He leaned down and spoke quietly. "I would take it as a favor if that did not get nosed around, Olive. You understand, of course. The ladies do not like it."

"Oh, certainly! Nothing easier to understand. I'll keep mum, never fear," said Olive reassuringly. He embarked on a long tale of his one visit to London and the pleasures that he had found there. It was told with much winking and snorts of laughter.

Even as Daggett maintained a polite expression of interest and made short comments when appropriate, his attention wandered. His eyes happened to rove over the people leaving the church. Suddenly he stiffened, his gaze riveted by one particular face. Brusquely interrupting Mr. Olive's climactic moment, he said, "Who is that getting into the rig with the gray cattle?"

Mr. Olive looked around. "Oh, that is Mrs. Townsend and her brother-in-law, the Viscount of Wythe. A regular London beau, is his lordship. I never learned the proper knack for tying a neckcloth, but his lordship is never seen abroad without an intricate design of some sort. I have been meaning to approach him, just in a friendly manner, and endeavor to find out his secret. But you never know—devilish high in the instep are some of these dandified gentlemen."

"Never mind the man's neckcloth, Ned! Who is that lady with his lordship and Mrs. Townsend?" asked Daggett impatiently. His eyes were still on the woman's face.

"Why, that is Mrs. Townsend's cousin, Miss Miranda Wainwright. She is an affable lady and her manners are quite good and surprisingly straightforward. Rather refreshing, actually, after some of our own ladies. She is visiting from the States, you know," said Mr. Olive. "What do you think, Daggett? Should I approach his lordship about his neckcloth and risk a setdown?"

The carriage containing the party from Willowswood passed. Daggett's hard glance followed the lovely, animated face of Miranda Wainwright. He could hardly believe that it was the same woman from the *Larabelle* and that she was in this neighborhood. The coincidence was extraordinary and it set his thoughts to spinning, especially the fact that Mr. Olive had called her "Miss" Wainwright. It was obvious to him that she had chosen to conceal her married state. Vivid to his mind came a recollection of boarding the *Larabelle* and of how she had protested the impressment of the sailors. He remembered in particular the protective clasp that her husband, Jeremy Wainwright, had had on her arm.

Daggett's lips lifted in an unconscious snarl. Jeremy Wainwright, the man who was responsible for his being under severe reprimand and stripped of his command! The deep hatred in him was like bile in his throat. "Do as you wish, Olive. I've no patience for neckcloths," said Daggett. He pulled his mount around and cantered off.

Mr. Olive regarded the captain's abrupt departure with astonishment. "No patience for neckcloths! My word!" he exclaimed.

Nineteen

Bertram Burton was well-known as a true sportsman. He often got up hunting parties that lasted for weeks. His acquaintance extended mostly to gentlemen like himself: horsy, loud outdoorsmen who often seemed to care more for their horses and hounds than they did for themselves or their families.

Miss Burton detested her brother's house parties but tolerated the company because the majority were male and occasionally there did appear an interesting face among them. Once there had been a Scottish laird, whose proposal she had declined only because she disliked the thought of being buried in the cold north six months out of the year. No, Miss Burton was looking for a gentleman of consequence who could provide for her expensive tastes and take her to London.

Bertram was well aware of his sister's ambitions. He did his best to bring fresh blood to her attention but thus far without noticeable luck. When the Viscount of Wythe had come into the neighborhood he had set out at once to make his lordship's acquaintance. He invited Lord Townsend to join in the sport to be had at Stonehollow whenever his lordship was so inclined and had sold one of his finest hunters to him. At first Bertram had been put off by Lord

Townsend's unconscious air of arrogance, but it was not long before a mutual interest in sporting had established a friendship between the two gentlemen. Bertram thought it was almost a pity to think of saddling his lordship with Mary Alice, but he was not long in realizing that there would be no such match.

After a particularly trying day dealing with another of Miss Burton's tantrums, Bertram wished that the London gentleman were not quite so cagey. He sat musing before the fire, wineglass in hand. "I've seen the look in his lordship's eyes when she plays her tricks. Lord Townsend laughs to himself, he does. He's too downy a one to be caught in Mary Alice's toils," he said with a sigh. A moment of thought and he slapped his thigh. "And damn if I don't admire his lordship all the more for it! There aren't many who see the sweetened trap for what it is."

His expression darkened as his thoughts carried him on to another gentleman who seemed impervious to his sister's manifold charms. "That Captain Daggett, now. I do not see what Mary Alice finds so fascinating in him. I don't like the look of him myself. Too twitchy by half and the way he sits that job horse of his is enough to turn a man's stomach with disgust. Aye, that fellow is not all that he is cracked up to be. He is the stuff one should never turn one's back on."

Miss Burton was aware of her brother's dislike for Captain Daggett. It but added to the naval officer's infuriating attraction. She had tried for weeks to break through the gentleman's formal manner toward her and spark some hint of admiration in his cold, derisive eyes, but to no avail. In the beginning it had only piqued her that Captain Daggett appeared immune to her beauty. Gradually, however, his disregard had become almost an obsession with her. She could not stand to be slighted by the gentleman. Gone was her original intent to make him beg for her favor. It was now she who schemed to solicit someone's interest. She did not recognize that Daggett had quite literally turned her own tactics against her.

Miss Burton made up her mind that Captain Daggett must be brought to recognize her. After much labor, she sent a carefully worded epistle to the gentleman. His answer was long in coming and at the end of two days she was on tenterhooks. When the letter finally arrived in the post, she seized on it and tore it open with impatient fingers. What was written there appeared to satisfy her, for she raised her eyes and slowly exhaled her pent-up breath. Tapping the letter against her hand, Miss Burton smiled in satisfaction.

That night Miss Burton drove her gig by a roundabout way to a little-used entrance to the rose garden at Willoughby Hall. She had disguised herself in a heavy veil and cloak, a wasted precaution since it had not occurred to her to use other than her own well-known gig and horse. Miss Burton alighted to the ground, then stood hesitantly. She stared at the garden wall, wondering if she was mad. Her nerves were stretched taut and she made a move to reenter her carriage. But the door in the garden wall opened and a man's silhouetted figure appeared in it. Miss Burton took a steadying breath, calling upon the steel and courage that a lifetime of jumping high fences and wide ditches had bred in her. She walked forward swiftly, not allowing herself another second to doubt her actions. Her hand was caught up and carried to the gentleman's lips as he drew her inside the garden wall. The door creaked as it closed behind them.

Captain Daggett led his private guest toward the gazebo that stood in the middle of the rose garden. The heady perfume of the roses was heavy on the night. They entered the mysteriously shadowed gazebo. Captain Daggett turned to her. With careful hands he put back the heavy veil and undid the ties that bound her cloak about her slender neck. His fingers paused at the pulse beating unnaturally swift in her soft throat. The cloak and veil slid away to the ground.

A shaft of moonlight reflected the uncertainty in Miss Burton's eyes. She was like a terrified hare, poised for flight and yet fascinated by the danger she sensed.

Captain Daggett ran his hand lightly up her bare arm. He felt her shudder but he knew it was not in revulsion. His thin mouth eased in a satisfied smile. He had deliberately chosen this spot for their assignation for its evocative atmosphere, and it was working its magic. Miss Burton was his at last.

He seized her by her hair and took her astonished lips with savage passion while his other arm pinned her to him. He gave no quarter, but demanded her surrender. Though often kissed, Miss Burton had never been treated to such a sensual onslaught. With the first flickering of her own awakening ardor, she was lost.

An hour later Miss Burton emerged from the garden. Beneath the concealing cloak she was disheveled in dress. There was a dazed expression in her eyes and she stumbled as she stepped up into the gig. With shaking hands she slapped the reins and the horse started up. A dense cloud passed over the moon as she drove off.

At Miranda's urging, Anne reluctantly agreed to accept an invitation to a small private dinner at the Earlingtons. Miranda had pointed out that Anne could not very well remain buried at Willowswood, if only for the sake of her own sanity. Mrs. Earlington had added her persuasions to Miranda's. "It is only the squire and myself, our daughters, and a few gentlemen to make up the numbers. You may rest assured, dear Mrs. Townsend, that our little potluck will be quite unexceptional."

Before dinner was served, the squire brought up the only gentleman unknown to the ladies and introduced him. Miranda met the gentleman's gaze and the shock of recognition drove the breath from her lungs. She stared at him unnerved. The dashing naval officer they had all heard so much good of was Captain William Daggett, the very same man who had created such hardship for her brother.

Anne was pleased to make the naval officer's acquaintance. She held out her hand to him. "Why, sir, I am honored. Indeed, I have looked forward to our meeting. Your reputation has preceded you, you know."

Captain Daggett bowed over her hand and retained it a slight moment. Though his eyes appeared a bit hard in expression, his smile was quite agreeable. "I hope that my reputation speaks well of me, Mrs. Townsend."

Anne laughed, her eyes dancing as she withdrew her fingers from his light clasp. "Quite well, Captain Daggett. I believe that you have garnered some sort of honor for not succumbing at once to Miss Burton's fatal beauty."

"I am prostrated at the mere sight of beauty, Mrs. Townsend. I acknowledge Miss Burton's loveliness, but I must also pay court to all the other charming ladies whom I have had the good fortune to have met," said Captain Daggett. He included Anne Townsend's silent companion in the compass of his smile.

Anne realized suddenly that Miranda had not offered one word since Captain Daggett had been introduced. She glanced at her cousin. Anne was startled by the hard look in Miranda's usually smiling eyes and the flush of color in her cheeks. Anne hurried into the lengthening breach. "My cousin and I were talking of you only a few days ago, Captain Daggett, and had wondered when we might have occasion to meet the neighborhood's latest guest. I am happy that we have at last done so, do you not agree, Miranda?"

"Quite," said Miranda shortly. She stared into the captain's cold blue eyes. She had listened to the exchange between her cousin and Captain Daggett with gathering anger. How dared the man behave so coolly when he must realize that she had recognized him. It was only deference for her hosts that prevented Miranda from delivering a blistering indictment of the naval officer's character.

She still remembered the tone of the last letter she had received from Jeremy only days before. Though he had obviously been happy about the outcome of the struggle, Miranda had been overwhelmed by the tired note that also came through. He had lost too much time in getting his cargo to market and had made far less profit than he had anticipated for his first voyage. He would be fortunate to break even on the return trip, he had written. Her heart had been wrung with sympathy for Jeremy. She knew how much hope her brother had placed on this voyage to establish him firmly in his life's calling. She had thought at the time that if ever given the opportunity she would happily draw and quarter Captain Daggett.

"Oh yes, Anne. I am indeed glad to encounter Captain Daggett. His presence in the neighborhood adds a distinctive odor to our circle of acquaintances," she said without any lightening of her cold expression.

Anne was appalled. She wondered wildly what to do. Miranda would never consciously insult someone on first introduction. Of course she would not, thought Anne loyally, but her choice of words was incredibly awkward. She was unutterably relieved when after the briefest moment, Captain Daggett began to chuckle. Anne uncertainly joined him in his laughter. Her eyes flew in appeal to Miranda's face, but her cousin's only response was to bestow a cool smile on them.

Captain Daggett bowed to Anne and Miranda. "I shall undoubtedly see more of both of the lovely ladies of Willowswood," he said with the faintest smile. His eyes rested deliberately on Miranda Wainwright's cool, dismissive expression. He read the scorn in her darkened eyes and took it as a sign of trapped defiance. "I am especially interested in pursuing my acquaintance with Miss Wainwright," he said quietly, his thoughts dwelling lovingly on the revenge he meant to take on Jeremy Wainwright. When next Jeremy Wainwright saw his wife, thought Daggett, he would learn that he had been cuckolded. He strolled away on the satisfying thought.

"How I detest that man!" exclaimed Miranda in a low, trembling voice. Her fingers were clenched on the ribs of her fan.

"But how can you say that? You have but just met him," said Anne. "I do not know what can possibly have gotten into you, Miranda. I have never before known you to deliberately offer unprovoked insult."

"Unprovoked? Little do you know of the matter, cousin! That man is the very same who unlawfully seized Jeremy's ship and impressed our American sailors. No, I do not offer unprovoked insult, Anne. If I had my way, Captain Daggett would be made to pay dearly for his temerity," said Miranda furiously.

"Oh!" Anne threw a startled glance after the departing officer. "That certainly puts a different complexion on the matter. But then how is it that Captain Daggett is so friendly? I would have thought that he would be appalled to be recognized by you."

"His arrogance carries him forward, Anne!" said Miranda in hasty judgment. "It is like taunting a gored bull. Captain Daggett obviously dares me to expose him for the cad that he is."

Anne shuddered. "Really, some of the things you say!"

Miranda looked at her a moment in bewilderment and then she laughed. "I am sorry, Anne. I did not realize that I was being indelicate. Come, let us forget the loathsome man and enjoy ourselves. There is our kind hostess free of her duties at last. I should like to discover which of the young ladies so effectively routed Miss Burton."

Anne gave a gurgle of laughter. "Indeed. Andrew said that Mrs. Earlington was puffed up like a partridge with pride. It was quite a triumph. I should have liked to have been present."

Mrs. Earlington received the ladies' attention with graciousness. She was particularly gratified when Mrs. Townsend complimented her on her daughter's extraordinary skirmish with the beauty. "Yes, it was quite a victory for my Tabitha. I don't mind telling you that it did my heart good to have a certain young lady set down for once," she confided. "I am sure I am as tolerant as the next person, but I have thought for quite some time that Miss Mary Alice Burton was too puffed up with her own consequence, if you will pardon the expression. And I am certain that you, Miss Wainwright, have every reason to feel pleasure. It is well known that Miss Burton bears you ill will, though I cannot think why, as kind and good-mannered as you are."

"I cannot say that I am sorry for Miss Burton, but it is an uncomfortable thing to have one's dignity cut up in public. To that extent at least I sympathize with her," said Miranda.

"That is just like you, I am sure," said Mrs. Earlington,

nodding. She turned to Anne. "Where is the viscount to-night, Mrs. Townsend? I had quite thought to see him with us."

Anne shook her head. "My brother-in-law is too consci-entious by half. He said that he wished to finish up some paperwork this evening that Richard's solicitor had brought. I never before realized how much was involved in—this sort of thing." Her voice cracked and tears entered her blue eyes. She reached quickly for a dainty handker-chief.

Mrs. Earlington was distressed. She certainly had not meant to discomfit Mrs. Townsend in any way, she stam-mered. Miranda eased smoothly into the breach. "Mrs. Earlington, perhaps you will be able to tell me. I have talked to the gardener and Mrs. Crumpet about candying violets, but they cannot agree on the best way to go about it."

Mrs. Earlington seized with relief on the change of topic. She spoke animatedly on the proper time to harvest the vio-lets and what she had discovered to be an admirable recipe for the delicacy. After a few moments Anne had recovered herself and was quite able to contribute to the conversation.

Dinner was announced and the small party of guests went in to a well-prepared repast of barley soup, meat pies, new potatoes, peas and scallions, and roasted game hens. Miranda and Anne partook of coffee afterward in the drawing room, but Miranda soon recognized that her cousin was drooping and it was not long afterward that the ladies took leave of Mrs. Earlington and the squire and re-turned to Willowswood.

Twenty

Lord Townsend heard their entrance from the study and opened the door. "How was the squire's dinner?"

"It was quite nice, for the most part. You were missed, however, and Mrs. Earlington read me a short lecture on allowing you to become a hermit," said Anne. She stood on her toes to place a kiss on her brother-in-law's cheek. "If you do not mind it, Andrew, I am on my way to bed. It has been a tiring evening." She turned from him and after a brief good night to Miranda, she went up the stairs.

Lord Townsend stared after his sister-in-law with a sudden frown. He glanced at Miranda, who was giving her cloak and gloves into Crumpet's care. "What happened to upset Anne tonight?"

"When Mrs. Earlington asked your whereabouts, Anne mentioned the papers that you were toiling over. It reminded her of Richard, of course, and overset her for a few moments," said Miranda.

"Damn! I had wondered if even attending a private dinner party was entering society too soon," said Lord Townsend.

"I do not think it would profit her to remain entirely secluded, my lord. She would dwell too much on her loss," said Miranda.

"You are right, of course. Anne needs the support of others when she is troubled," said Lord Townsend. "Do you also go up to bed, Miss Wainwright, or would you condescend to join me for a cup of tea?"

"I should like that very much, actually," said Miranda.

Lord Townsend glanced at the butler. "Crumpet, be so good as to bring Miss Wainwright and myself some tea. We shall be in the study."

"Very good, my lord," said Crumpet, and withdrew from the hall.

Lord Townsend gestured, inviting Miranda into the study. She walked inside and seated herself in a wingback chair. With a sigh Lord Townsend threw himself into the chair opposite her. He ran his fingers through his thick hair. "I did not realize the task Richard set for me when he named me executor of his will. It is a wretched business," he said.

"Is the will not clear, then?" asked Miranda with concern.

Lord Townsend gave a tired laugh. "Oh, it is clear enough. But other than naming Robert his heir and making me guardian until Robert's majority, Richard blithely left it to my discretion how the estate is to be handled and how Anne is to be provided for. He actually penned that he had no patience for such things and that I had a much better head for it than he," he said.

"Oh no. I cannot believe that Richard would leave such loose ends," said Miranda.

"I have discovered since coming to Willowswood that my brother was prone to leave any and all paperwork to others. Hence the mess that I found with the working papers of the estate and the discovery that his bailiff had been robbing him blind. I had hoped that the will, since it was drawn up with the guidance of Richard's solicitor, might be different. But Mr. Garrison informs me with much regret and obvious disturbance that Richard brushed aside his advice and would not add one more word than what he had written," said Lord Townsend. "These papers here involve Anne's future. I must make provisions for a pension for her out of the estate. But what with the estate tied up in trust for Robert, I do not yet see my way to how it is to be done."

The door opened and Crumpet entered with the teapot and cups on a tray. After serving them and accepting their murmured thanks, he left again.

"Surely there are other monies than those tied up for Robert," said Miranda.

Lord Townsend's eyes suddenly sharpened. "What did you say, Miranda?" She repeated herself, stuttering a little because he had used her Christian name. The viscount did not seem to notice her flush. "By God, you have hit it exactly! As Robert's guardian I may set aside proceeds from the estate for investments that are to his benefit. I think that a mother may be counted as a benefit for a small boy."

Miranda stared at him and then laughed. "I wish I may see Anne's face when she learns that you have invested in her as a mother."

Lord Townsend grinned. "It is an odd way of putting it," he agreed. "But I think that it may fly with Mr. Garrison, who is quite as anxious as I am to settle the question. He is a devout family man and it pained him that Richard made no clear provision for Anne other than to remand her to my discretion. I suspect also that he feared what form my discretion might take. I am a London gentleman and therefore must be assumed to be careless of life's more sober considerations."

"I cannot condemn Mr. Garrison for his prejudices. I

once thought you a cold and frivolous gentleman and took you in the greatest dislike," confessed Miranda.

"Good God! What had I done to warrant such an opinion?" asked Lord Townsend, disconcerted.

"It was your announcement that you had come down to Willowswood not in answer to your family's distress but because you were in disfavor with the Prince Regent," said Miranda.

Lord Townsend looked at her, his gaze suddenly intent. "And what is your opinion of me now, Miss Wainwright?"

Miranda felt a hint of danger on the air. She slowly replied, "I believe you to be a most caring gentleman, my lord. Certainly you have shown such consideration to Anne and Robert, and indeed to myself, that . . ." She could not continue then because the viscount had left his chair and come over to her.

He raised her out of her chair, his brown eyes holding her gaze. Still retaining a gentle grasp of her shoulders he stared intently into her eyes. "Your opinion of me is quite accurate, Miss Wainwright. I am definitely a caring gentleman," he said softly. He bent his head to kiss her with a tenderness that Miranda had never before experienced. It was like tasting a heady wine. Afterward Lord Townsend folded her quite naturally in his arms, his cheek resting on her hair.

Miranda blinked, coherent thought returning to her slowly. She felt warmed and secure. Something most important had just occurred between her and Lord Townsend. Before she could form the question that had risen in her mind, Lord Townsend had released her and gone over to the fireplace. He picked up the poker and prodded the burning log so that a shower of yellow sparks went up the chimney. "I did not ask you earlier, Miss Wainwright. How did you find Squire and Mrs. Earlington's dinner party?"

Miranda, of a sudden abandoned, had to gather herself together before she could reply. "As always the company was most pleasant," she said. "With the exception of one gentleman."

The quality of her voice was such that Lord Townsend turned his head, his heavy brows raised. "I discern a positive dislike for the gentleman. Who was he?"

"I met the naval officer that everyone has been speaking about with such approbation. I do not share the general favorable opinion of Captain William Daggett," said Miranda.

"So I gather," said Lord Townsend dryly. "What has Captain Daggett done to offend?"

"He was the commanding officer of the sloop that seized Jeremy's ship. I hope that I need not explain what my feelings were upon meeting him here," said Miranda.

"No, I can well imagine them. I wonder what the man is doing in this neighborhood? It strikes me as peculiar that he happens to appear in the same district as yourself," said Lord Townsend. "You did say, did you not, that in your brother's last letter he wrote that he had won his case? I wonder, did he happen to mention Captain Daggett in any regard?"

Miranda shook her head. "Jeremy said nothing. Why, should he have?"

"Perhaps it would have helped explain why Captain Daggett chose to take his holiday in this particular neighborhood. Miranda, I would prefer it if you gave Captain Daggett a wide berth. There is something about this that gives off a foul odor. And I think that you should write Jeremy. I am most curious to discover what was the outcome of the complaint against Captain Daggett," said Lord Townsend.

"Of course I shall write Jeremy. But I do not think that Captain Daggett poses much of a threat to me, as you so obviously fear," said Miranda with a smile. But in that she was to be proven wrong.

In the weeks that followed Miranda was surprised and angered when Captain Daggett seemed to single her out for attention. She could not understand his motive. It was as though he were taunting her to denounce him for the scoundrel that he was. This in itself made Miranda wary of doing so and so she kept her own counsel on what she knew of the naval officer. She had a strong wish that Jeremy would answer her letter so that she would know better what she ought to do; but Jeremy seemed to be in no hurry to reply.

Others noticed the dashing captain's attentiveness toward Miss Wainwright and began to speculate upon it, wondering if they were to see a match. Miss Burton was extremely disturbed by the gossip. After her clandestine rendezvous in the rose garden with Captain Daggett, and its unexpected intimate culmination, Mary Alice had assumed that the gentleman was a serious suitor for her hand. Since then she had shown him marked partiality over her other suitors, so much so that there had been several laughing remarks made even within her hearing that the capricious Miss Burton had at last been snared and not a title in sight.

It was a surprise to everyone, and no less to Mary Alice herself, that she did not care what was said. Her haughty pride seemed to have deserted her where Captain Daggett was concerned. She had eyes only for him. Her thoughts revolved around the maddening gentleman, who treated her with much the same negligence he had before that fateful assignation. But despite his unfeeling manner, Mary Alice gravitated to him at every function. Hers was not a particularly reflective nature and she accepted Captain Daggett's coldness as part of his personality.

However, the business of Miss Wainwright was more than she could stand in silence. Miss Burton decided that she had to confront Captain Daggett and discover exactly what his actions meant. She went boldly to Willoughby Hall under the pretence of issuing an invitation to one of her brother's sporting parties and requested a private interview with Captain Daggett. With a shrug, he led her outside to the gardens. Miss Burton waited only until her maid had discreetly dropped back before she taxed him over his attentions toward Miss Wainwright.

Captain Daggett laughed. "It is no concern of yours, Miss Burton," he said.

"But what of us, sir? Surely—" His glance silenced her for an instant, then she said in a pleading voice, "Captain Daggett—William, please! I gave all you demanded of me in this very garden. Surely I deserve an answer!"

Captain Daggett reached out to catch a blooming red rose between his thin fingers and plucked it from its stem. "A rose in full bloom is at its loveliest and most alluring. The bees hover about it in the warm sunshine, dipping to catch a taste of its sweet nectar." He dropped the rose and crushed it underfoot. He looked at Miss Burton, an edge of cruelty in his gaze. "The nectar has been collected, Miss Burton, and the rose is blown. Quite, quite blown."

Mary Alice's face flamed. She turned unsteadily and walked quickly away. Her surprised maid, who hurried to catch up with her, cast an uncertain glance back at the naval officer. Captain Daggett gazed after Miss Burton's exquisite form as she disappeared. He laughed softly and exited the garden.

Slowly a figure emerged from between the high hedges. He was frowning as he stripped off his pruning gloves.

Miranda continued to repulse Daggett's unwelcome advances as best she could so as to avoid any more gossip than was already circulating. But it went against the grain with her to be forced to receive the gentleman with any show of civility at all and she declined even such few invitations that were being received at Willowswood so that she would not meet Captain Daggett. On those occasions that she did encounter him, such as at church or during a morning call in the village, she managed to avoid him by never separating herself from the company of others.

However, the day came that Miranda ran into Captain Daggett without benefit of company. She had taken flowers to the church and arranged them on the altar, chatting in a friendly fashion as she did so with the caretaker of the cemetery. The man walked out of the church with her and tipped his hat as he said good-bye. Miranda stood pulling on her gloves. She was on the point of stepping up into the gig that she had driven from Willowswood when she became aware of a rider whom she recognized coming down the lane toward her. As the mounted gentleman approached she gave a cool nod but spared him no more than a glance. She was taken aback when Captain Daggett pulled up his mount and bade her good day.

"It is very well, thank you," said Miranda shortly, stepping up into the carriage.

Captain Daggett sat his horse in a negligent posture, one hand cocked on his thigh. "You do not care for me overmuch, my lady?"

Miranda paused to give him a straight stare before she seated herself on the carriage seat. "I have sufficient reason not to, sir."

Captain Daggett smiled. His smile did not quite reach his eyes. "Why, as to that I wouldn't be so certain. I have only to glance at a woman to know when she is restless. And I am very well able to satisfy that craving." His arm snaked out to catch Miranda about the waist and he half-lifted her out of the gig. His knee and topboot pressed against her thigh and his spur caught in the fabric of her skirt.

Miranda strained away from him, shoving with all her might at his chest. His arm was like a band around her and his wide-spread fingers pressed close the soft flesh of her waist. The contact was loathsome. For the first time in her life Miranda wished fervently that she wore a corset. "Unhand me at once, you cad!"

"You've a high and mighty way about you that appeals to a gentleman of my exacting character. Tell me, Miranda, when did you last feel the heat of passion a real man brings to a woman?" said Daggett. He caught her chin in a painful grip and brought his head down to hers.

Miranda twisted her head so that his kiss went awry. She cracked him across the face with all the strength in her arm. Daggett let go of her abruptly and she fell back onto the seat of the gig. She was breathing quickly and indignation colored her cheeks. Her eyes were flashing dark pools of fury. She grabbed the thin whip that lay on the leather seat and raised it. "I shall thrash you within an inch of your life if you dare to lay a hand on me, Captain Daggett!"

Captain Daggett rubbed his face where a red imprint was already visible across his cheekbone. His cold blue eyes were enraged. "You will regret your arrogance, madame. I promise you that!" He yanked his mount around and set spur to it, cantering off swiftly. Miranda sat stunned on the gig's seat, trembling in every limb. She attempted to catch her breath.

"Miss! Miss, be ye all right?"

She looked around to find the caretaker standing beside the gig, an expression of acute concern in his eyes. She straightened her posture and unnecessarily brushed a shaking hand across her smooth hair. "Yes, Jacob. I was— was taken unawares. But I am fine."

"That be a proper scoundrel, miss. I never seen a gentleman act so disrespectful," said the caretaker indignantly.

"Well, it is over now. I doubt that Captain Daggett will again be so bold. Let us simply forget the incident ever happened, shall we? I will come again next week with fresh blooms," said Miranda calmly. She picked up the reins and drove off. The caretaker looked after her, shaking his head in admiration for her composure.

Twenty-one

Miranda was not so composed as her bearing led the caretaker to suppose. Daggett's unexpected attack had revolted and appalled her, but she was particularly unsettled by his words. He had said something to the effect that he had detected a restlessness in her, obviously the sort of restlessness that led to such horrid advances. Miranda did not know what to believe. She had thought that the mask of content she wore was credible. She had taken such pains to cover her emotions from observant eyes. She had not even permitted herself the luxury of allowing her gaze to follow the viscount's tall figure when he chanced to walk past her. But it was now patently clear to her that she was unsuccessful in hiding her true feelings.

Miranda was surprised to find herself dashing away a few traitorous tears. The last time that Lord Townsend had kissed her she had been carried away by the most extraordinary anticipation. She had been so certain that he was about to declare himself. But he had only turned away to poke at the fire, and she had been left with her question unanswered.

"Oh, you fool! That was his answer and you have been unwilling to accept it," she exclaimed angrily. Lord Townsend did not love her or surely he would have said so in that sublime moment.

The tears fell faster and Miranda could no longer effectively dash them away. She relied on the horse to bring her safely to Willowswood and fought to regain possession of herself before the groom came to take the horse's head. She had halfway succeeded when she climbed down from the gig, but she knew that her control was fragile at best and that she was on the edge of a long-put-off bout of tears. "Thank you, Jenkins," she said, and hurried up the steps.

Crumpet opened the door to her and bowed her in with a smile. Miranda gave him a quick nod but did not exchange a few words with him as was her usual custom. She swiftly made for the staircase, wanting only to reach her bedroom and privacy. She heard a door open and a quick step. Miranda did not need to turn to know that Lord Townsend had come out into the entrance hall. "Miss Wainwright, I am happy to see that you have returned."

Miranda reached out for the newel post and stepped onto the stairs. "Forgive me if I do not stay to talk, my lord. I—I wish to see to the refurbishing of some gowns. The afternoon has gone so quickly, you know."

A strong hand caught her arm. "Come, Miss Wainwright. You can do better than that. If you wish to avoid me, tell me so and I will oblige you," said Lord Townsend in a teasing voice. He was startled by the quick glance that she sent him. In that brief second he became aware of an air of distress about her. His fingers tightened on her slender forearm. "Miss Wainwright, what has occurred?"

Miranda closed her eyes tight and swallowed. She shook her head. She was glad that her voice seemed almost natural when she spoke. "Why, nothing, my lord. Whatever are you referring to?"

"Perhaps the fact that you cannot look me in the face,

Miss Wainwright," said Lord Townsend. He did not give her the choice of leaving the stairs, but made her step down. He drew her hand over his elbow and walked her into the drawing room. He released his hold on her only to close the door, then turned to look at her.

Miranda had retreated across the room and now stood with her back to him as she lifted the curtain at the window. Her plaited crown of hair and slim neck and carriage were silhouetted by the late afternoon sun. Lord Townsend walked over to join her at the window. He set his gaze on her neat profile. "Now, Miss Wainwright, I wish to know what has so obviously upset you."

"It was nothing of great moment, truly. I would be too embarrassed to tell you," said Miranda with a small laugh.

Lord Townsend was not deceived. "You are not a lady easily intimidated or overset. Something has occurred that has shaken you and I demand to be told what it is."

"I have nothing to relate, my lord." Miranda turned away from him with the intention of quitting the drawing room, but he foiled her by the simple device of putting his arms about her and drawing her back against his chest. Miranda stood stiffly in the circle of his arms. She could feel the hot tears at the back of her throat. Why had he come out of the study at just that moment? she thought despairingly.

"Miranda, I do not intend to let you escape so easily." His breath ruffled her hair warmly.

Miranda made a small sound of protest to which Lord Townsend paid not the least heed. She put up her hand to dash away a tear. "Oh very well! It was Daggett." She felt Lord Townsend's body stiffen. "I was leaving the church and he said something—something despicable . . ."

She was turned swiftly about. Lord Townsend's fingers

flexed on her shoulders. His eyes were strangely alight and his expression was harsh. "Never mind what Daggett said. I know you better than to think mere words would upset you. Miranda, did Daggett dare—did he touch you?" The viscount read the answer in her eyes. Abruptly he let go of her. He strode to the drawing room door and wrenched it open.

Miranda realized his intent. She ran after him and put out a quick hand to catch his sleeve. "Andrew! It was not what you think! At least, not quite. I struck him so forcibly that he released me. I am quite all right, pray believe me. It was only a nasty incident. I do not think he will dare another."

"I assure you that he will not," said Lord Townsend harshly.

Miranda looked up at him, her hand still on his arm. "My lord, surely you do not intend to challenge him over it! Pray do not. The humiliation would be beyond anything. I do not desire that my name even be whispered in the same breath as his!"

Lord Townsend stared frowningly at her. After a moment his tight mouth relaxed. "You are right as usual, Miranda. For me to publicly confront Daggett would be the worst thing that I could do. Immediately tongues would be set wagging that there must be more than a private insult between us. Captain Daggett's attentiveness toward you is well known and it would be pointed out that I am your cousin. In the end your reputation would suffer, my dear Miss Wainwright."

Miranda would recall that conversation with a sense of irony. Not many days passed before she noticed that ladies who had treated her with friendliness now turned away from her when she chanced to encounter them in the village. Their demeanor was cold, their greetings if spoken at all were reserved and contemptuous. Miranda did not know what to think. She had done nothing to bring down on her head such universal dislike and there grew a sinking feeling in the pit of her stomach. The situation struck her as similar to that which she had left behind in Massachusetts when she had broken her engagement to Harrison Gregory and had been treated to an incredible snubbing. What troubled Miranda most was that this time she had no clue of how she had sinned.

Miranda was distressed enough that she was driven to confide in Anne. "I do not understand it, Anne. I have told you what happened when I jilted Harrison Gregory and the resulting scandal. I was practically ostracized from polite society. This has the same feel to it and yet I do not know why it is happening," said Miranda. She brushed her hand across her aching brow. "I don't know that I can go through it again. I truly don't."

Anne's pretty face was puckered in a frown. "It is outrageous. I, too, am certain that something has happened, for at chapel conversations end abruptly whenever I approach. I am at as much a loss as you." She looked over at her cousin with a sudden air of determination. "I shall get to the bottom of it, Miranda, I promise you. I shan't stand by and watch you shunned and snubbed. There is one lady whom I can trust to tell me the truth. I shall visit her this very hour."

"If you do not mind, I shall not accompany you. You will undoubtedly be received more graciously if I am not present," said Miranda with a bitter twist to her lips. Anne nodded in agreement. Before she left the drawing room she paused to give Miranda a fierce hug.

As Anne hurried away, Miranda was surprised by the

rush of tears to her eyes. She had not thought that she was so vulnerable, but apparently her spirits were lower than even she had known. "This will not do," she said aloud. She straightened her shoulders and left the drawing room with the thought of taking refuge in the herb garden. There she could be assured of virtual privacy and only the flowering shrubs and sweet-smelling herbs would be witness to her perturbation.

Anne returned to Willowswood some time later. She was in a state of high indignation and could hardly remain silent until she was private with Miranda. "I went to call on Mrs. Averidge. I knew that she would be unable to withstand my entreaties and so it was. She was very reluctant to spread gossip, as she put it, but I finally won her over," said Anne swiftly, pulling off her bonnet and gloves with jerky movements.

Miranda was alarmed by her cousin's high color and unusually agitated movements. "Anne, pray calm yourself. You are not well enough that you should let yourself be distressed."

"Bother my distress!" exclaimed Anne, rounding on Miranda. Her blue eyes sparkled with fury. "Miranda, I was told that Captain Daggett has put it about that you are secretly married to a bounder and a scoundrel named Jeremy Wainwright. Furthermore, Captain Daggett has dared to hint that you are no better than you should be and that he has made a conquest of you."

"What!" Miranda was startled into laughter. It was so outrageous as to be ludicrous. She abruptly stopped laughing when she saw that her cousin's face remained grim. "You are serious, Anne. This—this ridiculous farrago is what has caused me so much anxiety. Why, how can anyone believe such nonsense?"

"So I asked Mrs. Averidge. I told her that Jeremy Wainwright is your brother and that I have known him for years. As for Captain Daggett's heavy hints that he has had an affair with you, I denied it strenuously. But she shook her head, saying that she did not know how such a mistake could be made. But I could see that she did not quite believe me. When I took my leave I pleaded again for her understanding of the truth. She patted my hand with a pitying look and said that my loyalty to you did me credit, if you please! I was never more infuriated in my life," said Anne.

Miranda stared into the air. "He said that I would regret my arrogance, you know." She glanced at her cousin. "I did not tell you before, Anne. When I took flowers to the church two weeks ago, Captain Daggett chanced to ride up. He made horrid advances to me and I rebuffed him quite strenuously. He threatened that I would regret what I had done, and I suppose this is his way of revenging himself on me."

"It's despicable! But why did you not tell me before, Miranda? Between us, we might have foreseen what he meant to do, especially after receiving Jeremy's letter and learning that Daggett was disciplined for actions unbecoming a King's officer. Perhaps I could have discreetly made it known what a blackguard he is and thus saved you this heartache," said Anne.

"I did not think, I suppose. I honestly thought that would be the end of it," said Miranda. She wavered on the point of confessing to Anne that Lord Townsend had learned of Daggett's advances and had almost issued a challenge to the man, but she dreaded Anne's exclamations. Little as she wished to be thought infatuated with Captain Daggett, it would be infinitely worse to have even her beloved cousin begin to speculate that Lord Townsend might

200

care for her. She knew the truth of the matter and it pained her too much to wish the question explored by a third party.

"I mean to inform Andrew of this preposterous tale the moment that he returns from the hunt. Then we shall see how Captain Daggett is to be dealt with," said Anne, a martial light in her eyes.

Miranda's cheeks flamed. "No! I could not bear—"

"Do not be ridiculous, cousin!" said Anne sharply. "Andrew will be as furious as I that your reputation has been so infamously besmirched. And he is a gentleman. Gentlemen have ways of dealing with their own who cross the line."

Lord Townsend had enjoyed the hunt. He was leading his horse back to the hunting lodge at Stonehollow for some well-earned refreshment when Miss Burton pulled up her mount to walk beside him. "Good afternoon, Miss Burton," said Lord Townsend.

She smiled at him. "And to you, my lord! I have never enjoyed anything half as much in my life," she said, her violet eyes sparkling. Her color was becomingly high and the wind had loosened a few curls and blown them about her face.

Looking up at her, Lord Townsend had to admire such an abundance of beauty. Miss Burton was a spoiled young woman and at times spiteful, but much could be forgiven such a face and figure. She was a regular goer at hounds as well and had gained his respect for her smart riding. "I am impressed with your style, Miss Burton. I have seldom seen such clean jumping executed by a lady," he said.

Miss Burton preened herself a little. "Thank you, my lord. I have always adored horses, so naturally my mounts all respond handsomely. And today's hunt was particularly invigorating, do you not agree?"

Lord Townsend laughed up at her. "Quite. It but needed the rest of the neighborhood to become a regular circus."

"Oh, I don't suppose we could have gotten Miss Wainwright to join us," said Miss Burton with a slight titter. "Poor thing, she is quite out of favor these days. I am certain that it must be a trial to her."

Lord Townsend glanced up at his beautiful companion with a slight frown. "What do you mean, Miss Burton?"

Miss Burton eyed him in surprise and then with speculation. Of late Lord Townsend had been more than normally inclined to appreciate her company. She had assumed that he was influenced by the gossip circulating about Miss Wainwright, but apparently that was not so. Perhaps he was simply beginning to come around. She had always thought of Miranda Wainwright as her true competition for the viscount and conceivably she had just been handed a golden opportunity to deal her rival a fatal blow. "Surely you have heard, my lord. Why, Miss Wainwright's name has been linked with Captain Daggett's. I myself do not indulge in gossip, of course, but I must say that the story is heard everywhere," she said indifferently. She bent to pat her mare's sweating neck. She was startled when her wrist was caught between steely fingers.

Lord Townsend stared into her astonished eyes. "What story do you refer to, Miss Burton?" he asked pleasantly.

Disliking the viscount's ungentle hold, Miss Burton glanced deliberately at her imprisoned wrist. "My lord, you are hurting me," she said. But she discovered that she was not always to be indulged. The viscount was not thrown in to discomfiture by her displeasure. If anything, Lord Townsend's eyes hardened. Of a sudden, his tight-lipped expression rather frightened her.

"I wish the round tale, Miss Burton."

Miss Burton cast her eyes about for possible succor, but the field was deserted of fellow huntsmen. She looked down again at Lord Townsend. "It—it is merely a rumor, my lord. Miss Wainwright is said to have succumbed to Captain Daggett's blandishments. What is considered equally shocking is that Miss Wainwright supposedly hides a secret marriage in her past. I am certain there is nothing in it, truly."

Lord Townsend's smile was not pleasant. "I trust that I know Miss Wainwright too well to believe such evil of her. I hope you do not think me ungentlemanly, Miss Burton, but I must insist upon knowing who originated this rumor. Ah, I can see in your eyes that you do know! Who was it, Miss Burton?" His fingers tightened about the lady's wrist.

Miss Burton winced. Suddenly her temper flared. She had never been treated with such disrespect. Recklessly she threw discretion to the winds. "If you must know, it was Captain Daggett himself! And I would not be so sure that your precious Miss Wainwright is innocent. Captain Daggett is quite the lady's man, as I have occasion to know, and he tells a vastly pretty tale regarding Miss Miranda Wainwright!" She tore free from the viscount's loosening grip and plunged her spur into her mount's side. The mare snorted and bolted away, its hooves throwing great clods of earth into the air.

Lord Townsend did not look after Miss Burton. She was already forgotten. He threw himself into the saddle and spurred his own horse into action. He thought he knew where Captain Daggett might be found. His dark eyes glittered. The naval officer would not find their upcoming meeting a pleasant one.

Twenty-two

A few weeks before, Captain Daggett had formed the pleasant habit of holding court at the local inn during the late afternoons. It gratified him that the young gentlemen, and some of the older ones as well, gravitated to him in the informal surroundings to solicit his opinion on everything from politics to agriculture. He held forth on every topic, shrewdly drawing out his listeners to discover their leanings and then feeding back their own beliefs to them. As a consequence, most of his listeners nodded contentedly and with awe spoke among themselves of the naval officer's extraordinary intelligence. There were a few here and there who did not share the general opinion of Captain Daggett's worth, but their cynicism and snorts of derision were whisperings in the wind.

Surprisingly enough, one of the stronger dissenting voices was that of Mr. Willoughby, who had gradually become disillusioned with his guest. Little by little the captain's activities had begun to impinge on Mr. Willoughby's chosen isolation. He found within himself a growing dislike for Captain Daggett that both surprised and distressed him. But he had come to the conclusion that the fault did not lie in his own character, but rather in Captain Daggett. The last straw for Mr. Willoughby was the discovery, quite by accident, that Captain Daggett had seduced Miss Mary Alice Burton, and that the assignation had taken place in his own garden, which revelation scandalized him to a shocking degree. He had been at work on his roses, hidden between the hedges, when he overheard the conversation between Captain Daggett and Miss Burton. Though he was quite aware that Miss Burton had freely chosen her course, he blamed Captain Daggett the more for not having enough strength of character to deny his lust and thus protect the lady from hers.

Mr. Willoughby had given the situation considerable thought and he had concluded that in all honor he could not condone his guest's actions, so he had requested that Captain Daggett leave his roof. The naval officer had laughed with contempt. "Assuredly I shall, Willoughby. Your company has always been deadly boring. But I've used your hospitality, such as it was, to good advantage. I suppose I must at least thank you for that much," he said.

"Pray spare me such mouthings, sir. I have no need of hypocrisy. I am only sorry that I allowed such a one as yourself into my house," said Mr. Willoughby. "You have brought disrespect and licentiousness to my home and the homes of my friends and neighbors. I urge you to leave our district behind."

Captain Daggett looked coldly at his former host. "Never fear, Willoughby, I have no intention of rotting much longer in this backwater. I will soon have my ship returned to me and then—" He realized by Mr. Willoughby's altered expression that he had let drop more than he intended. He waved a thin hand. "My plans can be of no possible interest to you. I shall take myself off to the inn in the morning. I trust that will satisfy you?"

Mr. Willoughby bowed stiffly. "Quite." He turned on his

heel and strode away, leaving Daggett looking after him with an unusual feeling of defeat. But he was quickly able to shrug it off and went upstairs to pack his belongings. The gentlemen did not speak at dinner that night but maintained a mutual stony silence. At daybreak, Captain Daggett removed himself to the local inn where he took rooms.

The break between Mr. Willoughby and Captain Daggett was obvious and thorough. It was observed that Mr. Willoughby did not vouchsafe the naval officer so much as a nod when they happened to meet on the street, but rather stared at his former guest with a sternness of expression that was positively astonishing. As a witness of one such exchange put it, "For a pleasant, vague sort of fellow, Willoughby is exhibiting extraordinary hostility. I wonder what happened between the two? I'll warrant it was a rare falling out, given Willoughby's easy nature!"

Mr. Willoughby was not one to betray his own counsel and so the curiosity of his friends and neighbors went unsatisfied. He was aware that he was attracting notice, however, and he discovered that he was not adverse to the increased social interaction that his decision to break with Captain Daggett had caused. However, he did not forget that there was one other person involved in the breach with his former guest. His reflections on Miss Mary Alice Burton would have appalled that young woman if she had been privy to them. On the day that Lord Townsend was told of the rumor regarding Miss Wainwright's character, Mr. Willoughby came to his decision. He borrowed a friend's gig and set out for Stonehollow to call on Miss Burton.

When Miss Burton reached home, she was in a flying temper. The confrontation with the Viscount of Wythe had gone completely awry. More than that, she had betrayed herself with her reckless speech. She could only hope that Lord Townsend was so wrapped up in his precious Miss Wainwright that he had not caught her stupid reference to herself and Captain Daggett.

By the time that she had bathed and changed, Miss Burton felt more in control of herself. But the conversation with Lord Townsend ran around and around in her thoughts, occupying her so unduly that when the butler announced a visitor it never occurred to her to wonder why this particular gentleman had chosen to call on her. Miss Burton had long ago dismissed Mr. Willoughby as not worth the effort to entice into her court. As far as she had ever discovered, Mr. Willoughby had never shown the least interest in anything beside his doves and roses.

Miss Burton greeted Mr. Willoughby graciously, inquiring if he had had tea. Mr. Willoughby declined tea and came directly to the point of his visit. "I have come on a matter of grave importance to you, ma'am, as I am certain you will agree when I have divulged it to you," he said soberly.

Miss Burton put up her delicate brows. "Indeed, Mr. Willoughby?" She waved her hand in dismissal of the butler. When the door had softly closed, she turned to her unexpected guest. She bestowed an encouraging smile on him, her violet eyes warm with curiosity. "We are quite private now, Mr. Willoughby. You may feel free to unburden yourself."

Mr. Willoughby tugged at his cravat. It was one thing to make a decision based on one's code of honor and quite another to follow it through when the lady in question sat across from one, he discovered. "A fortnight ago I requested Captain Daggett to remove himself from my house," he said abruptly.

Miss Burton sighed, her smile fading a little. "Yes, Mr. Willoughby. The entire district is aware of the breach between you and Captain Daggett. What can this possibly have to do with me?"

"It has everything to do with you, ma'am. It was on your behalf that I ordered Captain Daggett's removal from my house," said Mr. Willoughby.

Miss Burton was taken aback. Then she threw back her head in a peal of tinkling laughter. When she glanced again at Mr. Willoughby, her eyes were coy. "Why, Mr. Willoughby! I did not know that you harbored a jealous streak. I am flattered, truly I am. But there was no need to throw Captain Daggett out in the streets on my account! He is but one of my several admirers, you know."

Mr. Willoughby reddened. "You mistake me, Miss Burton. I am not a jealous rival for your favors." He was appalled by the word he had chosen and hastily tried to retrieve himself. "I intend no disrespect, I swear! I meant to say— Oh, the devil with it! Miss Burton, the sum of it is that I overheard the conversation between you and Captain Daggett in my garden. In view of that intelligence, I could not in all honor allow that gentleman to remain in my house."

All color was driven from Miss Burton's face. She attempted a light laugh that fell dismally short. "Why, I do not know what you are referring to, Mr. Willoughby. Captain Daggett simply showed me the lovely roses you cultivated," she said with desperate calm.

But the expression on Mr. Willoughby's face showed him unconvinced. He slowly shook his head. "I am sorry, Miss Burton. I was between the hedges and as close to you then as I am now. I did not mistake a word of that shocking exchange, believe me."

Miss Burton jumped hastily to her feet. Her cheeks blazed a poppy pink. "You are a filthy eavesdropper! I despise you, sir!" She picked up a vase handy to her hand and threw it in Mr. Willoughby's direction. It missed his head by a good two feet to crash against the wall. She stamped a dainty foot and hurled shrill insults at her open-mouthed, astonished guest.

Mr. Willoughby rose. Quite deliberately he slapped the beautiful Miss Burton across the face. She was shocked into silence. Her widened gaze fastened on his calm countenance. "Now I will continue, Miss Burton. I know what took place in my garden between you and Captain Daggett, for it was quite obvious from your conversation with him. His lack of honor cannot have come as anything but an unwelcome surprise to any lady, let alone one as beautiful and willful as yourself. I have given the matter considerable thought. You should not have to bear such dishonor even in the privacy of your thoughts. I am therefore prepared to offer for your hand in honorable marriage. I do not pretend to love you, nor even to like you overmuch. I think that for the most part I have ignored you; but then you have done much the same by me. It is perhaps not much to base a marriage upon, but I believe that we could learn to deal well together."

The door to the drawing room opened and the butler tentatively put in his head. He kept hold of the door as a precautionary measure in the event his appearance provoked some flying missile. He had had too much experience with Miss Burton's tantrums to be overly anxious to expose himself to her capricious temper. "Do you wish anything, miss?"

Miss Burton stared at the servant with a strangely blank expression. Then she shook her head. The butler was happily surprised by his mistress's unusually placid manner and retreated, gently reclosing the door.

Miss Burton turned to look again at Mr. Willoughby, but still she did not speak. He understood that she was in shock. "I shall not press you for an answer now, Miss Burton. A decision such as this needs time to be considered. I wish you good day," he said. He bowed to the still immobile lady and strode out the door.

When he had gone, Miss Burton sank once more onto the sofa. She was shaking. She could not believe the interview that had just taken place. Her eyes wandered about the familiar drawing room. Nothing had changed and yet everything had. She had received a proposal of marriage from a gentleman who knew of her foolhardy assignation, her intimacy with Captain Daggett. The gentleman wished to salvage her honor, but in the same breath had announced that he did not like her overmuch. "How dare he," she murmured, but there was not much fire behind it. She was still spellbound by Mr. Willoughby's unsuspected strength of character and felt a dawning respect for the gentleman. For the first time in her life someone had done something for her without being first biased by her beauty. She thought about Mr. Willoughby for quite some time.

Lord Townsend found Captain Daggett at the inn. He strode inside the taproom, pausing just long enough to allow his eyes to adjust to the darker interior smoke. He did not reply to the greetings that his appearance engendered but went directly over to the naval officer seated negligently at a round table in the middle of the room. "Stand up, Daggett!" The general buzz of conversation abruptly died. Every face turned, expressing its owner's astonishment at the viscount's harsh voice.

Captain Daggett stiffened instinctively. He met Lord Townsend's gaze and a frisson of shock went through him at the patent rage in the gentleman's eyes. "What can I do for you, my lord?" he asked with outward calm.

"I ordered you to stand, Daggett," said Lord Townsend through his teeth. He flexed his gloved hands, the twist of leather sounding loud in the suspended silence.

Daggett's attention was captured by the movement and he saw that the viscount carried a small whip. His expression when he looked up was perceptibly warier than before. "I do not pretend to understand your obvious agitation, my lord. But I am a King's officer and I will not be browbeaten, even by a gentleman of your social standing and exalted birth. Therefore I request that you state your grievance without these histrionics."

Lord Townsend put his hands on the table and leaned toward the naval officer. His voice was quiet and measured, but was heard quite distinctly in every corner of the taproom. "I have learned that there is a distasteful rumor circulating about concerning my sister-in-law's cousin, Miss Miranda Wainwright, and that you are its author. I take exception to such fictions being woven about a member of my family, Captain Daggett. I demand satisfaction." He slowly straightened, never removing his gaze from Daggett's face.

Captain Daggett rose from his chair. He knew from the rapt faces around the taproom that his erstwhile companions waited to see how he would handle the Viscount of Wythe's challenge. He affected an arrogant pose, one hand cocked on his hip. He eyed Lord Townsend with calculation. "I fear that you have been misinformed, my lord. There is no fiction, as you so delicately put it. I suggest that you apply to *Mistress* Wainwright regarding the assignation between her and myself."

There was a gasp of disbelief at the naval officer's open admission of responsibility for the rumor. Lord Townsend smiled but there was no amusement in his expression. "I have known the truth from the day that the incident occurred, Daggett. Do you think that Miss Wainwright would not immediately inform her cousin and me of your attack upon her? You forced your attentions and she retaliated by striking you in the face. You could not hide the mark, Daggett. I saw it myself two days later when I met you at Burton's hunt."

There were murmurs about the room and Daggett saw a few nods of agreement at Lord Townsend's statement. He could see his position slipping and quickly said, "If what you say is true, my lord, why have you waited so long in confronting me? I find that vastly peculiar." His face took on a sneer.

"It was only Miss Wainwright's intervention that saved you then, Daggett. The lady assumed that you would not again be so bold. She did not count on your incredible lack of honor. But you prove yourself a scurrilous dog, sir, unworthy of the King's uniform that you hide behind!" said Lord Townsend, raising his whip.

Captain Daggett flinched away, throwing up an arm to protect his face. But the whip did not strike. Daggett saw the viscount's derisive smile, the utter contempt in his dark eyes. There were snickers about the taproom. Deep color stained Daggett's cheeks. He was neatly trapped, he realized. He was compelled to accept the Viscount of Wythe's challenge if he were to salvage any part of his dignity. "You have insulted me unpardonably, my lord. Name your seconds," he said hoarsely. Lord Townsend swiftly named two of the gentlemen present, who agreed to accept the duty. Captain Daggett looked about him, only to read the uncertainty in the faces of his former admirers. Several pairs of eyes slid away rather than meet his gaze. His thin lips tightened. "Ned Olive, will you stand for me?" he asked brusquely.

Mr. Olive appeared startled, then dismayed, to be singled out. He threw a wild glance about him, but he received no help. He squared his shoulders. "Very well, Captain Daggett. A gentleman must have a second, after all."

It was not an enthusiastic response, but Daggett was forced to accept it. He turned back to the viscount. "My second will call upon yours to set the time and place, my lord!" He strode out of the taproom, his boots beating a hard tattoo on the wooden plank floor.

Captain Daggett took dinner in his rooms that evening. There was nothing unusual in that, he told himself. But he knew that it was more his usual custom to descend to the taproom. There he had always been assured of convivial company and the opportunity to smack the ample bottom of the serving wench. She always squealed in mock protest, but there was a distinct invitation in her eyes that he had rarely passed on.

With the thought, Daggett threw back his brandy in a single swallow. He saw now that he had wasted his time. He had been obsessed with the beauteous Miss Burton to the exclusion of all others. He should have taken all that the district had to offer and not counted the cost if whispers had reached Miss Burton's fair ears. She might have repulsed him at first, but his understanding of her character would still have won her in the end. His thoughts recalled for him their interlude in that fool Willoughby's garden. A smile formed about his mouth. For the first time since his fateful confrontation that afternoon with the Viscount of Wythe, the tension that Captain Daggett had been experiencing began to dissipate.

There was a knock on the door. Captain Daggett stood up, once more all too aware of his situation. "It is open," he said. He was relieved to see that his visitor was only Mr. Olive, who entered almost reluctantly. "Close the door, Ned," said Daggett with a note of impatience. He could feel his muscles tensing again. He gestured at the bottle of brandy on the table, but Mr. Olive shook his head.

"I won't stay but a minute, Captain Daggett. I've come to tell you of the arrangements made for the duel," said Olive unhappily.

There was a sinking feeling in the pit of Daggett's stomach. "I take it that the viscount did not wish to call off the unfortunate necessity," he said coolly. He uncorked the bottle of brandy and made a show of pouring himself a glass.

Mr. Olive stared at him queerly. "No, sir, he did not. In fact, his lordship was adamant that the duel take place at once."

Captain Daggett nodded, still retaining his expression of calm. The weight in his guts grew. "Quite admirable to wish to have the affair done and over with as soon as possible. I agree with Lord Townsend on that count. When is it to be?"

"Tomorrow morning."

The bottle jumped in Daggett's hand, clinking against the wineglass. "Tomorrow! But that is preposterous," he exclaimed.

Mr. Olive shrugged. "I fear that the Viscount of Wythe was insistent, sir. The place is to be the small meadow back of the churchyard cemetery. You naturally have the choice of weapons since it was his lordship who challenged."

Captain Daggett's mouth twisted. "The meadow back of

the churchyard cemetery! How incredibly practical of his lordship. One or the other of us shall not have to be carried far, that is certain." He laughed shortly and tossed back the glass of brandy. He picked up the bottle again and slopped another drink into his glass.

Mr. Olive eyed Captain Daggett with misgivings. He thought the naval officer must be quite mad to accept the communication just relayed with such abandonment. He knew that if he had been in the same shoes, he would have been quivering with fear. Mr. Olive edged slightly toward the door. "What weapon shall I tell his lordship's seconds that you favor, sir?"

"What?" Captain Daggett stared at his former friend. "Oh, as to that I hardly think it matters. Shall we say pistols, Mr. Olive?" And he laughed again. Mr. Olive bowed and hastily took leave of what he considered a deranged man. Captain Daggett toasted his exit with raised wineglass. "To you, Mr. Olive, and to all in this provincial neighborhood! Good riddance to every one of the idiot bumpkins." He stood while he finished off the bottle of brandy. Then he quite calmly packed his valise and waited for the black of night.

In the small hours of the morning a slight figure stealthily emerged from the inn and made for the stables. Shortly thereafter a rider cantered out of the inn yard and turned his mount away from the village.

Twenty-three

"Quite, quite shocking. And to think that the assignation took place in this very church! It is unthinkable!"

The caretaker was disturbed by the conversation that he overheard. He approached Mrs. Averidge and her guest. Twisting his cap between his fingers, he said, "Begging yer pardon, m'ladies, but that ain't the way it happened."

The ladies looked at him, surprised. "What do you mean, Jacob?" asked Mrs. Averidge.

"I was not ten feet from the miss when it happened. Miss Wainwright had brought flowers for the church. She was getting into her gig when the captain fellow rode up. He put his great bloody paws on her and tried to steal a kiss off her," said the caretaker.

Both ladies gasped sharply, their horrified eyes riveted on his face. " 'Tis the truth I be telling you," said the caretaker. "Miss Wainwright hit the fellow such a blow that he dropped her quick-like. Then she told him to be off or she would thrash him with her whip. An' I believed her, too, for there was such a look in her eyes! The scoundrel threatened Miss Wainwright would regret what she done. Then he hauled his nag around and left in a fury. It was then I asked the miss if she were all right. Miss Wainwright was feeling peaked, I could see. But she spoke very composed and

216

drove off for Willowswood."

Mrs. Averidge drew a breath. "Thank you, Jacob. What you have related is most enlightening," she said quietly. The caretaker bobbed his head and shuffled away. Mrs. Averidge and her guest looked at one another. "I am distressed, Amelia. That young woman has been subjected to a gross injustice. I feel it acutely that I did not pay more heed to Mrs. Townsend's testimony on her cousin's behalf," said Mrs. Averidge.

"It was not you alone who persecuted the young woman. Why, I cut her direct on the main street of the village!" exclaimed Mrs. Heatherton. "I should like to have my hands on Captain Daggett for just one moment. Why should he wish to destroy a lady's reputation in such a despicable fashion?"

Mrs. Averidge shook her head. "I fear it must have been vanity, my dear. Pride goeth before a fall, you know, and undoubtedly Captain Daggett was treated to a fall by the redoubtable Miss Wainwright."

"Indeed! I quite sink to recall how I have treated Miss Wainwright this fortnight. We must make amends, Mildred, and the first step is to inform our husbands and friends of the true tale," said Mrs. Heatherton, drawing on her gloves.

"It does not reflect well on Captain Daggett," said Mrs. Averidge.

Mrs. Heatherton's eyes were surprisingly hard. "How little I care for that! I do not appreciate being played for a fool, and that is certainly what Captain Daggett has done to us all. Believe me, he shall rue the day that he ever set foot in this district."

In the company of her maid, Miss Burton paid a call on Mr. Willoughby. She was shown out to the gardens by a wondering footman. Her maid walked away a few discreet steps and bent to sniff at the roses, which were in riotous bloom. Mr. Willoughby brushed the leaves from a stone bench and Miss Burton seated herself with a quiet word of thanks.

She was pensive and stared out over the quiet garden. The strong perfume of the roses hung on the air, recalling to her mind a certain night that she would prefer to forget forever. Miss Burton listened to the bees buzzing and the soft cooing of doves and found that the tranquil sounds did much to steady her nerves.

Mr. Willoughby waited patiently. At last he was rewarded when Miss Burton turned her gaze on him. She said, "Mr. Willoughby, I have thought long on your proposal. Before I give you an answer, I wish to relate to you something that happened very early this morning. I was in my bed when I was awakened by a rain of pebbles on my window. Curious, I arose and opened the casement. You may imagine my astonishment upon seeing Captain Daggett on the lawn below. I was further amazed when Captain Daggett expressed himself to me in quite passionate terms and pressed me to fly with him that very moment." She glanced at Mr. Willoughby to gauge his reaction. There was a tightness about his mouth, but otherwise he gave no indication of his feelings. Miss Burton said with the flicker of a smile, "I must confess that I was very rude to the gentleman. I threw my water pitcher down and he staggered off with a cracked head."

Mr. Willoughby's mouth quivered. "Indeed, Miss Burton. A worthy shot, surely."

Miss Burton dropped her eyes to gaze at her hands, which were at rest in her lap. "I wished you to know particularly so that you may better judge what I have next to say."

She raised her head. Mr. Willoughby was surprised to observe a blush in the redoubtable beauty's soft cheeks. Miss Burton said steadily, "I have a strong partiality for roses, Mr. Willoughby. And I find that I am willing to learn an appreciation for doves."

Mr. Willoughby felt as though he could not quite catch his wind. He was surprised to discover that her answer had been so important to him. He raised one of Miss Burton's hands to his lips. "You have honored me more than I can say, Miss Burton. I assure you that you will come to love roses and doves as much as I do myself."

"Angus, I believe that we may be a little less formal on this occasion," said Miss Burton softly.

Mr. Willoughby reddened. Casting a glance after Miss Burton's maid, he was reassured to see that the woman had continued down the path out of sight. He lowered his head to meet Miss Burton's waiting lips.

When it was learned that Captain Daggett had abandoned the inn in the dead of night, leaving his bill unpaid, it created a sensation. The fact that the naval officer had fled rather than face the Viscount of Wythe in a duel branded him a coward and plunged his name into final and irrevocable disrepute. Those who had idolized him were furious with themselves and spoke the most bitterly of him. Those who had never liked the man had the satisfaction of being proven correct concerning his character.

Bertram Burton in particular crowed that he had known all along how it would be. "I observed many times that one could not trust a fellow who sat a horse as badly as Daggett did," he said. He could not wait to relate the news to his sister. Mary Alice would have to rethink her idiotic infatuation with the bounder, he thought complacently. But it was

Bertram who received the shock of his life, when his sister calmly informed him that she had accepted an offer. "Angus Willoughby! But how—" Bertram recovered himself and enthusiastically embraced his sister. "I couldn't have chosen a better man for you, Mary Alice. When did you say the wedding is to be?"

Mrs. Averidge and Mrs. Heatherton lost no time in spreading what they had heard from Jacob the caretaker and Captain Daggett was at last seen in his full colors as an absolute scoundrel. Miss Wainwright garnered much sympathy and many sheepish apologies, which she was very gracious in receiving.

It had not gone unnoted that the Viscount of Wythe had been prepared to defend her honor to the death. His championship refueled once-dead conjectures that he and Miss Wainwright were more friendly than cousins should be. But in light of the debacle over Captain Daggett, most were unwilling to pry any closer. However, there were always the diehard gossips who could not resist putting their heads together. "But really, the Viscount of Wythe and Miss Wainwright are not related at all. It would be extraordinary if she did not set her cap for his lordship. I would certainly do so were I in her shoes," declared one lady.

"So should I. But living in the same house like they are, it is scandalous to think of it. They were virtually unchaperoned for weeks while Mrs. Townsend was ill. Do you think . . ."

The thought was left unspoken but speaking looks were passed. Thus slowly grew a fresh rumor coupling Miss Wainwright and the Viscount of Wythe. There was not a malicious tone to the gossip, not after the unfortunate affair with Captain Daggett. The general feeling was that Miss Wainwright deserved some happiness, though opinion differed whether living in the Viscount of Wythe's pocket was the proper course for her to pursue. There was no question of impropriety, of course, what with Mrs. Townsend up and about and a new household staff in place. However, what had gone before was quite a different matter. The conclusive opinion of the good ladies and their gentlemen was that Lord Townsend ought to do the proper thing by Miss Wainwright and marry her.

Lord Townsend was the first to become aware of the new gossip. He had been waiting to hear just such rumors, having realized almost from the moment of leaving the inn after issuing his challenge to Captain Daggett that he had exposed himself and Miss Wainwright to that sort of speculation. But he did not regret his actions in the slightest. His rage in learning Miss Wainwright had been pilloried in such an infamous manner had known no bounds. If Daggett had appeared on the field of honor, the viscount thought that he would have had no compunction in blowing a neat hole straight through the blackguard's heart. Instead, Captain Daggett had chosen to run like a rat in the night, convincing all in the neighborhood of his guilt and Miss Wainwright's innocence. That suited Lord Townsend perfectly. He had only to deal with the fresh gossip and all would be made comfortable.

Lord Townsend had long since realized that his feelings for Miss Wainwright were strong. In fact, he had come to care for her more than he had thought possible. He wanted to care for her as she deserved, and shield her from the capricious winds of society.

Most of all, he wanted to share his days and his nights with her. He could not recall a single moment in her company that was other than stimulating. Her quick wit and tongue, her silvery laugh when she was amused, the teasing light in her eyes, had all gone far to bind him to her. The fact that she was also beautiful merely capped her perfections as he perceived them.

Lord Townsend had come to the decision that he wanted to marry Miss Wainwright before the gossip linking their names arose. The talk merely braced his determination. He thought that if for no other reason he would offer for Miss Wainwright to protect her from further distress. With that thought in mind he requested a private interview with Miranda.

Miranda wondered at Lord Townsend's serious demeanor when she entered the drawing room. She paused at the door and looked across the room at him. He stood at the mantel, one arm laid along its edge, and the expression on his face was pensive. He met her gaze and his countenance was lightened by the sudden spark of warmth in his brown eyes. Miranda moved to seat herself on the settee, remarking, "You are very sober today, my lord."

Lord Townsend removed his arm from the mantel, turning his back on the fireplace. "Am I? Perhaps I seem so because of my thoughts. I have come to a momentous decision, Miss Wainwright, one that concerns yourself."

Miranda's heart beat a little faster. She could not imagine what Lord Townsend was talking about, but nevertheless she instinctively felt a sense of anticipation. "Yes, my lord?"

"Miss Wainwright, I have come to appreciate your strength of character. I learned early a high regard for you, and my opinion has only been strengthened through the experiences we have shared. I think now is a most appropriate time to declare myself." Lord Townsend came over to sit beside her on the settee. He raised one of her hands to his lips in a brief salute and, retaining her fingers in a light clasp, said, "Miranda, I wish for you to become my wife."

Miranda sat quite still. She could not believe that he had declared himself. She had known herself to be in love with him for some time, but she had not actually seen much sign that he returned her feelings. At turns he had been both impersonal and tender. She did not know how to take his proposal. She did know, however, that she could not marry him if he did not love her. Once before she had made that mistake and it had been a bitter, disastrous affair. "My lord, why do you offer for me?" asked Miranda quietly.

Lord Townsend was taken aback. He had expected quite a different response. "It is as I have told you, Miranda. I have come to hold you in high regard," he said, puzzled.

"Yes, you mentioned my strength of character," said Miranda, nodding. "But is there any other reason?"

Lord Townsend shrugged, somewhat at a loss. "Well, I must admit I have been made to realize how vulnerable you have been to gossip, not only in connection with that blackguard Daggett, but to myself as well. I very much want to spare you any future distress of that sort, Miranda."

Miranda felt her throat tighten. She also had heard the gossip concerning herself and the viscount. It had been told to her by three kind ladies, who took it upon themselves to assure her that it would naturally be quite a feather in her cap if she were to become affianced to the Viscount of Wythe. Miranda had brushed aside the ladies' speculative glances with a laugh. After the trouble over Captain Daggett she had believed herself immune to the bad effects of any further gossip.

But now she was not so certain. Lord Townsend had just proposed to her out of chivalry, to spare her what he so obviously perceived as the ignominious effects of this most recent rumor. The gossips had hinted strongly that they thought the viscount ought to offer for her. Now he had done so, no doubt influenced by what was being said in the district. Miranda would have given her soul if Lord Townsend had only come to her with his heart instead of his sense of honor.

She rose from the settee and walked a few steps away. Her head bent, her hands clasped tightly before her, she said, "I naturally thank you for the honor, my lord. But I cannot accept your offer."

Lord Townsend could not believe his ears. It had never occurred to him that she might reject his suit. He stood up quickly. "Miranda! I do not understand. After what we have experienced together, what we have meant to one another!" His hands descended onto her shoulders.

Miranda turned quickly at his touch. His words released a well-spring of emotion in her. She stared up at him with sparkling eyes, but whether from anger or from tears he did not know. "I asked you not to refer to that regrettable incident, my lord!"

Lord Townsend's face registered open astonishment. For a moment he did not understand what she was referring to, since he had been thinking of the entire span of their relationship over the past months. But as he absorbed her meaning, his features set in grim lines. His fingers tightened on her shoulders. "Regrettable? Is that how you recall it, Miranda? It is passing strange that I do not share that opinion."

Miranda turned her face away. "Pray let me go, Andrew. It will not do either of us a service to continue this discussion." She did not struggle, but merely waited.

Lord Townsend was infuriated by her passivity. Instead of releasing her, he shook her forcefully. "Now listen to me, my girl! I'll not allow you to refuse me because of some misguided, missish notion that you have taken into your head. I do not make such a decision lightly. I have made an honorable offer for your hand and by God you'll accept me."

Miranda was at last made angry. "How dare you dictate to me, Andrew Townsend! Are you so arrogant that you cannot accept anyone's daring to refuse the Viscount of Wythe? I think I know what is in my best interests, and it is certainly not marriage to you, or to anyone else at the moment. I have a mind and heart of my own."

Lord Townsend stared down at her. There was an arrested, angry look in his eyes. "What was that you said? A heart of your own? Does that mean you care nothing for me, Miranda? Is that why you refuse my suit?"

Miranda seized on the excuse. She tossed her head. "Why should you be so surprised, my lord? *I* do not consider duty or gossip or past follies reason enough to entertain the thought of wedlock. I cannot imagine why you should."

Lord Townsend released her suddenly. His eyes were hard, but were shadowed with some emotion that Miranda could not fathom. "I understand you, I think. Forgive me, Miss Wainwright. It was not my intention to trespass upon your independent spirit. It quite slipped my mind that you are not English-born and might be expected to view certain matters in a different light."

The reasons given by the viscount in offering for her hand and her previous disastrous experience with romance whirled chaotically through Miranda's mind. "Indeed, sir! I do not know how it is with your English ladies, but I certainly would not enter into a contract of marriage without those feelings of affection necessary for a comfortable existence between the parties. As I have cause to know, a high regard for one another is not sufficient," retorted Miranda.

Already horribly wounded that she had so baldly stated that she cared not at all for him, Lord Townsend positively pounced on her last words. "Are you admitting that Daggett's allusions to a secret marriage had truth?"

Miranda laughed scornfully. "Of course not! But I was once engaged to a worthy sort of man whom I held in respect. I discovered that my respect for him did not fill the differences between us. I cried off, my lord, and braved the censure of the world."

"Upon my word." Lord Townsend stared at her. He shook himself free of the astonishment and disillusion that pervaded his thoughts and straightened his shoulders. His voice was cold. "Perhaps I am well out of it, then. You appear to invite scandal of the worst kind."

Miranda was cut to the quick by the distant expression of disapproval in his eyes. "It is the price a woman must pay to exercise independence of thought and feeling, sir!"

"I must express my gratitude for this enlightenment, Miss Wainwright," said Lord Townsend. He made a sharp bow to her and strode quickly to the drawing room door. A second later the door banged shut behind him.

Miranda felt the tears rush to her eyes. She hastened out of the drawing room and ran up the stairs to her bedroom. After turning the key in the lock, she threw herself across her bed to enjoy in private a hearty bout of tears.

Twenty-four

When next Miranda saw Lord Townsend, it was at dinner. His very demeanor was arrogant and he treated her with the same haughty manner that she had received at his hands upon their initial acquaintance. Miranda could hardly bear the change in the viscount's attitude. Gone were his warm friendly glances, his bantering words, his easy laughter. She withdrew into a shell of studied politeness, never allowing the hurt she suffered to show by so much as a glance.

Anne was astonished and bewildered by the sudden cold antagonism between her cousin and her brother-in-law. When she and Miranda had left the dining room so that Lord Townsend could enjoy his wine, she at once taxed Miranda about it. "Miranda, you must tell me what has happened between you and Andrew. It was horrible to listen to the cold, indifferent exchanges that were hurled between you this evening," she said.

Miranda glanced at her as she seated herself on the settee before the fireplace. "Why, I do not know what you mean, Anne." She picked up a copy of *The Ladies' Magazine* and began to flip rapidly through the pages.

Anne sat down beside her and pulled the magazine down. "I shall not be put off, Miranda! Something terrible has happened and I insist upon knowing what it is."

Miranda stared at her cousin. She saw the determination in Anne's eyes and the firmness about her mouth. Miranda sighed. "Very well, Anne. If you must know, the viscount made an offer for my hand this afternoon, and I rejected his lordship's proposal."

"Miranda! But how wonderful. I had hopes—" Anne abruptly realized what her cousin had said. "One moment! How could you reject Andrew's suit? I do not understand. Surely you are in love with him. I quite thought you were. Come, I know that I am not wrong!"

Miranda could not bear her cousin's quick rush of words. She covered her face with her hands. "Please do not, Anne. It is not my feelings, but his, that are wanting. He offered for me out of chivalry, Anne." She let her hands drop to show an anguished countenance. "Anne, he had heard the gossip linking the two of us. He offered for me to spare me any further distress, if you please! I cannot marry him knowing that he feels only pity for me!"

"Oh, Miranda, I am certain that you are wrong. Andrew is not the sort of gentleman to do such a thing. I know that he must harbor affection for you," said Anne sympathetically. She was overwhelmed by the despair evident in her cousin's quick headshake. She seized Miranda's hands. "I shall speak to him, Miranda, and discover—"

Miranda tightened her fingers on Anne's. She said fiercely, "No, no! You must not. I do not want to deepen his pity for me. Anne, promise me that you will not."

Anne began to protest, but Miranda was so emphatically against it that she reluctantly agreed to abide by her cousin's wishes. "But I do think that you are wrong, Miranda. Why, I know Andrew better than anyone, I should think, and I quite thought he exhibited a partiality for you."

"Pray do not say another word, Anne. I do not wish to discuss it any further," said Miranda, her voice ending on a quiver.

Anne realized that Miranda was on the verge of tears and sighed in defeat. "As you wish, dear cousin. I shall not refer to it again."

She was to regret many times over her promise to Miranda. The next week saw increasing distance between Miranda and Lord Townsend. The atmosphere of frost was of such intensity that it made all around them uncomfortable, from Robert and Anne down to the servants. Miranda thought she must go mad before the month was out. For her, the last straw was Robert coming to her with a terrible frown marring his features and asking, "What is wrong with you, Cousin Miranda? You never smile or look happy anymore. And I don't like you half as well as before."

Miranda felt as though her heart was breaking a second time. She knelt and wrapped her arms around the boy in a fierce embrace, which he returned. She looked into his eyes and managed to smile at him. "I know that I have been a positive bear, Robert. I shall try to do better, I really shall." He nodded, satisfied, and ran off to play.

But Miranda stood for several minutes staring into space, grappling with her feelings and her thoughts. Finally she came to the decision that had been in the back of her mind for days. She went to the study, hesitating before she entered. But fortunately Lord Townsend was not in the room and Miranda sat down at the desk. She hurriedly scrawled a short letter to her brother, Jeremy, to tell him to await her in London; she had finally decided to leave Willowswood.

Once the decision was made and the letter sent, Miranda discovered that she was strangely reluctant to put her resolve into action. She went several days just floating in a sort of limbo, going through the motions of her usual activities. But the characteristic interest that she brought to whatever task she took on was now lacking. Her preoccupation was commented on by some of the servants and it began to be wondered if Miss Wainwright was coming down ill, so pale and lackadaisical as she was becoming. Anne well understood the cause of Miranda's lethargy and though it took an exercise of will, she did not tax her cousin about it.

The one person who seemed not to notice nor care about Miss Wainwright's sharp decline was Lord Townsend. But then he made certain that he was not often in her company, preferring instead to be about estate business. Some time before he had discovered plans drawn up by his brother for the renovation of the ruined section of the house and now spent much of his time conferring with the builders whom he had hired to begin the renovations. If Lord Townsend did chance to come face to face with Miss Wainwright, he retained his air of distant arrogance and spoke to her as little as possible.

Finally Miranda shook herself free of her melancholia enough to begin making preparations for the trip to London. She chose not to reveal her decision to anyone but Constance until she had already made arrangements for a post chaise to come for her at Willowswood. Constance disliked the suddenness of the move, but she did not question it. She thought that even if she were blind, she could not have failed to notice the marked coldness between her mistress and the viscount. "Ah, a lover's quarrel," she sighed. She quietly began to pack away gowns and dresses. Constance could only shake her head over the unfairness of it all. Miss Miranda had been unlucky in love once before and she appeared to have lost again. Constance knew herself to be friend and confidante, but she saw something in Miranda's eyes that warned her that this time even sympathetic words would not be welcome.

Miranda announced to the family late on a Thursday evening that she would be leaving the following day for London. There was an immediate outbreak of protests from Anne and Robert, who had been allowed to come down to the drawing room for an hour before his bedtime. "You cannot be serious, Miranda!" exclaimed Anne.

Robert stared at Miranda with a mutinous expression in his eyes. "I shan't let you go, Cousin Miranda. I don't want you to go. Mama, make her stay!"

Anne put her arm around the upset child. She threw a glance of rebuke at her cousin. "Really, this is too sudden. Miranda, you must give this decision more thought. What are we to do without you?"

Miranda dug her nails into her hands. She did not glance toward Lord Townsend, who stood silent and motionless at the mantel. "Forgive me, Anne, but I really must go. I have not seen Jeremy in ages and London not at all." She managed a smile for her cousin and the boy, whose small face was streaked with tears. "I shall come back one day, you know. I love you too well not to." Her voice choked then and she could no longer face their accusing, sorrowing eyes. Blindly, she turned to the drawing room door and hurried out.

It was not until she had gained the hall that Lord Townsend went after her. "Miss Wainwright!"

She did not heed his call, but only walked more quickly toward the stairs. Her arm was seized in an unfriendly grip. She cast a hunted look up at him. His expression was exceedingly grim, his eyes hard. "You will grant me an audience, I know," he said harshly. He pulled her into the study and shut the door with decided force. Miranda had flown to take refuge behind the desk as he turned to look at her. "Miss Wainwright, I do not like the distress that your resolve to leave Willowswood so unexpectedly has brought to my sister-in-law and nephew," he said ungently.

Miranda clutched hard the top of the desk chair, her knuckles whitening. "It pains me as much as it does you, my lord. However, my decision has been made. Jeremy will already be expecting me. I am quite looking forward to seeing London."

"Let us put an end to this polite bilge, Miranda! It is not the lure of London that has inspired your decision, but the differences between you and me," said Lord Townsend with harsh emphasis. He advanced until he could place his hands on the desk and leaned over it toward her. Miranda instinctively drew back from his angry expression. "I should have seen this coming. But fool that I am, I ignored all of the signs. You are not leaving Willowswood, Miss Wainwright. I am. I have decided to buy a commission in the army."

The color drained from Miranda's face. "But you cannot!"

Lord Townsend slowly straightened, his eyes never leaving her face. "Since I am leaving, you may feel comfortable in awaiting Jeremy here at Willowswood. I hope that you will, for your presence will go far in soothing Anne and Robert over my leavetaking."

"But how can you join the army, when you know what such a step must mean to them?" asked Miranda. Without realizing it she came from around the desk, holding out her hands in appeal. "My lord, you know that it will devastate them."

"Nonetheless, that is the decision I have made," said Lord Townsend inexorably.

Miranda flushed. "You are selfish and hard, my lord! I find you contemptible. How dare you turn your back on those who love you and depend upon you!" In her fury she slapped him full across the face.

Lord Townsend caught her wrist. When she struggled against him, his fingers tightened painfully about her slender bones. There was a red imprint from her hand rising on his lean cheek, but he did not seem to notice the sting. He looked down at Miranda with an odd expression in his eyes. "Why should it matter so very much, Miss Wainwright?"

"You will likely be killed, you fool!" exclaimed Miranda. Her throat tightened at the thought. She turned her head quickly aside as tears pricked her eyes.

The intentness of his voice sharpened. "Would that be such a bad thing?"

"It would leave Anne and Robert alone, so very alone. You are too well loved," said Miranda, her voice muffled. She raised her free hand to shadow her eyes. The fear and grief she felt was growing like a hard ball in her chest.

The viscount drew her close to him, his hold becoming astonishingly gentle. He asked softly, "And what of you, Miranda? Do you love me also?"

His tenderness completely overset her. She pounded on his broad shoulder with her fist. "Yes! But I hate you, too!" She burst into tears and hid her face against his coat.

Lord Townsend folded his arms about her. After a moment he reached up to cradle her head, murmuring, "Oh, Miranda, what you have put me through. I thought I had lost you forever, my love. Sweetheart, pray do not cry."

His endearments eventually penetrated Miranda's consciousness. With a watery sniff, she raised her head. "What did you call me?" she stammered.

Lord Townsend smiled faintly. "I believe that I referred to you as my love. I do, you know. Even when you show me the reddest nose I have ever seen on a female." He pulled out a handkerchief and inexpertly dabbed at her wet face.

Miranda took the linen square from him and dried her eyes. She blew her nose and put the handkerchief in the pocket of her gown. "Why did you never tell me before that you loved me, Andrew? It would have made such a difference," she said.

Lord Townsend regarded her in open astonishment. "I thought it obvious. I am not in the habit of declaring myself to just any female I chance to meet!"

Miranda gave him a wavering smile, shaking her head at his idiocy. Her eyes danced with a little of her old spirit. "I am glad we have resolved at least that question between us, my lord."

"Miranda, will you marry me?" asked Lord Townsend.

She shook her head. "No, I will not," she said decidedly. Lord Townsend swore comprehensively. Miranda waited until he was done, then said quietly, "I shall not marry a soldier, my lord. I do not wish to be a young widow like my cousin." Lord Townsend stared at her in astonishment. Then he threw back his head and laughed uproariously. Miranda frowned at him, drawing away to the extent that his arms would allow. "I fail to see the amusement in this, Andrew."

Lord Townsend looked down at her again, still chuckling. "Do you not know, my love? Then I shall tell you. I never had any intention of going into the army. I only resorted to that ploy out of desperation. You have been so cool and indifferent toward me that I despaired of breaking

down the walls between us. Yet I hoped that with time . . .
But then you announced that you were leaving Willowswood. I could not allow you to walk out of my life without
discovering what you felt for me. So I attempted to shock
you into betraying your true feelings."

Miranda stared at him. Her eyes darkened with indignation. "You tricked me. You actually set out to trick—"

Lord Townsend realized his danger and quickly pulled
her close. His lips descended on hers before she could utter
another word. The kiss was long. When at last Miranda was
permitted to emerge from it, she was breathless. The viscount regarded this circumstance with approval. "I have at
last discovered a way to effectively silence you, Miss Wainwright. I shall exercise it most freely, I warn you."

The door to the study opened abruptly and a gentleman
attired in traveling dress entered with a hasty step. His
browned face taughtened at sight of Miranda and the Viscount of Wythe, who turned their heads to regard the in-
truder with astonishment. "Unhand my sister at once, sir!"

"Jeremy!" exclaimed Miranda. She did not attempt to
withdraw from Lord Townsend's embrace, nor did he seem
in the least inclined to remove his arms from about her.
"Whatever are you doing at Willowswood?"

"I came in answer to your last letter, Miranda. It was unduly agitated and now I fully understand the reason. A
vastly pretty scene, I swear!" Jeremy left the door and
strode forward. His hard eyes bored into the viscount's mild
gaze. "You will have the goodness to name your seconds,
sir."

Miranda was stunned. When at last she moved, she flew
over to her brother to clutch his arm. "Jeremy, what are you
doing? You cannot challenge Lord Townsend! Why, he is
your cousin!"

"Cousin or not, I'll defend my sister's honor," said Jeremy grimly.

"What!" Miranda stared at her brother as though she thought he had gone mad. Her hand dropped numbly from his sleeve.

Lord Townsend sat down on the corner of the desk. He contemplated the toe of his boot, then glanced across at Miranda with a faint smile. "I think Mr. Wainwright believes that I have compromised you, Miranda. What did you pen in your letter?"

"Why, only that circumstances were such that I thought I would be more comfortable in London," said Miranda. Her eyes suddenly widened. "Oh!"

"You did not convey the information that Captain Daggett had left the neighborhood," said Lord Townsend dryly, nodding.

Jeremy looked from one to the other with an uncertain frown. He did not quite know what to make of the easy concourse between Miranda and the Viscount of Wythe, who he instantly concluded had seduced his sister.

Miranda went into a peal of laughter. She shook her head at her brother, her eyes still shining with amusement. "I am sorry, Jeremy. I did not think. And you have charged down from London to save me! I assure you, Captain Daggett is long forgotten."

"That is all very well, Miranda. But what of this bounder? If Daggett was already gone, then I would be a fool to believe his lordship had nothing to do with your state of mind when you penned that letter," said Jeremy, gesturing at the viscount.

Miranda colored. Her glance flew to meet Lord Townsend's amused glance. "His lordship had everything to do with my agitation, actually. And you are quite right,

Jeremy. I have been compromised—oh, beyond redemption!" She could not help laughing as Lord Townsend's expression altered to one of consternation. She went to him and laid her hand along his hard jaw. "Forgive me, Andrew. I could not resist teasing you but a little."

"When we are wed, I shall beat you for it," he growled, catching her fingers to his lips.

Jeremy realized that he was quite forgotten. He swore pithily and the two at the desk turned in surprise. He bowed to the Viscount of Wythe, then flashed a dazzling grin at him. "I beg forgiveness for my misapprehension, sir. It becomes obvious that I am meeting my future brother-in-law. I am happy to make your acquaintance, my lord. Evidently my sister intends to lead you a pretty dance. I hope that you are equal to the task of taming her."

Lord Townsend glanced down into his betrothed's dancing eyes. He slid his arm around her neat waist and drew her closer to his side. "I admit to reservations, Wainwright. However, I consider myself a relatively brave man and—"

"Oh! You are horrid!" exclaimed Miranda, starting to draw back, but his arm only tightened about her. She appealed to her brother. "Jeremy!"

He shook his head, his grin growing wider. "No, dear sister. I believe that this time you have met your match. I shall leave you to it, my lord!" He bowed once more and then left the study. He firmly closed the door behind him.

Lord Townsend's eyes were warm as he smiled down into Miranda's indignant face. He caught her chin with his free hand. "I discovered an effective means of silencing you, Miss Wainwright. I wonder if it works equally well in disarming you?" He kissed her thoroughly. It was but seconds before Miranda's arms slid around his neck.

Several moments later, the viscount raised his head. His breathing came more rapidly than before. He stared down at her suspiciously. Becomingly flushed, Miranda chuckled. "You see, my lord, it is a double-edged sword!"